Dear Parent:
Your child's love of reading starts here!

Every child learns to read in a different way and at his or her own speed. Some go back and forth between reading levels and read favorite books again and again. Others read through each level in order. You can help your young reader improve and become more confident by encouraging his or her own interests and abilities. From books your child reads with you to the first books he or she reads alone, there are I Can Read Books for every stage of reading:

SHARED READING
Basic language, word repetition, and whimsical illustrations, ideal for sharing with your emergent reader

BEGINNING READING
Short sentences, familiar words, and simple concepts for children eager to read on their own

READING WITH HELP
Engaging stories, longer sentences, a[nd language play] for developing readers

D0973165

READING ALONE
Complex plots, challenging vocabula[ry, and high interest] for the independent reader

ADVANCED READING
Short paragraphs, chapters, and exciting themes for the perfect bridge to chapter books

I Can Read Books have introduced children to the joy of reading since 1957. Featuring award-winning authors and illustrators and a fabulous cast of beloved characters, I Can Read Books set the standard for beginning readers.

A lifetime of discovery begins with the magical words **"I Can Read!"**

Visit www.icanread.com for information
on enriching your child's reading experience.

I Can Read!

READING 2 WITH HELP

THE DARK KNIGHT RISES™

Batman versus Bane

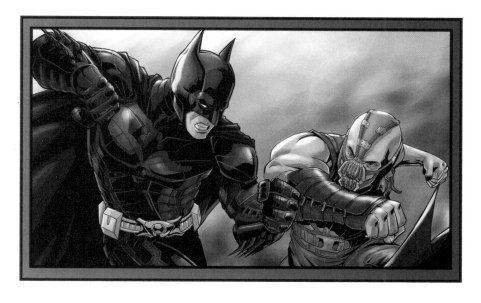

Adapted by Jodi Huelin

Illustrated by Andie Tong

INSPIRED BY THE FILM THE DARK KNIGHT RISES
SCREENPLAY BY JONATHAN NOLAN AND CHRISTOPHER NOLAN
STORY BY CHRISTOPHER NOLAN AND DAVID S. GOYER
BATMAN CREATED BY BOB KANE

HARPER
An Imprint of HarperCollinsPublishers

I Can Read Book® is a trademark of HarperCollins Publishers.

HARP5000
Printed in the United States of America. No part of this book may be used or reproduced in any manner whatsoever without written permission except in the case of brief quotations embodied in critical articles and reviews. For information address HarperCollins Children's Books, a division of HarperCollins Publishers, 10 East 53rd Street, New York, NY 10022.
www.icanread.com

Library of Congress catalog card number: 2012930073
ISBN 978-0-06-213224-6

Book design by John Sazaklis

13 14 15 16   LP/WOR   10 9 8 7 6 5 4 3
❖
First Edition

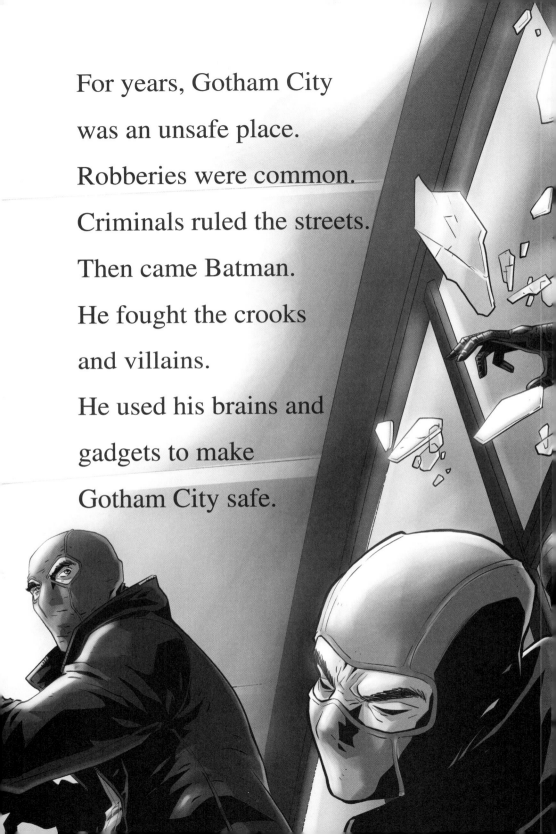

For years, Gotham City
was an unsafe place.
Robberies were common.
Criminals ruled the streets.
Then came Batman.
He fought the crooks
and villains.
He used his brains and
gadgets to make
Gotham City safe.

Even the police relied on Batman.
Police Commissioner Gordon would shine
a special light into the sky
whenever he needed Batman's help.

Then, one day, Batman vanished.

Gotham's protector was gone.

There is a new villain in town.

His name is Bane.

His goal is to destroy

Gotham City.

The Gotham police are helpless.

Bane is too strong to stop

and too smart to catch.

To show how dangerous he is,
Bane kidnaps Commissioner Gordon
and holds him in his secret lair
deep in the underground tunnels.

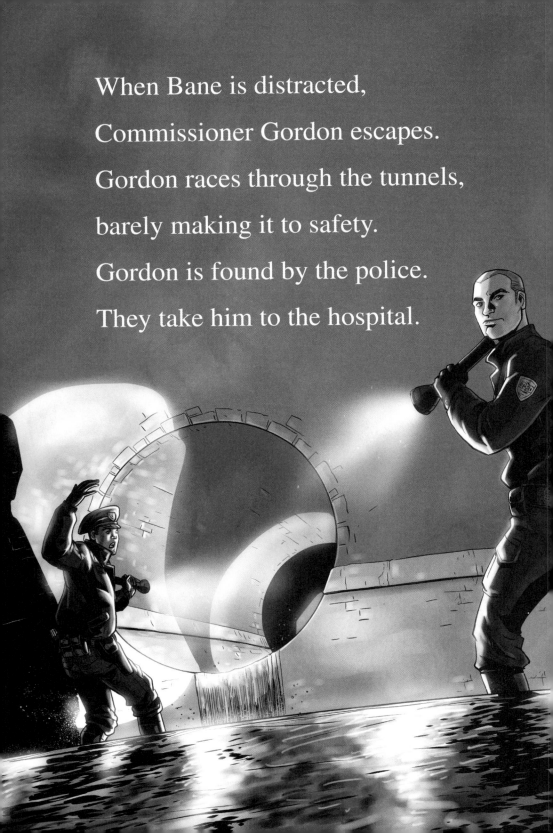

When Bane is distracted,
Commissioner Gordon escapes.
Gordon races through the tunnels,
barely making it to safety.
Gordon is found by the police.
They take him to the hospital.

That night, Batman sneaks into Gordon's hospital room.

"You're back?" Gordon asks.

"Gotham needs me," Batman says.

Gordon tells Batman

where Bane is hiding.

Batman promises to find

this new foe and to stop him.

Batman zooms off on the Bat-Pod.

He meets Alfred back at the Batcave.

Together they form a plan.

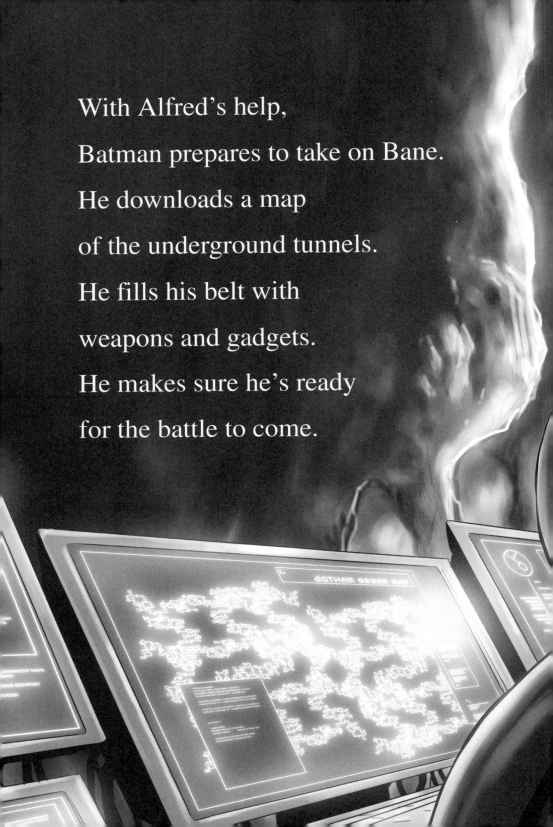

With Alfred's help,

Batman prepares to take on Bane.

He downloads a map

of the underground tunnels.

He fills his belt with

weapons and gadgets.

He makes sure he's ready

for the battle to come.

GOTHAM SEWER MAP

Batman enters the tunnels.

He winds his way down into the darkness and finds Bane's headquarters.

Batman watches as Bane and his men discuss their latest crime. Batman hides in the shadows, waiting for his chance.

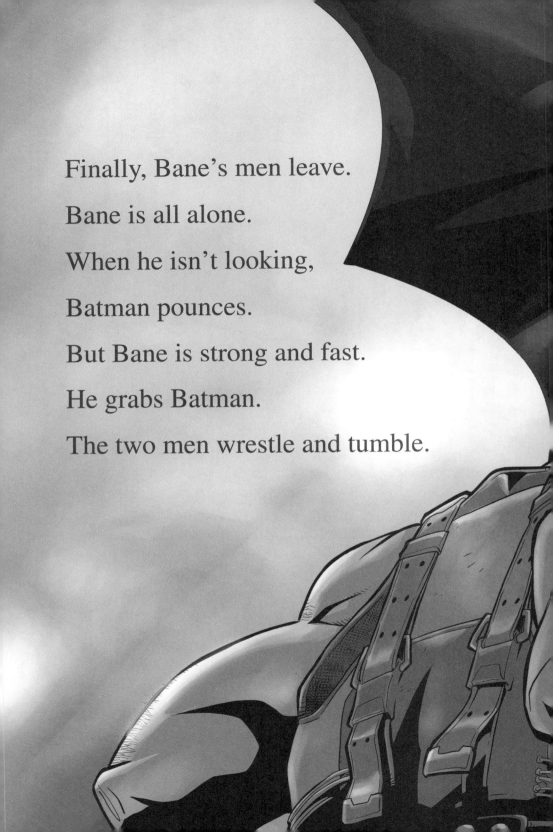

Finally, Bane's men leave.

Bane is all alone.

When he isn't looking,

Batman pounces.

But Bane is strong and fast.

He grabs Batman.

The two men wrestle and tumble.

The Dark Knight jumps to his feet
and lunges at the villain.

They fight and struggle.

Bane and Batman are equally matched.

Batman grabs Bane

and pushes him into the wall.

Bane breaks a pipe.

Water shoots at Batman!

The blast catches Batman off guard.

He doesn't see what happens next!

Bane uses the shadows against
his opponent and knocks Batman out.
After a while, Batman wakes up.
He's alone in a strange place.
There is no sign of Bane or his men.

Batman vows that this is not the end.

He will bring Bane to justice

and save Gotham City!

LET ME SEE YOUR BODY TALK

Jan Latiolais Hargrave, Ed. S.

KENDALL/HUNT PUBLISHING COMPANY
4050 Westmark Drive   Dubuque, Iowa 52002

TABLE OF CONTENTS

PREFACE

You Must Have Graduated From The University of Heaven

As I approached the podium, my knees began to shake, my throat tightened and my stomach began to churn. I first looked out into the huge gymnasium, with its high ceilings and massive windows, then peered at the sky outside, and it was as if someone greater than I, were looking down upon me, confidently guiding me. I stared at the huge audience, the men in starched whites and the women in their Sunday best, and I began to question, "What am I doing here?" "What gives me the right to tell these people to look forward instead of backward concerning all that has happened in their lives?" "Am I really qualified?"

And then, by some kind of magical strength, I began to quote from Og Mandino's *The Greatest Salesman In The World* about living this day as if it were our last and committing ourselves to excellence in everything we do. I stressed to that wide-eyed audience, eagerly anticipating my every word, that we've only just begun and that the troubles in our lives are intended to make us better instead of bitter.

The presentation continued, and as I felt my audience respond, my own excitement and enthusiasm grew. After several inspiring messages, I approached the end of my talk and noticed a gentleman in the audience, overcome with emotion, wipe away a tear. I took a deep breath and gave a sigh of relief as I ended the speech, almost happy that it was over. Then, to my surprise, the cheering crowd gave me a standing ovation.

After the commencement, a man of about twenty-two forced his way through the crowd and tapped me on the shoulder. I turned around, surprised at his youth, his intensity in trying to reach me, and to this day am still astounded by his words. He said to me, "Most people think all of us here are losers, but you made us all feel like winners. You must have graduated from the University of Heaven."

Tears welled in my eyes, I could not contain myself, and began to repeat. "We've only just begun. Let's look forward to what we can change, instead of backward to what is beyond our control." Overwhelmed with emotion, I hurried then to reach my car, and as I opened the door and sat inside, I began to cry uncontrollably. As the tears streamed down my face, I knew I had done what I had set out to do. I had wanted to make a difference, and by all accounts, I had. This commencement exercise, imbedded so deeply in my mind, was not a high school graduation, nor a college commencement. It was held for the Texas State Department of Corrections. Wherever that inmate is today, I say to him, "Thank you. Whether you ever know it or not, letting me know that I made a difference in your life has made a tremendous difference in mine."

If my words, my thoughts, my ideas help to make a difference in YOUR life, then my mission will have been accomplished.

Jan

ACKNOWLEDGMENTS

To my Father in Heaven, and my father and mother in Louisiana.

To Virginia Cambron whose creativity, editorial expertise and feedback, added rhythm and music to my words.

To my silent partner, in appreciation for his constant encouragement, devoted friendship and borrowed time.

I am truly blessed.

INTRODUCTION

Mama, Mama, he winked at me! What does that mean? I suppose it began for me at any early age. I was four when I first noticed that grownups slightly nodded their heads at each other when meeting on the street. But it even goes back further than that. The warmth I felt when my mom smiled at me or the excitement when my dad raised me high, high into the sky, above his head, were also nonverbal clues that I read before I could speak. Babies communicate nonverbally with their parents and all those around them until they are able to talk. How does a baby let others know he is content, full, or ready for a nap? He coos. He smiles. He cries. Parents read their children from the moment of birth. Maybe that's why it's almost impossible for children to lie to their parents and get away with it.

While we cannot read minds, we can read and understand certain body movements. We watch a conversation taking place inside a telephone booth and without a sound escaping, sense the mood of the conversation. The caller tells all with facial expressions and body posture. Through the silent, yet expressive, language of our gestures, posture, gaze, expression and appearance we demonstrate our innermost thoughts and feelings.

This book will provide answers to key questions about the effective use of body language at work and play, and will serve as a manual for your journey into self discovery concerning living, loving, learning and growing. It can serve as a practical guide to help you become a better business associate, lover, mate and social partner.

To make it as immediately useful as possible, I have grouped the chapters into two sections: one that relates to personal information concerning nonverbal communication, and one that relates to useful knowledge about effective use of body language in professional settings.

Let Me See Your Body Talk is a book that can and will, literally, change your personal and professional life for the better. Its purpose is to make you more aware of your own nonverbal cues and signals and to demonstrate how people communicate with each other using this medium. It is my hope that it will help us to raise a new generation of people who are more successful and more comfortable in face-to-face encounters.

When it comes to success or failure, *WHAT* you say often matters far less than *HOW* you say it.

Note: For ease of reading, general use of "he", "his", and "him" throughout the book is in reference to women and men alike.

Section I

PERSONAL

CHAPTER 1

Let Me See Your Body Talk

Let me
see your
body talk, read
the rhythm of
your walk, learn
the language of your
sighs, for you
speak poetry
to my
eyes.
Although your
posture gives commands, you
speak gentleness with your hands.
Your emotion is softly heard, without
the need to say a word. In the way
you look at me, there's so
much that I can
see; I can
tell if
your
tears lie,
or if caring
makes you cry. Even
in the way you sleep,
I know secrets dark and
and deep, or in the magic
of your touch, that you love
me very much. Hold me, kiss me,
hug me, squeeze me; get to
know me; learn to please
me. It's as easy
as A, B, C;
Body Language
holds the
key.

Welcome to the world of BODY LANGUAGE. Your body speaks to the world around you. The way you cross your arms, fold your hands, tilt your head, even how you blink your eyes communicates a secret language. Every movement reveals underlying thoughts. Mouths lie, but bodies don't. Decoding this unspoken language leads to understanding and success.

I will help you discover if someone is lying when he says, "Ooooh, you've never looked better," or if he is telling the truth about their feelings when he plays with the stem of a wine glass while saying, "I love you." The importance of nonverbal communication is evident in the frequency with which we hear expressions such as: "Actions speak louder than words;" "Talk is cheap;" or "It's not what you say that counts." Body Language, nonverbal communication, is the silent language of power, success and love. Let us explore it together.

Olivia Newton John said it in her song: "I've been patient, I've been good; trying to keep my hands on the table. It's getting hard, this holding back. I want to get physical; LET ME SEE YOUR BODY TALK!"

After my professor said to me time and time again, "I know what you're thinking, Jan Hargrave, and you better stop!" I became obsessed with body talk. So obsessed, that I researched everything and everybody I could get my hands on . . . ooooops!

The research has been fun and fascinating. While teaching "Body Language" classes at the University of Southwestern Louisiana, I put my study into action. I taught my students signs to watch for in a person's body movements, then conducted "To Tell The Truth" sessions to which I invited two imposters and a true professional, and had my students ask all of them questions. I often brought in Catholic nuns. My students had fun asking questions: "How many beads are there on a rosary?" "How much does that hat really weigh?" "Do you really get together with the priests for wine after mass?"

After a timed period of questions and answers, my class then voted on whom they believed to be the real Sister Mary Theresa, and nine out of ten times they picked the correct professional. Body language works. Let's prepare you for your own "to tell the truth" experience.

To begin our thinking processes for learning nonverbal communication, answer true or false to the following questions:

1. If you are talking with someone and he continuously puts the tips of his fingers together, almost like in prayer, it is a sign that he lacks confidence.
2. Our eyes are the most descriptive of all of our body parts. They tell almost everything about us.
3. Dangling of a shoe by a woman when seated near a man that interests her is a sign of nervousness.
4. If someone crosses his arms across his chest as he is listening to you, it means he agrees with everything you are saying. Get ready for number five, it's frightening!
5. People who tend to use their left hand a lot, tend to lie a lot.
6. When men turn chairs around and straddle them, putting each leg on the sides and resting their chest against the inside of the chair, they are displaying a sign of agreement.
7. How about this one? If someone you don't know gets too close to you for comfort, you feel he/she is invading your space.
8. The most aggressive sexual display a man can make is the thumbs-in-belt, "cowpoke" stance.
9. The type of clothing we wear tells something about us.
10. Placing your right hand against your upper chest as if you were reciting the Pledge of Allegiance, shows dishonesty.
11. Tapping on a desk with your fingers means boredom.
12. Whistling is a sign of nervousness.
13. Touching gestures, gently patting someone on the shoulders, patting on the upper arm, or even patting on the hand, are gestures often used to emphasize a point.
14. When an interviewer throws his glasses on his desk and begins to point a finger at you, he is expressing a sign of confidence.

15. Stroking the chin with thumb and pointer finger indicates contemplation.

Actions have always spoken louder than words, and still do! Picture a woman sitting with her attorney, talking about her upcoming divorce. When her attorney asks, "Do you still love your husband?" The woman nods her head "yes" but responds "no." Bodies don't lie; they give us away. You have read the actions of others all your life and intuitively understood many. If I thrust my thumb and index finger in a circular formation, you know it stands for "OK." If I make a fist and raise my thumb, you presume it stands for "no worries," and if I sensuously pucker my lips and kiss the air in your direction, hopefully you know what that means too.

Our analysis of body language will begin with our heads, and end with our toes. Stopping longest at the most interesting places, I'll work my way slowly down the body to show you unmistakable signs that reveal exactly what we're thinking.

We will first analyze space utilization. Studies on body language indicate that we need three feet in front of us, three feet behind us and three feet on either side of us. We live in an imaginary bubble. Each day as we pass each other, our bubbles touch. When a person you don't know very well gets inside your bubble, you think, "What is this person doing this close to me?" It makes us feel uncomfortable. Only on rare and wonderful occasions do we see someone we wish would invade our bubble.

We tell people how much space we need. If you enter a library and spot a guy at a table alone with his books spread all over the table, you presume he is sending the message, "This is my table and don't you dare sit with me!" Or you may see others sitting at tables with their books placed very close to them. It is as if they are saying, "I am sitting here, but won't you please join me?" When we get food in shopping malls and try to find a place to sit, we look around for someone safe to sit with; that is, all of their belongs are very close to them. Cafeteria tables provide us with imaginary lines that divide two people sitting across from each other. Would you ever think of taking a sip of your milk and then putting it down across that line?

Would you ever consider breaking your bread and putting the remainder of it down across that line? I didn't think so. But you know what? If you don't like the people sitting across from you, you can get rid of them by simply invading their space. Put your milk close to them; enter their space! Replace your leftover bread across the table. They do not quite understand what's going on; they begin to feel intimidated, to eat quickly and are in a hurry to leave. Right now, if there's someone sitting next to you and you don't care for him, begin to invade his space, move your things closer, and eventually he, too, will leave.

We have long used space and size to indicate power. The more space someone needs, the larger the desk is, the larger the office is; the more powerful that person seems. If you were to see three limousines driving down the highway, and one was larger than the other two, wouldn't you presume that the most important person was in the largest of the three? People who tend to need a large amount of space also tend to think they are very powerful. People like to brag on their big cars or big corner offices with windows. Space indicates status.

Every nationality uses a different space distance when conversing. Some nationalities (Germans, British, Austrians) are more comfortable talking with a large distance between them. Others, such as the French, the Arabs, the South Americans and the Italians, are more comfortable with less distance between them and their conversational partner. When people move away from us it does not necessarily mean they do not like us, only that they are not comfortable with the specific space distance we have created.

Touch is an important part of communication. We shake hands, we pat shoulders, we hug people. Touching can be the most rewarding of our nonverbal communication process. Caring touches help us develop mentally and physically. Research indicates that the more a baby is cuddled and comforted, the better adjusted that baby will be. People who commit crimes and commit suicide are perhaps reacting to the attention they did not receive when they were young. We can never hug a baby enough or child too much if we want them to feel loved and wanted.

In business, the area from your wrist to your upper arm is considered "the safe area." When we touch there, it is as if we are saying, "I like you as a person."

It's alright to touch in a good way. Know what else is alright to do? It's "OK" to tell people that you like them! We live and work all of our lives with people we care about who make us happy, but we never say, "Gee, I like you!" or "Gee, you make my days a lot happier!" Sometimes we spend more time with our peers at work than with our spouses, yet we never mention to them how we feel. How many times have you discovered that someone you've been interested in has also been interested in you, yet both of you said nothing? How many times have we found ourselves wishing, "If only I had known." If someone makes you happy, tell them! When things are going right and you feel those special feelings, let the other person know. Not only will it make them feel good, it will make you feel good too.

Sometimes we postpone telling others how we feel about them too long. Someone important to you could die before you ever get to tell them how you really feel. If you practice this thoughtful lesson throughout your life that will never happen to you and you will have no regrets: "I will say the things I meant to say to you when we grow old today, not only because we may not grow old together; but because we may not grow old at all!"

The following story, which I present on stage in a Jamaican accent, reinforces my beliefs concerning feelings:

"I am a little gul from Jamaica. I am certain dat it is hard for you to tell because I have lost a lot of my accent, but I must tell you dis story of what happened while I lived dere. I had what day call a currio stan. You know a currio stan—we sold dose big, long wooden pencils—dose dancin girls swinging from dose plastic palm trees—we sole dat newspaper and dat chewing gum. Everry day, people came to my stand to buy dat newspaper, and den dey just go away.

Well, child, one day I am at my little stan and I am cleaning and I looked up, and I see a mon coming towards me and I say to myself, 'What kind of a mon is dat?' His skin was verry tan, verry dry and verry wrinkled and I said to myself, 'He looks like an ole dried raisin; if I had an irron, I would prress that mon's skin rright out.' He come to my stand, he buy dat newspaper and den he go away.

I said to myself, 'Surely I will neverr see dat ugly ole dried raisin again.' But, I was incorrrect, da next day he was rright back dere. He buy da newspaper again, and den he go away and again I said to myself, 'now, surely I will neverr see dat ugly ole dried rraisin again.' But I was incorrrect cause he come back to my stan, everryday, for about two weeks.

Afta a week he began to talk to me, child, I tink he even began to get a crrush on me. I was very prretty Jamaican gul. He said to me one day, 'You ever been to Amerrica?' I said, 'No.'

He said, 'You ever tought of going?'

I said, 'Not rreally.'

He said, 'Why don't you come with me to Amerrica?'

I said, 'Why?'

And he said, 'You would love it in America; you could be my companion, I have a wonderful home and you would have a wonderful time.' Den he says to me, 'Listen, I have a lot of money!'

Well, my eyes got verry big den, and I said, 'Ooops, I might have to tink about dis trrip to America. I tought to myself, 'Not bad adventure for Jamaican girl; when dat ole man ask me again, I will tell him yes.' Well, he ask again and I said, 'alrright.' He bought everryting dat I had in my stan, and he said for me to meet him at the airrport tomorrrow morning.

Next day I get up and I put on my best drress; I did not have many good drresses, because I am verry poor Jamaican girl. I go down to da airrport and I am embarrrassed to be seen with dat ugly, ole dried rraisin, but he found me and we get on dat aerroplane and we fly to Amerrica.

As we began to fly, he began to tell me some storries and some storries, and I say to myself, 'What did I get myself into, this mon is coo coo!' He talked about a verry big house, wit white columns and some rred land and I tought to myself, 'This poor ole buzzard has been reading *Gone With the Wind!* If Scarlet O'Harra answers dat door, I am not going in dat house.' But we lan in Amerrica, and a big limousine come to pick us up and I said, 'Ooooh, dat ole drried rraisin might have some mooney!'

We drrive and we drrive and we see dis big house, and he said, 'Jamaican gul, dat is my house.' It was the most beautiful ting I had ever seen. Da big white house, da big white columns, and da rred land; it was da most beautiful house I had ever seen. The good ting for me, dough, was dat da batrooms was inside da house. I like dat a lot.

You know dat ole drried rraisin and I lived togeda for fourr years. We not talk a lot. He's verry busy man; he trravels all of da time and he is always on dat telephone. He does not talk to me dat much. I do not talk to him much eida, but a verry, verry good man he was. I neverr did say, 'Tank you,' because I prresume he knew I was MOST, MOST grrateful to him, to be in America. I did not tell him dat I was having a verry good time because I prresumed he could see dat in my face.

Child, once for my birtday, I go to my room, and on my bed was a prresent wit a card dat read, 'To you from Frredrricks of Hollywood.' I know no Frredrricks of Hollywood, but it said to you, so I prresume dat it is for me. I opened dat ting up, and, child, in dere was the prretiest little black nightgown . . . dat ole drried rraisin was having some silly, silly ideas. I was verry happy gul in Amerrica.

One day, dough, I did not hear dat ole drried rraisin in his bedrroom and I say, 'What is the matterr wit the ole man; he is usually stomping arround in dere, making all kinds of noises. I betta go in dere and see what is da matter.' Well, mon, I opened da doorr and the ole man was not on his bed and so I began to look arround in the room. I looked and I looked, and den I looked on da floor and da ole mon was dead; child, dead as a do nail. I even had to close his mouth. Well, I got on da telephone rright away, and I called dat attorney and I said, 'I tink da ole man has died.'

He said, "We were expecting dat;' you come to my office in fourr days and I will take carre of you.'

I said, 'Alrright.'

Den he said to me, 'Don't you steal anyting from dat house.'

I said, 'O.K., dat piano dat I have in my purse upstairs, I will take it out; you ole buzzard.' Den I hung up that telephone.

On dat fort day, I decided I betta go get my ticket. So I get up and put on a good dress. Da ole man saw dat I had some good clothes. I was getting rready to walk out of da house and I tought to myself. It is verry, verry quite in here; I kind a miss dat ole drried rraisin. But, it is too late to tink of dat; I must go get my ticket. Well, child, I went down to dat attorney's office and I sit in dat room where dey tole me to sit; and dere are trree people in dat room, too. Dose trree people began to look at me and so I tought to myself, I gonna look at you! When I looked at dem rreally well, I said, 'Oh my God; dey look just like dat ole drried rraisin.' So, child, I call dem da raisinettes.

I looked at dem some more and they looked at me and prrobably said to demselves, 'What is a Jamaican gul doing here?'

And I said to myself, 'What are dose raisinettes doing here; dey had neverr come to da house in dose fourr years dat I lived dere?' But I said 'never mind; I will take my ticket and I will be out of here. I will let dat attorney talk to da raisinettes alone.'

Well, child, dat attorney began to rread the will and when he began to rread, the strrangest ting happened. He not look at da raisinettes, but looked strraight at me. He looked rright at me and said, 'To you Jamaican gul, dat ole mon leave $20 million dollars and dat big house.'

I said, 'To me? To me?' And den I said to myself, 'I neverr even tole dat ole drried rraisin dat I liked him. I neverr even tole him, I was having a verry good time. And, I neverr even hugged dat ugly, ugly silly, ole drried rraisin.'"

That story teaches a good lesson. Our lives are much too short not to tell special people that we like them. Please take a lesson from my story about the "Ole Drried Raisin."

We said we'd study body language from head to toe. Here goes! We'll begin with the four kinds of smiles we use every day. The first one is called, "Just to be polite." Sometimes while walking down a hall at work, we come across a colleague we really dislike. We're thinking to ourselves, "I better smile at this old girl, because I may have to work with her later." This "Just to be polite" smile is accomplished when our top lip is very, very tight across our face and just our top front teeth are showing. We usually nod our heads in politeness and mutter the words, "How do you do?"

I bet you have the second type of smile on your face right now. It is called the "Typically nonsense" smile. Typically nonsense smiles indicate you are enjoying something inside. You drive down the highway tuned in to your car radio and the disc jockey says something funny; a little smile begins to form on your lips. In "Typically nonsense" smiles, no teeth are showing, and the corners of the mouth are slightly turned up.

The third smile is the biggest and the best. It is called the "Broad smile," and is accompanied with a laugh from way down in the tummy. Our teeth, our cavities, our gums; everything shows. It is the most wonderful smile. If we had a laugh like this every day, one so joyous that it made us cry, life would be much better. Laughter can be as powerful as medicine. Funny movies are now being played in hospitals to make patients laugh. It lets out a wonderful, healing enzyme. We are blessed by being the only species on the face of this earth capable of laughter. Monkeys can grin, but only people can laugh. So I say to you LAUGH, LAUGH, LAUGH! Did you know that every time you laugh whole heartedly, you add three years to your life?

Our fourth smile is the specialty of ladies. But be careful ladies; it is the smile Marilyn Monroe used when she was out to catch a guy. This smile is accompanied with a "breathy," sentence of "Hi-ya Baby." Let's practice. Your shoulders should be back, your chest out, head tilted to the right side, lowered just enough that you can look seductively upward from eyes cut to the extreme left. Now here comes the important part. Lick your lips lingeringly with your tongue until they are glistening and wet. With mouth slithtly open, tongue barely visible, smile a gentle invitation. Baby, if that don't bring them in, they're dead.

It's always hard to leave good lips, but let's go on to our hands. How many times have you said, "If I couldn't use my hands, I couldn't talk?" Much of what we communicate to others, we communicate with our hands and our arms. Let's begin our study by inspecting the inside of our palms. Lifting the insides of our palms means acceptance. When we hug someone, they see the inside of our palms. When we shake someone's hand, they see the inside of our palms. Jesus is on the cross with both his hands open to us as if to say, "I accept you, I don't care what you have done; I take you as you are." If insides of palms show acceptance, think of what happens when two people shake hands. The more the insides of palms touch, the more acceptance is felt between the two people. Ordinarily, handshakes require the right hand from each person to securely clasp.

Politicians, sales people, and corporation executives pay large sums of money to understand the value of various handshakes in nonverbal communication. They often ask, "When I shake someone's hand, how can I appear more honest, more genuine and more accepting?" How does a politician shake hands? He grabs your right hand with his right hand and then coming with his left, he cups your one hand between his two. He is thinking, "The more I can get my palms on you, the more genuine you will think I am." They sometimes even shake your right hand with their right hand and then use their left hand to grab your right arm.

The manner in which we extend our hand to someone reveals our level of control in that particular situation. Some of us extend our hands with our whole palm facing toward the ground; some of us reach with only a little of our palms facing the ground. Some of us extend our hand in a straight up and down movement, and sometimes we extend our hands with our palms facing toward the sky.

Whether a palm is flat facing downward or just slightly facing downward, it shows control and dominance. A person in this handshake position is thinking, "I am going to control you and anything that we're deciding here." Hands that come to us with palms facing the sky indicate submissiveness. They seem to be saying, "Whatever you decide is fine with me."

In a job interviewing situation, if an interviewer comes to shake your hand with his palm facing the ground, you should grasp his hand and turn it straight up and down as you are shaking. This movement gives a message indicating that both of you have a fifty-fifty chance in the outcome of the meeting.

Arms crossed in front of the body and legs crossed at the knees are nonverbal signals indicating the thoughts, "I am very defensive and I am not listening to a word you're saying." This defensiveness is shown in varying degrees. The tighter the fists, the tighter the arms across the body, the more opposed the listener is to conversation. Anger is shown when the hands grip the upper arms tightly. It is a sign that says, "I am not listening to you and I am angry with what you are saying." The opposite position, arms resting at sides and legs partially open, signifies openess to ideas being expressed by both parties.

Next, let's study signs of lying and telling the truth. Three gestures performed with the left hand and the left side of the face indicate "I am lying to you." Before we go into those gestures, let's mention the role our eyes play in lying. Eyes are the windows to the soul; they show fright, happiness, sadness, excitement, even tiredness, and play a big part in lying and telling the truth. When people can look at you the entire time they are talking with you, it is an indication that they are being very honest with you. Darting eyes indicate avoidance and nervousness; telltale signs of lying.

Using the left index finger to rub up or down the left side of the nose while talking is the number one sign of lying. Imagine someone doing this while saying, "You look reeeeal good." Don't go for it; they are lying to you.

The second sign of lying is when someone uses their left index finger to slightly tug at their left eye while talking with you. This seems to indicate, "Do not look too closely at what I am saying, because I am lying to you." Haven't you seen people do this while saying, "Yeah, I'll be there about seven o'clock." You will never see them; they're lying to you.

The third sign of lying is when the left index finger and thumb are used to tug at the left ear. This gesture indicates, "Do not listen too clearly to what I am saying; because I am lying to you." These left-hand gestures are used to distract the listener. When someone places somthing in his face while talking with you, you tend to not pay full attention to what he is saying. We focus on their fingernails, rings, and watches. They are distracting us and telling us anything that they want. How do people rob stores? They distract you and then take whatever it is they're after. Same way with liars; they are also distracting you.

Placing the entire hand over the mouth when talking is an even greater sign for lying. It is a coverup for an untruth. Unnecessary yawning, while in an important conversation, is also considered a sign of lying.

Honesty is conveyed when one takes his right hand, palm open, and places it on his chest as if he were ready to recite the Pledge of Allegiance. Since it is the single sign for honesty, it would be wise if you wanted that special guy or girl to place his right hand on his chest when they whisper "I Love You."

Confidence and lack of confidence are next. The steeple (hands as if in prayer with finger tips touching) is the most powerful sign of confidence. We watch attorneys use this gesture in courtrooms; we see teachers steeple in classrooms and we observe preachers steepling in pulpits. It does not have to be done at chest level. Steepling can be accomplished by hanging our arms down and folding our thumbs together, while touching our two pointer fingers or folding all our fingers together and just touching the thumbs together at chest, waist or hip level. Students in classrooms show confidence before exams by sitting in their chairs, placing their elbows on their front desks and resting their chins on their clasped hands.

Another powerful sign of confidence is the clasping of hands behind the head. It is as if someone were saying "I think I am better than you are." Accompanying this, we often see people prop their feet up on desks; another powerful sign of confidence. These two gestures combined are too strong; too powerful.

Presenters on stage should never fidget with clothing. This fidgeting, or rearranging of clothing, gives a strong message that the speaker is nervous. The fewer times a speaker arranges his clothing while in front of an audience, the more confident he will appear. The fewer times he adjusts his tie or rearranges his shirt in his pants, the more confident he can appear. In James Bond movies, the directors and producers display the suave confidence of Mr. Bond by never allowing him to touch himself throughout the movie. Every move he made was so smooth that moviegoers envisioned him as cool and collected.

Whistling is a sign of nervousness. It is not necessarily negative; it can be a sign of positive nervousness or positive energy that must be released.

Nervousness is also expressed while smoking cigarettes. Observing the direction smoke is exhaled during a conversation gives hints concerning the direction the dialogue is headed. Smoke that is blown upward is an indication that both feel relatively good about what is being said. Smoke that is exhaled downward indicates dissatisfaction about what is being said, and smoke that is being blown down and through the side of the mouth usually indicates anger about the conversation.

Nervousness concerning financial matters is expressed when men jingle their money in their pockets. Either they are financially well off and thinking of ways to increase their wealth, or they hardly have any money and are concerned about where their next pennies will come from.

Chewing on pencils, pens, or paperclips shows nervousness. "Chewing" is indicative of a person in need of nourishment. Not in the way of food, but in the way of words or love. We tend to put things in our mouths when we do not know exactly what to say. In classrooms when students do not know answers to a question, they usually stick pens or pencils in their mouths to send a message that says, "Don't call on me; I don't know the answer."

Let's examine courtship signs. What are signals sent from men and women that say, "I like you; you make me soooo crazy?" Lets study men first.

A guy walks into a room and sitting there is that wonderful girl who makes his heart skip a beat. He approaches her and begins a conversation about nonsense issues; the weather, the time, her watch, etc. He'd like to ask her to go out, but does not know exactly how to do it. He fumbles with his words, then here comes the give-away; he begins to pull at his socks. I have seen men dig in cowboy boots for socks or even pull the hair off of their legs if they don't have socks. Ladies, if you see a guy pulling up his socks in your presence, go over to him and say, "I know it's me, Honey, come over here!" Gentlemen, if you catch yourself pulling your socks up, you may want to look around the room and say to yourself, "Who's in here that I may be interested in?"

The cow-poke stance, originated in Texas and Oklahoma, is a primary male courtship gesture. In this stance the male locks his thumbs in his belt, points his fingers down and around his zipper area, slightly spreads his legs apart, and tilts his head to one side. It carries with it a seductive message that says, "Hey Baby, come over here!"

Excessive buttoning and unbuttoning of a suit jacket, in the presence of his love interest is a male nonverbal gesture indicating, "You're making me nervous." If after playing with the buttons of his jacket for a some time, the male unbuttons the jacket entirely and holds it open on both sides at the waist, he is saying to his partner, "You're making me a little more nervous." Lastly, if he takes the jacket completely off, after completing steps one and two; he is yours, "hook, line and sinker."

Squeezing cola cans, stems of glasses, or pens in the presence of a love interest are also courtship gestures. Let's examine "can-playing." Can-playing begins when someone turns the can to the right, then to the left. If he begins to slightly squeeze the can and let it go again and again, he is sending a message that says, "I'd like to squeeze you, Baby."

Interest in another is often indicated when one glances at another's body and lets the other person see them glancing. We tend to get upset and say, "Did you see the way he looked at me!" I think it's because our Moms drilled the fact in us that we had to "act" like we didn't approve of it, but we like it. Let's not forget May West's suggestive motto: "It's better to be looked-over, than over-looked."

Women, in the presence of someone who interests them, will deliberately cross their legs slowly at the knees and begin to swing the upper leg. After spotting a mate that interests them, women begin to dangle the shoe that is on their upper crossed leg. Women courtship signs send a message that says, "Please notice me; I like you!"

For either sex, it is feet that play a major part in courtship. We do not realize the importance of our feet. They have long been associated with sexual fetishes; they are the last things to touch the earth before we die; they serve as our support systems while we are here on earth. Shoes are strung from the back of wedding limousines; Cinderella dropped her glass slipper! I've overheard young girls say to each other, "You need to see this guy; he'll knock your socks off," and I know exactly what they're thinking.

Women also tend to clasp their knees, calfs or thighs with both hands in the presence of a potential mate. It is as if they were saying, "Gee, I'd love to hold him, but instead, I'll hold on to myself and give the message that I'm prim and proper." Sitting on a crossed leg is also a sign of courting. It is as though the woman were thinking, "I feel very comfortable with you; I'd like to get to know you better."

Hair tossing, rearranging, and curling, express an extreme desire to be noticed. Not only do women play with hair, men also adjust their tresses in the presence of a love interest. Ladies, if you pass up a gentleman while driving in your car and he thinks you are nice looking, look in your rear view mirror and you will be able to catch him slicking back his hair. I've seen men who must have slicked back their hair one time too many, because there is isn't any left. My thoughts concerning lack of hair go back to my roots. In Louisiana, we say that men who don't have hair in the front of their heads, those are thinkers; men who don't have hair in the back of their heads, those are lovers; and men who don't have any hair on top of their heads, those are the ones who just think that they are lovers.

Let's close Chapter 1 with some "Life Lines" for you.

1. Most of what we worry about, NEVER happens! We worry ourselves silly and the worrying really never solves anything. Direct action does.
2. Success depends upon our ATTITUDES and how good we are to other people. When it is all said and done, we will not be measured by how much money we made or the type of job we had, but how good and kind we were to others. Harvard University revealed that 85 percent of people who get and keep their jobs do so because of their ATTITUDES, not intelligence or job skills.
3. Almost ANYTHING, ANYTHING, that we really, really want, we can get. Each of us is filled with so many talents, abilities and skills that we can achieve anything we set our minds to. Unused and undiscovered talents and abilities die when we die. Discover you.

In closing and in reference to the above statements, I give you my thoughts for life: "God took ORDINARY people and gave them EXTRAORDINARY skills and talents. He then put them in ORDINARY places to do EXTRAORDINARY things." Do we know our missions?

TEST ANSWERS

1.	F	9.	T
2.	T	10.	F
3.	T	11.	T
4.	F	12.	T
5.	T	13.	T
6.	F	14.	F
7.	T	15.	T
8.	T		

CHAPTER 2

You've Come a Long Way Baby: Gender Differences Between Men and Women

"Sugar and spice, and everything nice . . .
that's what little girls are made of."

"Frogs and snails and puppy dog tails . . .
that's what little boys are made of."

Even though we've come a long way, our past conditioning and socialization have created many problems for both men and women. From the soft, gentle manner in which little girls are talked to, to the gregarious way in which little boys are thrown up into the air and teased; there is a difference.

Nothing is wrong with the fact that men and women are different, or that they communicate differently. The problem arises only when men and women become insensitive to this difference.

The way to win the battle of the sexes and close the communication gap forever is to understand the differences between men and women, to develop a sensitivity to the differing behavior patterns and to compromise or ask for help when miscommunications occur.

Male and female brains develop at different rates. This can account for some perplexing differences between the sexes. Boys tend to develop speech and language skills at a slower rate than girls. Research shows that the left side of a girl's brain develops more rapidly than a boy's, explaining why little girls learn to talk sooner than boys, excel in memory at a younger age, and learn foreign languages more rapidly than boys of the same age.

It must be pointed out though, that these brain differences eventually level-out as people age, and men eventually tend to

21

favor the left side of their brains whereas women tend to eventually favor the right side of their brains.

Since the primary functions of the left side of the brain are analytical thinking, factual thinking, interest in facts and figures, and logical thinking, and the primary functions of the right side of the brain concern more emotional, romantic, expressive feelings, it is easy to understand why communication differences exist between men and women. Women also are more bilateral in their thinking processes (switch easily from right brain to left brain as needed), whereas men are predominately lateral in their thinking (many times using only one side of the brain).

To prove just how much men favor the left side of their brains, and how women favor the right side, let's use the brain that I have provided for you and take the following brain-dominance test.

Darken the correct side of the brain that corresponds to the question asked. Then total up the number of circles that you have darkened on each side of the brain. The side with the most darkened circles is your brain dominance side when communicating with members of the opposite sex.

LEFT/Analytic   **RIGHT/Global**

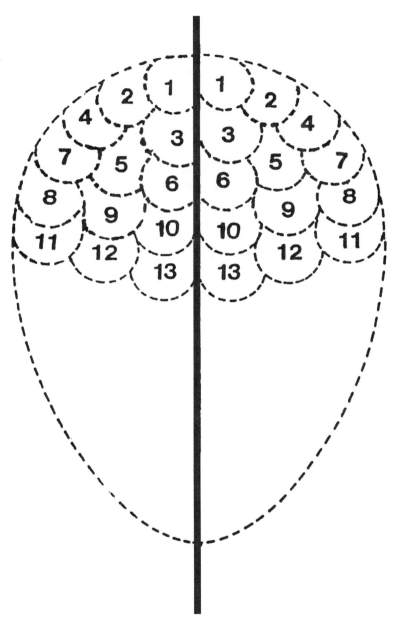

Chap. 2, Fig. 2

Brain Questions:

1. I tend to remember people's names. (L)
    I tend to remember people's faces. (R)

2. I like to let people know how I feel. (R)
    I keep my feelings to myself. (L)

3. I come up with ideas best when I lie flat on my back. (R)
    I come up with ideas best when I sit straight up in a seat. (L)

4. I am good at solving crossword puzzles. (L)
    I am not any good at solving crossword puzzles. (R)

5. I get lost very easily. (L)
    I can find my way around, even in strange places. (R)

6. I always seem to know what other people are thinking. (R)
    I never know what someone is thinking until they tell me. (L)

7. My idea of a romantic evening is a candlelight dinner. (R)
    My idea of a romantic evening is lying on the couch, watching TV with my mate. (L)

8. Sometimes I talk without thinking. (R)
    I always analyze everything before I speak. (L)

9. I love to tell people about my family and children. (R)
    I love to tell people about my work and my accomplishments. (L)

10. I am very competitive. (L)
    I don't particularly care who wins if I'm watching a sport. (R)

11. My conversations are usually dialogues (back & forth). (R)
    My conversations are usually monologues (lecture type). (L)

12. It's easy for me to say, "I love you." (R)
    It's hard for me to express my feelings and say, "I love you." (L)

13. When making love, I like to be told that I am loved. (R)
    When making love, I like to be told that I am a good lover. (L)

How did you score? Are the two genders looking at the world from totally different angles? Let's begin at the beginning.

Just as the rhyme at the beginning of the chapter revealed, we are all exposed to stereotypic situations early in life. Do you see any stereotyping in the following story?

Just two hours ago, Mary Jane gave birth to her twins, Jess and Jessica. Her two babies were identical except one was wrapped in a blue blanket. The other was in a pink blanket and had a tiny pink bow attached to her little tuft of brown hair. When Mary Jane's husband, Jess, Sr., arrived to visit his wife and the new babies, he went directly to little Jess, picked him up, waved his little arm in a "hello" gesture and began to poke Jess, Jr.'s little tummy, exclaiming that he would grow up to be the best football player because he had such broad shoulders. He then went over to his new daughter's bassinet. His tone immediately changed. He spoke softly and more gently to her as he lightly touched her cheek and cooed, "You're so beautiful" in a barely audible tone. There was no lively bouncing tone or "tummy-poking" with little Jessica.

A study conducted at Harvard University, revealed that children are conditioned by their parents and that conditioning remains with them a lifetime. Boys are handled more physically, picked up, bounced around and tickled more than girls. Whereas the girls are caressed and patted more, boys are told things like, "Hey, little man," or "Hey, big guy." Voices soften when speaking to little girls, and comments such as, "You're so pretty," or "You're a little sweetheart," are the ones most often used with female infants.

As children grow older parents still tend to socialize their children differently. Fathers often use more "command" terms than mothers. Also, men give more commands to their sons as opposed to their daughters.

Parents will even tolerate certain behaviors from boys that they would never tolerate from girls and vice versa. A two-year old little girl would be stopped and reprimanded for hitting another child and earnestly told why her behavior is unacceptable, whereas a two-year old male would be stopped, reprimanded, and told that his behavior is unacceptable, but, in the second instance, the male child's parent would be subconsciously thinking, "Tough guy, they'll learn not to pick on you."

As children and throughout their socialization period as young adults, boys not only play differently but talk about different things than little girls. Early on in life, little girls tend to talk about people—"Who is mad at whom?"; "Who's the prettiest?" or "Who likes whom?" They will usually talk about their friends. Since most little girls tend to play together in two's or small groups, (maybe that is why they still seem to always want to go to the restroom in pairs) they will usually tell one another "secrets" in order to bond their friendship. These "secrets" are usually about people, their wishes and their needs.

On the other hand, little boys will talk about things and "activities." Little boys are usually socialized in groups and mostly talk about what they all are doing and who is "best" at the activity. Since young boys are introduced to sports and games at an early age, their socialization concerning "winning" begins to form. The positive outcome of this competitiveness in young boys is that they tend to hold fewer grudges, both as young men and adult men. Boys and men are taught that when the "game's over, it's over; let's learn from our mistakes and look forward to the next game." Even as adults, when a confrontation before lunch begins between two men and one woman, the men tend to be able to end the disagreement peacefully, and even go off and have lunch together. The woman, however, tends to hold a grudge and cannot see an immediate settlement to a disagreement.

Studies also reveal that while little girls have conversations, little boys seem to enjoy making noises like "uhmmmmmm uhmmmmmmm" or "urrrrrrrrrk." In fact, in taped conversations of two year olds, 100% of a little girl's conversation is words, and 60% of a little boy's conversation is words while 40% of his conversation is sounds. Perhaps it is easy to see how this can cause problems later in life. For example, a wife asks, "Honey, do you like my dress?" and the husband answers, "Uhmmmmmmm uhmmmmmmm, of course, I do!"

Observations indicate that as teenagers, girls seem to talk mostly about boys, clothes and weight, while teenage boys talk about sports and the mechanics or functions of things.

Surveys reveal that the biggest event for girls is to have a boyfriend and "make out." Research in turn found that even though boys were equally interested in girls, they were also equally interested in cars and in sports.

These differences often carry over through puberty and adulthood. In adulthood, the content of a woman's talk usually centers around people, relationships, diets, clothing, and physical appearance. On the other hand, according to psychologist Dr. Adelaide Haas of the State University of New York, adult males usually talk about activities such as sports or what was done at work, cars, news, music or the mechanics of things.

A similar study by sociolinguist Dr. Cheris Kramarae of the University of Illinois further illustrates this point. She found that "male speech" is characterized as being more forceful, dominating, boastful, blunt, authoritarian and to the point than "female speech," which is perceived as friendlier, gentler, faster, more emotional, more enthusiastic, and tends to focus on more "trivial" topics.

With such vast differences not only in how they talk, but in what they talk about, it stands to reason that when they become adults, men and women have such a difficult time talking to one another.

How well do YOU really know the opposite sex? Try the following quiz to see how much you actually know about the way men and women communicate. There are fifteen statements. Place a True to indicate the statements with which you agree. Place a False for the statements with which you disagree. After you are through, check your answers to determine how well you do know the opposite sex.

He Says, She Says Quiz

_____   1. Co-workers are more likely to listen to men than they are to women at business meetings.

_____   2. Women are more complimentary; they give more praise than men.

_____   3. In general, men and women laugh at the same things.

_____   4. Men interrupt more and will answer a question even when it is not addressed to them.

_____   5. When making love, both men and women want to hear the same things from their partner.

_____   6. Men ask for assistance less often than women do.

_____   7. Men are harder on themselves and blame themselves more often than women.

_____   8. Through their body language, women make themselves less confrontational than men.

_____   9. Women tend to touch others more often than men.

_____ 10. Men and women are equally emotional when they speak.

_____ 11. In general, men and women enjoy talking about similar things.

_____ 12. Women tend to confront problems more directly and are likely to bring up the problem first.

_____ 13. Men tend to favor the right side of the brain, whereas women tend to favor the left side of the brain.

_____ 14. Men speak approximately 8,000 words per day, while women speak approximately 25,000 words per day.

_____ 15. In the book, Men Are From Mars, Women Are From Venus, John Gray compares men to waves in the ocean and women to rubber bands.

Answers to the He Says, She Says Quiz:

1. TRUE — Men are listened to more often than women. An explanation for this may be in the more authoritative nature that is presented by a male figure, i.e., suit, deep voice, physical statue. Women can attempt to achieve this authoritarian manner by wearing dark suits and making a conscientious effort to display the qualities of confidence as they approach the platform or enter the room where the meeting is held.

2. TRUE — Studies show that women are more open in their praise and give more "nods of approval" than men. Women also tend to use more complimentary terms throughout their speeches and often interject "uhm uhms" as indicators of approval when listening to either sex. Both men and women should never overlook the 'Power of Praise.' Praising someone for a job well done is a basic requirement for a healthy relationship. If one wants something done for him, whenever the other person begins to almost do the chore correctly, the other party should begin to praise and soon the chore will get done correctly.

    In a study at a college on the West coast, students in a Psychology 101 class decided to experiment with their instructor. Every time the instructor approached the radiator in the room, the students began to nod their heads in approval, looked very interested in the lecture and even took notes. When he moved away from the radiator, the students began to pretend to nod, stare into space, and doze off. Within three weeks, the professor was sitting on top of the radiator for every lecture.

    I cannot leave the area of praise without making one other comment. It has been always known that we honor the priceless Stratavaros violin or a unique Picasso drawing, but we never honor the actual things/people that make our lives so very happy. Imagine the sound that you would expel if someone laid a $100,000 Stratavaros in your hands; you would say something like, Aaaahhhh. Try honoring your mate the next time you see that person by truly showing him how much you value him and say, "Aaaahhh, I can't believe I'm in the same room as you; how magnificent, how priceless." Learn to honor the people that you love. It can make life much more pleasant.

3. FALSE — Men and women definitely differ in their sense of humor. Women tell jokes less frequently than men and usually only to small, non-mixed sex groups. Men are more likely to tell jokes in a larger, mixed sex group and their humor tends to be more hostile, abrasive and sarcastic than women's humor. Men also tend to joke around with one another as a "bonding" technique or to establish camaraderie with one another.

4. TRUE — A University of California study revealed that 75% to 93% of all interruptions were made by men. It was found that often after being interrupted by the man, the woman became increasingly quiet, pausing more than normal after speaking. It is believed that the reason men interrupt is because interrupting may be a way of establishing dominance. This dominance is also verified by the fact that men are more likely to answer questions that are not even addressed to them and their answers tend to be lengthier and more involved than the questions they were asked.

5. FALSE — In general, women want to be told that they are beautiful and loved, while men want to hear how good their performance was and how they pleased the woman. Not only what each sex wants to hear is different, the thinking that precedes lovemaking is also different. When it gets to cooking, as when it gets to loving, "women often can be compared to crock pots and men often can be compared to microwave ovens."

6. TRUE — Men usually will not ask for help by asking directions, while women will. This is due to men usually being perceived as "givers" of information, while women are often thought of as "takers" of information. As "givers" of information, men tend to think that they are experts in specific areas and do not need the input of others.

7. FALSE — Women tend to be more self-critical and more apt to blame themselves than men. Women tend to be more apologetic when things go wrong. Women also often personalize a problem, take responsibility for it, or blame themselves when they may not ever have instigated it. Women also tend to use more apologetic phrases in their conversations such as, "I'm sorry," "I didn't mean to," "If I can't return it, it's OK," or, "Excuse me."

8. TRUE — Women tend to cross their legs at the ankles or knees and keep their elbows close to their sides; they take up less room in terms of body language. Space and size have always been associated with power and status; therefore, by women keeping their limbs close to their bodies, they tend to make themselves less available for confrontation than men, who always seem to spread their arms across the backs of chairs and cross their legs in more open positions.

9. FALSE — Men tend to touch more than females. According to several researchers, women are more likely to be physically touched by men who guide them through the door, assist them with jackets and coats, and help them into cars. Men also tend to touch one another (i.e., backslapping and hand-shakes) during participation in various sports.

10. TRUE — Men and women are equally emotional when they speak. However, women appear to sound more emotional because they use emotional verbs, such as: I feel, I think, I hope and I wish. Women also have a greater variety of vocal tones when expressing themselves. Women use approximately five tones when expressing themselves, while men only use three tones. This makes men sound more monotonous and unemotional than women. Also, men have been observed to express their emotions through increased vocal intensity such as loudness, yelling, or by using swear words. Women, on the other hand, express themselves by getting quiet, exhibiting a shaky voice quality, or letting out tears.

11. FALSE — Men and women usually talk about different things. Studies indicate that women enjoy talking about personal relationships, personal appearance, clothes, self-improvement, children, marriages, personalities of others, actions of others, relationships at work, and emotionally charged issues that have a personal component. Men, on the other hand, enjoy discussing sports, what they did at work, where they went, news events, mechanical gadgets, latest technology, cars, vehicles and music.

12. TRUE — Even though men make more direct statements, women tend to confront and bring up a problem more often than men. When confronting a problem, though, women tend to be more indirect and polite. As goes the story, a passerby in a little town where a local funeral was going on noticed that all the pallbearers were women. When he asked if all the men in town were busy and couldn't do it, the local answered, "Oh no, it's a woman in that casket and she always said, 'Men didn't take her out while she was alive, then they sure weren't going to take her out once she was dead.'"

13. FALSE — Men tend to favor the left side of the brain (factual, conquering, analytical, objective), while women tend to favor the right side of the brain (feeling, intuitive, less

aggressive, more romantic, more personable). For this reason, sometimes Dads tend to give lectures to kids and Moms tend to give sympathy to kids. A perfect example of this is when the college student calls home and gets Dad on the phone. Dad asks about the car insurance or the checking account balance, and when Mom gets on the phone, she asks about the new friends that you've met, what foods are you eating, or whether or not you remembered to take your vitamins.

14. FALSE — Men speak approximately 12,000 words per day, while women speak approximately 25,000 words per day. I suppose sometimes men wish their wives would have spoken their limited 25,000 words by the time 5:00 p.m. rolls around.

15. FALSE — In John Gray's book, he compares men to rubber bands stating that "when they pull away, they can stretch only so far before they come springing back." Even when a man loves a women, periodically he needs to pull away before he can get closer. Mr. Gray states that, "It is not a decision or choice; it just happens; it is neither her fault or his fault; it is a natural cycle." A man automatically alternates between needing intimacy and independence. In *Men Are From Venus, Women Are From Mars*, John Gray states that, "A woman is like a wave. When she feels loved, her self-esteem rises and falls in a wave motion." A woman reaches a peak when she is feeling good and feeling that she looks good, but when her mood shifts, the wave crashes down. The crash is temporary, because when she reaches bottom, suddenly her mood shifts and she will again feel good about herself, and her wave begins to rise back up. When a woman crashes down, what she needs is someone to be with her as she goes down, to listen to her while she shares her feelings and to empathize with her, not someone telling her why she shouldn't be down. Even if a man can't fully understand why a woman feels overwhelmed, he can offer his love, attention, and support.

If you scored incorrectly on any of these questions, then, perhaps learning more about the differences between men and women can help you when communicating with your spouse, lover, friends, and even business associates.

Let's first take a hard look at all the different ways men and women communicate. Effective communication is the answer. Ninety percent of all people in prison say, "I am here because I just cannot communicate." Sixty percent of all managers that fail, fail because they say, "I'm not any good at communicating; I can't tell people when they have done something well, and I can't tell them when they have done something poorly," and we know that 50% of all marriages that fail, fail because the couple just can't communicate. Take this instance:

Friday afternoon, the husband is in the living room reading the paper and watching television; his wife is in the laundry room doing the laundry. She runs into the living room and yells at her husband, "Quick, get in here, the washing machine just broke."

He looks at her dumbfoundedly and says, "What do you think I should do about it?"

She then replies, "Well, I think you should get in here and fix it!"

He says, "Do you think I look like the Maytag repair man?"

Needless to say, she was angered, and believe me, there was no communication in that house for the entire weekend.

On Monday afternoon, the husband comes home from work and finds his wife happy, and bouncing off the wall with excitement. He looks at her and says, "What is wrong with you?"

She replies, "George from next door came over."

Her husband then says, "Well, what did he want?"

She says, "He really didn't want anything, but he fixed our washing machine."

The husband says, "Gee, that's great!"

She says, "Yeah, that's great, but he wanted a little payment."

He asks, "Well, what did he want?"

She replies, "He didn't want much; he either wanted me to bake him a cake or he wanted a little kiss."

He says, "I bet you baked him a darn good cake."

She then replies, "Do you think I look like Betty Crocker?"

Like it or not, there are basic sex differences which do exist. I will attempt to expose you to these differences by subdividing them into the four basic areas of communication. Those four areas are:

1. Body Language
2. Facial Language
3. Speech and Voice Patterns
4. Behavioral Patterns

BODY LANGUAGE

MEN	WOMEN
1. take up more space	1. take up less space
2. gesture away from their body	2. gesture toward their body
3. gesture with fingers together or point their fingers	3. gesture with fingers apart and curved hand movements
4. assume more reclined positions when sitting and lean backward when listening	4. assume more forward positions, lean forward when listening
5. use arms independently	5. move their entire bodies from their neck to their ankles as a whole

FACIAL LANGUAGE

1. tend to avoid eye contact and do not look directly at the other person	1. look more directly, have better eye contact
2. display frowning and squinting when listening	2. display smiling and head-nodding when listening
3. open jaw less when speaking (tight lipped)	3. open jaw when speaking

SPEECH AND VOICE PATTERNS

1. interrupt others and allow fewer interruptions	1. interrupt less and allow more interruptions
2. mumble words more and have sloppier pronunciation	2. have more precise articulation and better pronunciation

3. are more likely to leave off "ng" from words (comin' and goin')

3. are more likely to include "ng" on words (coming and going)

4. have more monotonous speech when speaking (use approximately 3 tones when speaking)

4. sound more emotional (use approximately 5 tones when speaking)

5. talk at slower rate of speech

5. talk at faster rate of speech

6. monopolize conversations about activities such as cars, jobs, and mechanical things

6. talk about people, relationships, clothes, diets, feelings and children

7. make direct accusations (You don't call.)

7. make indirect accusations (Why don't you ever call?)

8. say "right" or "ok" as interjections

8. say "um hum" as interjections

9. give more direct command (Get me the paper.)

9. use softer command terms and more tones of politeness and endearment (Honey, would you mind getting me the paper?)

10. make declarative statements (It's a nice day.)

10. use "tag endings" on statements (It's a nice day, isn't it?)

11. use fewer emotional verbs

11. use emotional verbs such as (I feel, I love, I hope)

12. when answering questions, offer minimal responses, i.e . . . (Yep, Yes, Fine)

12. when answering questions, elaborate more, explain more, use more adjectives

13. tend to lecture more . . . monologue

13. use give and take more in conversation . . . dialogue

BEHAVIORAL PATTERN DIFFERENCES

1. have analytical approach to problems (left brain)

1. have emotional approach to problems (right brain)

2. use teasing and sarcasm to show affection	2. are openly direct in showing affection
3. are less aware of details (Am I supposed to be a mind reader?)	3. appear more intuitive, more aware of details
4. are more argumentative	4. are less argumentative
5. hold fewer grudges (When the game's over, the game's over.)	5. hold more grudges
6. in an argument, rarely bring things up from past, stick to problem at hand	6. in an argument, bring up from the past
7. are less likely to ask for help, try to figure things out on their own	7. are likely to ask for help when lost
8. do not apologize after a confrontation	8. often apologize after a confrontation
9. tend to take verbal rejection less personally	9. tend to take verbal rejection more personally

Based on all of these findings, it is no wonder that men and women have difficulty communicating with one another on a personal level. Since that is the case, let's examine what men and women need to do to have better personal, social and business relationships with each other.

The following pointers could help MEN better communicate with women:

1. Sit in an upright position instead of reclining in a chair. This gives men a more interested appearance.
2. Gesture closer to the body to appear more intimate and sensitive.
3. Smile more; look directly into a woman's eyes. If you're interested in someone, let them know it.
4. In conversation, respond to topics which a woman brings up. Interject immediate feedback by using "uhm hums" and nods. When men interrupt or change the topic, it tends to make the woman feel

that what she has to say is not important. Remember to make it a dialogue conversation, not a monologue conversation.

5. Get excited when you really like something. Don't be stingy with compliments. Use more adjectives and intensifiers like, "wonderful," "absolutely," "grrreat," and so forth; this makes you sound more interested, sensitive and aware of what the woman is saying.

6. To stimulate conversation, ask about her "feelings" on a certain topic. Doing this makes you appear more sensitive and more attentive. Learn to talk about personal issues and don't be afraid to cry; you'll always win our hearts when you appear more "human and sensitive."

7. Don't ever use command terms with a woman. Never say, "Do this," "Get me that!" Using warm, sincere terms of endearment such as "honey" or "darling" and words of politeness will work wonders with women.

8. Do not be afraid to ask for help. The sooner you ask for assistance, the quicker you will receive it and accomplish what you have to do. Forget about the male ego for a while.

9. Do not yell or curse to release frustration at work. Instead, control your temper and handle yourself in a professional manner at all times.

10. Look directly at the woman you are speaking to and do not look at her from an angle or off to the side. Making direct facial contact gives a person the impression that you are giving your full attention and that you consider what she has to say is important.

The following pointers could help WOMEN better communicate with men:

1. Don't permit a man to interrupt you. If he does, interject and say, "Excuse me, I'm not finished saying what I have to say."

2. Keep abreast of news items and talk about more things men enjoy discussing such as sports, news events, automobiles, the arts, and music.

3. Don't be afraid to approach a man and ask him out, especially if you are interested in him. They, also, need to know that we like them.

4. Don't keep bringing up the past. If problems arise, stick to the matters at hand and try to resolve them.

5. Be comfortable talking about your accomplishments and yourself. Doing so, gives your partner more insight into you and gives him a true sense of who you are and what you are all about.

6. Help a man open up by encouraging more free-flowing conversation and talking about things he is interested in.

7. When talking with male co-workers, make direct statements. Discuss what you did, where you are going and where you went, not how you feel. Try to use words such as, "It is," "We will," or There are," instead of "I feel," "I wish," and "I hope."

8. In business meetings, try to take up more space; spread out your books and papers. Walk around when making a presentation; it gives you a more powerful presence.

9. Slow down your talk; don't be a chatter-box. Never use "tag endings," which make you seem unsure of yourself, such as, "That's a nice car, *ISN'T IT?*"

10. Use stronger quantifiers like "always," "none," or "never," and fewer qualifiers like, "sort of" or "kind of." Strong quantifiers make you sound more confident, factful and less tentative.

11. At work, look at situations and events more critically, objectively and less emotionally. Do not respond to a male's use of swearing unless it is directed to you, then put a stop to it by using a firm tone and letting the man know his behavior is unacceptable.

12. If you have a major disagreement with a co-worker, maintain your professionalism and don't

hold a grudge. Whatever you do, do not cry in front of others. Doing so may make you lose your professional credibility.

13. Do not apologize unless you are wrong. Stop saying "I'm sorry" just to be polite.

The only way you can win the battle of the sexes and close the communication gap forever is for men and women to learn to become each other's best friend. This means understanding one another and being sensitive to and respectful of one another's needs.

The traits of tenderness, gentleness, softheartedness, aggressiveness, and lightheartedness, do not belong to any one gender, but rather they are human traits that are possessed by both men and women. It's quite simple; we all have the same fears, desires, and needs. We all fear rejection and alienation and we all want to be loved, respected, and admired.

We HAVE come a long way, BABY; we now realize and understand that there is nothing particularly wrong with the fact that men and women are "different" and that they communicate "differently." In fact, this "difference" is a blessing that helps make the world a more interesting, beautiful and exciting place to be . . . would we have it any other way?

As a tribute to the women who will read my book, I have incorporated the thoughtful, inspiring manner of Maya Angelou's poetry in MY poem to you.

Beautiful, intelligent women wonder what's my story,
I'm not super smart, but I've definitely experienced glory.
When I start to tell them
They think I'm telling lies.
I say,
It's in the sincerity of my eyes,
The enthusiasm of my smile,
The smoothness of my style,
I'm a woman
Incredibly.
Incredible woman,
That's me.

Men, I'm quite certain, have also wondered
Why they fell in love with me,
My explanations are simple
But they can't find the key.
I say,
It's in all I want to be,
An original sense of fashion,
The spirit of my passion,
The yearning of my mind,
Their need for my kind,
I'm a woman
Incredibly.
Incredible woman,
That's me.

Maybe you now understand
How I can think I'm grand,
I don't need to boast or lie
I know how to reach the sky.
I say,
It's in the languor of my sigh,
The laughter of my lips,
The joy in my hips,
The peace that's in my mind,
The sureness of my kind,
Cause I'm a woman
Incredibly.
Incredible woman,
That's me.

As a tribute to the inspiring, remarkable men that have
touched my life and to all men reading this passage, what
follows is for you.

Beautiful, wondrous, warm and caring,
Thank you for giving to me,
Your mind, your spirit, your laughter, your love,
Those are the ingredients others sometimes never see.
I say,
It's in the warmth of your arms,
The broadness of your chest,
The passion of your kiss,

The giving of your best,
Cause you're a man
Remarkably.
Remarkable man,
That's you.

My respect for men goes back to my grandfathers,
Their courage, their wisdom, their charm,
Second to none,
They were my first loves, when they opened their arms.
Then came my Dad, finally loving, exceedingly strong, exceedingly laid back,
I love him so much, he'd blush at the fact.

Young men, old men, wise men, eager men,
Past men, future men,
I'll dim the light as we begin,
Perhaps surrender to a whim,
And pretend you're one of them.
I say,
It's in the smoothness of your hand,
The emotion you command,
Your soft whisper or caress,
Urging me confess, confess.
The provocative sexiness of your dance,
Daring me to take a chance,
Cause you're a man
Remarkably.
Remarkable man,
That's you.

CHAPTER 3

Reading Others Right: Nonverbal Communication Differences in Personalities

She was a real looker. She sported bouncy red hair, twinkling eyes, a cinched waist and puckered red lips. We worked in the same building, and although we never spoke to each other, we certainly eyed each other. She always appeared peaceful, relaxed and self confident. I wanted to get to know her, wanted to meet her, wanted to see what she was all about.

I asked her friends about her, but they, too, didn't have much information. I even asked to take her home on several occasions, but was told that she still had work to do and couldn't get away. She worked tirelessly, endlessly. When I arrived at work in the mornings, I always noticed her, busy at work. At closing time, she was still at it.

A year after I spotted her on the job, her supervisor, Xavier, informed me that he had had just about enough of her. He said she was getting too old for the job and her replacement would be there within a week. I felt sorry for her, and thought if I tried to console her, it might be my chance to get to meet her.

The day arrived, her position was filled by her replacement, and it was time for goodbyes. As I walked into the room, I saw her sitting quietly, peacefully, with a serene smile on her face, and thought to myself, "What a gal, they'll never get her down."

To my surprise, Xavier said I could take her home if I wanted. I began to grin from ear to ear, eagerly anticipating my chance to get to know her. When I approached, she just sat there, no movement at all, and let me pick her up without

43

hesitation. As I left the room with her, Xavier yelled out, "Jan, you forgot the bottom half of her. It's here in the closet." I thought to myself, "Wow, a closet case, my kind of girl!"

I loaded her into my baby blue Volkswagen Beetle bug convertible, head and bust in the front seat, and spread her legs across the back seat. She seemed quite happy to be going for a ride. On our drive home, I noticed several people looking strangely into my car. I just waved and merrily drove off. She was mine! I had my new friend in tow. My mind raced for a name for her. What was I to call her? Mary, Jane, Susan, Betty, Veronica? Yes, that's it, Veronica. I baptized my new friend, Veronica Mannequin Hargrave, as we sped to our destination.

Veronica and I drove through Houston and once we arrived home, I introduced her to my neighbors. They were quite surprised by how pretty she was, but found her quite withdrawn. She and I toured my apartment. She peered in each of the rooms, but my bedroom was her favorite.

After Veronica settled in, she began to wear my clothes. Oooooh, she loved my pink and black aerobics outfit. She liked it so much, she once kept it on for an entire week. Veronica was easy to get along with; never complaining, always agreeable. She kept to herself. My family and friends took quite a liking to her, too. She became so popular, friends often called to take her out or to line her up with one of their friends. And sometimes, she got better Christmas presents and nicer dates than I did.

Veronica was a dedicated sun worshiper. She loved the pool and the beach, but the sands of time were not ready for her the day my friends propped her head first in their five-foot sand castle. The roaring ocean waves engulfed her, yet thanks to an alert lifeguard, Veronica was saved. It was strange. She'd lie on a floatie in the water for hours and never get burned. I never understood that. She had the best skin, flawless and peachy pink.

Once she came with me to school and helped teach a lesson on Dress for Success. Veronica looked great. She wore a double-breasted black suit. During the presentation, we added pearls to her outfit to give her a professional look, then added a colorful scarf to give her a more casual look. My students fell in love with her. They asked if she could return and wanted her to wear one of their Cheerleader uniforms. She did, was a real trouper, and, of course, had the best pom poms.

During Homecoming week, Veronica was placed alongside our school's mascot to add a dramatic effect to the celebration. If I didn't feel like packing her up, she'd stay at school overnight. I didn't worry much about her. I knew she could take care of herself, but several times when I arrived in the morning, she wasn't in the same position that I had left her in the day before. This seemed to be happening more and more. In fact, I think the cleaning staff was having their way with her in the evenings.

The last straw, though, was when I arrived at school early one morning and found Veronica humped over the copy machine with one hand nearly torn off. It was the worst thing I had ever seen. I soothed her, bandaged her hand (it never healed completely) and made up my mind that day. She was coming home with me and was never to leave my sight.

Veronica and I lived together eight years. She wasn't much of a conversationalist. I'd speak to her on occasion, but she never uttered a word, not even a sound. She just stood there with that peaceful smile on her face. How could she have always been so happy? Nothing upset her. Veronica was agreeable, never left my side and respected anyone I ever brought home. She watched everything I did, knew all my bad habits, and still hung-out with me. Wow, that's a true friend.

Then it happened. While cleaning my house one afternoon, I became startled at what I found. Veronica had never talked, never used the restroom, or even spit, in all the years I had known her. She seemed so delicate, so pure. That hot August afternoon, though, my opinion of Veronica changed. While intensely vacuuming back and forth with my Hoover, making certain that I got every corner of the room, I saw it. It was at her feet. I closed my eyes, opened them wide in disbelief, and stared at it again. Lo and behold, there at her feet was a teeny-tiny ca ca. Yes, a ca ca! Veronica had used the bathroom right there on the floor. I was astonished; who else could it be but her? I hadn't done it! I had no dog, no cat. I delicately picked it up with pink tissue (everything's pink and soft in my house), and ran out my door. I began yelling to my neighbors. "Look what Veronica did!" I screamed, "I can't believe it!" Amazed and disbelieving, we began to analyze the situation.

She wasn't alive, couldn't breathe, yet she had made a ca ca. We analyzed, contemplated, backtracked. Finally, it became clear. I took a sigh of relief, apologized to Veronica, and reaffirmed my belief in my friend. It wasn't Veronica's ca ca at all. It belonged to my neighbor's dog who had visited me earlier in the day. Forgive me, Veronica, I should have never doubted you.

After that incident, her life became more difficult. She suffered a bad fall and split the top of her head from ear to ear. Such pain she went through with that splitting headache, but never complained. She spent time in a casket during a Halloween party, never uttering a word as the guests laughed and merrily carried on around her. Veronica's and my biggest disappointment, though, was that we never found a stiff rod for her to use as a supporting device. She always had to prop herself up against a wall. Certainly that was no indication that she was a wallflower. Not Veronica, she was too entertaining.

I remember the day we parted. I carefully reclined her, smoothed her dress, arranged her hair, and crossed her hands one over the other as if in prayer. Tears flooded my eyes as I kissed her goodbye. She lay in the trunk of my Mom's car, still so peaceful, so calm. I hated to see her go, but our time to part had arrived. Although she now lives in Louisiana, with my niece, I visit her every chance I get. We catch up on gossip, men, and talk about the good old days.

I share my life with Veronica Mannequin Hargrave with you because, although she was not a living person, she had a dynamite personality, a healthy self-concept, and a style all her own. She was different. In fact, she was unique. I know living human beings that are frightened of their uniqueness, and suppress their individuality and personality. Learn a lesson from my friend who became popular and memorable with nothing more than an agreeable and a pleasant expression. Appreciate your differences; be yourself, and trust that your assets will work in wonderful ways to insure your personal and professional success.

Each of us is different. Our uniqueness, like Veronica's, consists of self-concept and personality. How you perceive yourself is your self-concept. How you relate to others, including all the different traits that influence your behavior, defines your personality. These are closely related concepts. How you act toward others is greatly influenced by how you feel about yourself. How you feel about yourself is also determined to a great extent by how others act toward you and by what you believe to be their opinion of you.

If someone were asked to describe the kind of person you are, he probably would describe you in terms of characteristics. He might describe you as sincere, considerate, boastful, stubborn or shy. There are hundreds of additional traits, and variations for each one. Individuality lies in the uniqueness of the combination and degree of one's behavioral traits.

In the 1920's, Carl Jung, the famous Swiss psychiatrist, developed his concept of "personality typing" to explain human differences. "Typing" celebrates healthy differences. It has become an increasingly useful tool for marital therapy, career counseling and management counseling. Thousands of companies use personality testing each year to gather information about themselves and their employees. Organizational tendencies, leadership skills, and communication styles can be determined through these tests.

According to Jung, each of us has two opposite attitudes or ways of looking at the world (extroversion or introversion), and four functions or preferred ways of gathering information and making decisions (feeling, judging, thinking, perceiving). Not being aware of "typing" during a conversation can make a person feel that he is having a talk with someone who speaks a different language. If a feeler, for instance, is asked about the rainy weather, he'll comment, "The sun will be out any minute now. This rain is just about finished."

A thinker would say, "This weather is so gloomy, it makes me feel like not doing a thing." It's similar to a German and an Italian engaged in a conversation, each speaking his own language. They're both talking, but neither is understanding.

Each type has advantages and disadvantages; none is better, worse, or ideal. No one is 100 percent extroverted or introverted, thinking or feeling, judgmental or perceptive. We are a unique blend of all the personality traits.

For my purpose in discussing personality and temperament, I will define each. Temperament is the combination of inborn traits (nationality, race, sex and other hereditary factors) that subconsciously affect our behavior. These traits are passed on by the genes. Personality is the outward expression of ourselves. It is the "face" we show to others. It is the clothes we wear, the smile on our faces. Sometimes it is used as a pleasing facade for an unpleasant or weak temperament.

"I've Got To Be Me," the title of a song that was popular in the 1960's, contains some useful information for the work place. All personality types can get along together if each allows the other to maintain his natural temperament. While we generally like people who are like us, the ones we often fall helplessly, hopelessly in love with are our opposites. Opposites attract. We seek partners who make us feel complete. We look for in others what we lack in ourselves. A thinking, sensing man may be enchanted by the warmth and creativity of a feeling, intuitive woman. She, in turn, may admire his logical head and practicality.

Marriage between polar opposites tends to be exciting, and explosive. These relationships can work if both parties have opportunities to be themselves and both compromise their differences by working on their weaker functions.

The personalities, Sanguines (who exude enthusiasm), Cholerics (who are born leaders), Melancholies (who strive for perfection), and Phlegmatics (who are always calm, cool, and collected), go back as far as 400BC. They are based on the studies of Hippocrates. His philosophy stated that we are born with one basic temperament (personality) and possess some characteristics of a secondary one. This blending of these temperaments identifies our dominant personality style.

An understanding of the personalities provides us with two basic advantages:

1. By examining our own strengths and weaknesses, we learn how to accentuate our positive traits and eliminate or censor our negative traits.

2. By possessing a thorough understanding of others, we realize that because someone is different, his difference is not an evil. It is merely a difference.

Before I describe the four different types of temperaments, take a few moments to check off the Personality Traits document that follows. When you have completed the thirty questions, transfer your marks to the score sheet and add up your totals. Your score will give you a basic view of your primary and secondary personality styles.

PERSONALITY TRAITS

DIRECTIONS: Place a check mark by the *ONE* word in each of the following rows of words that best describes you. Continue through all thirty lines. If you are not sure as to which word best applies to you, ask a spouse or a friend.

STRENGTHS

1.	_____	Precise	_____	Entertaining
2.	_____	Enthusiastic	_____	Dry Humor
3.	_____	Analytical	_____	Hesitant
4.	_____	Courageous	_____	Musical
5.	_____	Smart	_____	Cheerful
6.	_____	Loyal	_____	Leader
7.	_____	Brave	_____	Outgoing
8.	_____	Active	_____	Winner
9.	_____	Objective	_____	Kind
10.	_____	Faithful	_____	Firm
11.	_____	Serious	_____	Supportive
12.	_____	Resourceful	_____	Calm
13.	_____	Gracious	_____	Planner
14.	_____	Indifferent	_____	Comical
15.	_____	Motivating	_____	Cultured

WEAKNESSES

16.	_____	Demanding	_____	Compassionate
17.	_____	Careless	_____	Impatient
18.	_____	Frank	_____	Relaxed
19.	_____	Modest	_____	Unforgiving
20.	_____	Informal	_____	Passive
21.	_____	Materialistic	_____	Spiritual
22.	_____	Unorganized	_____	Suspicious
23.	_____	Worrier	_____	Intense
24.	_____	Explosive	_____	Workaholic
25.	_____	Grateful	_____	Rambler
26.	_____	Moody	_____	Forgetful
27.	_____	Sensitive	_____	Volunteers
28.	_____	Bold	_____	Accidental
29.	_____	Insecure	_____	Possessive
30.	_____	Vindictive	_____	Touchy

TRANSFER ALL YOUR CHECKS TO THE MATCHING WORDS ON THE PERSONALITY SCORING SHEET AND ADD UP YOUR TOTALS

STRENGTHS

_____	Agreeable	_____	Direct
_____	Efficient	_____	Accurate
_____	Decisive	_____	Expressive
_____	Animated	_____	Accommodating
_____	Reserved	_____	Confident
_____	Quiet	_____	Spontaneous
_____	Respectful	_____	Factual
_____	Idealistic	_____	Conforming
_____	Reassuring	_____	Intellectual
_____	Influential	_____	Undemonstrative
_____	Encouraging	_____	Independent
_____	Ambitious	_____	Disciplined
_____	Inoffensive	_____	Work-horse
_____	Competitive	_____	Persistent
_____	Outspoken	_____	Considerate

WEAKNESSES

_____	Exaggerates	_____	Cautious
_____	Bashful	_____	Scheduled
_____	Innocent	_____	Judgmental
_____	Boastful	_____	Interruptive
_____	Critical	_____	Opinionated
_____	Content	_____	Wild
_____	Shy	_____	Domineering
_____	Obsessive	_____	Loud
_____	Procrastinator	_____	Particular
_____	Unemotional	_____	Detailed
_____	Stubborn	_____	Unsure
_____	Easygoing	_____	Candid
_____	Self-conscious	_____	Inflexible
_____	Emotional	_____	Determined
_____	Standoffish	_____	Soft spoken

PERSONALITY SCORING SHEETS

STRENGTHS

SANGUINE		*CHOLERIC*	
1.	_____ Entertaining	_____ Direct	
2.	_____ Enthusiastic	_____ Efficient	
3.	_____ Expressive	_____ Decisive	
4.	_____ Animated	_____ Courageous	
5.	_____ Cheerful	_____ Confident	
6.	_____ Spontaneous	_____ Leader	
7.	_____ Outgoing	_____ Brave	
8.	_____ Active	_____ Winner	
9.	_____ Reassuring	_____ Objective	
10.	_____ Influential	_____ Firm	
11.	_____ Encouraging	_____ Independent	
12.	_____ Ambitious	_____ Resourceful	
13.	_____ Gracious	_____ Work-horse	
14.	_____ Comical	_____ Competitive	
15.	_____ Motivating	_____ Outspoken	

Totals _____   _____

WEAKNESSES

SANGUINE		*CHOLERIC*	
16.	_____ Exaggerates	_____ Demanding	
17.	_____ Careless	_____ Impatient	
18.	_____ Innocent	_____ Frank	
19.	_____ Interruptive	_____ Boastful	
20.	_____ Informal	_____ Opinionated	
21.	_____ Wild	_____ Materialistic	
22.	_____ Unorganized	_____ Domineering	
23.	_____ Loud	_____ Obsessive	
24.	_____ Explosive	_____ Workaholic	
25.	_____ Rambler	_____ Unemotional	
26.	_____ Forgetful	_____ Stubborn	
27.	_____ Volunteers	_____ Candid	
28.	_____ Accidental	_____ Bold	
29.	_____ Emotional	_____ Determined	
30.	_____ Touchy	_____ Standoffish	

Totals _____   _____

Combined
Totals _____   _____
     (Praise)   (Power)

STRENGTHS

MELANCHOLY	*PHLEGMATIC*
_____ Precise	_____ Agreeable
_____ Accurate	_____ Dry Humor
_____ Analytical	_____ Hesitant
_____ Musical	_____ Accommodating
_____ Smart	_____ Reserved
_____ Loyal	_____ Quiet
_____ Factual	_____ Respectful
_____ Idealistic	_____ Conforming
_____ Intellectual	_____ Kind
_____ Faithful	_____ Undemonstrative
_____ Serious	_____ Supportive
_____ Disciplined	_____ Calm
_____ Planner	_____ Inoffensive
_____ Persistent	_____ Indifferent
_____ Cultured	_____ Considerate

Totals _____   _____

WEAKNESSES

MELANCHOLY	*PHLEGMATIC*
_____ Cautious	_____ Compassionate
_____ Scheduled	_____ Bashful
_____ Judgmental	_____ Relaxed
_____ Unforgiving	_____ Modest
_____ Critical	_____ Passive
_____ Spiritual	_____ Content
_____ Suspicious	_____ Shy
_____ Intense	_____ Worrier
_____ Particular	_____ Procrastinator
_____ Detailed	_____ Grateful
_____ Moody	_____ Unsure
_____ Sensitive	_____ Easygoing
_____ Inflexible	_____ Self-conscious
_____ Possesive	_____ Insecure
_____ Vindictive	_____ Soft spoken

Totals _____   _____

Combined
Totals _____   _____
    (Perfection)   (Peaceful)

PERSONALITY SUMMARY

	SANGUINE	*CHOLERIC*
How he sees world	Extrovert	Extrovert
Handles problems	Reacts	Practical
Handles others	Manipulative	Dominates
Others see them	Outgoing	Pushy
At work	Enthusiastic	Organizer
Emotionally	Demostrative	Controlled
Makes friends	Easily	Difficultly
Professions	Public Relations Salesmen Entertainers Preachers Politicians Realtors	Teachers Entrepreneurs Military Service Sports Figures Salesmen Attorneys
Conflict resolution	Charms	Attacks
Social style	Tells	Controls
Falls in love	Easily	Infrequently
Organizational tendencies	"Let's get it done"	"Let's change it"
Comes to a conclusion	Intuitively	Judging
Manages by	Frequent contact with others	Perseverance and one-to-one discussion
Type of car	1935 Brashmobile, fog lights, 16 speaker stereo, wet bar and water bed	Continental or Mercedes black or gray, 500 H.P., steel belt radials and a 60 lb. air horn
Family	3 wives, 27 children, (scattered)	1 wife, 3 children (boys first then 1 girl)
Dog	1 Saint Bernard with Poodle cut, trained to tap dance	200 lb. Shepherd with license to kill
Recreation	Hand buzzing and back thumping	Skiing Mount Everest, swimming Lake Mead

MELANCHOLY	PHLEGMATIC
Introvert	Introvert
Persistent	Permissive
Inflexible	Conforms
Critical	Hesitant
Planner	Agreeable
Deep	Sympathetic
Cautiously	Easily
Accountants Musicians Inventors Doctors Engineers Architects	Retail Bankers School Administrators Therapists Librarians Psychologists Craftsmen
Negotiates	Avoids
Asks	Listens
Cautiously	Eagerly
"Let's look at it another way"	"Let's keep it"
Logically	Perceiving
Perseverance and personal distance	Laid-back, flexible
Chrysler Imperial or New Yorker, computerized ignition, full set of design specs and testing data	American Motors Station wagon, beige with factory recommended tires, no horn, 140 H.P.
1 wife, 2.3 children	½ wife, 1 or 2 children (if it's OK)
2 Standard Poodles with papers	A Cocker Spaniel with paper fetching permit
Counting the bulls in a Merrill Lynch ad, correcting the encyclopedia	Whatever everybody else wants to do

Now that you have taken the test, how do you feel? Did you know all that about yourself? Probably no one else has ever come up with the exact blend of strengths and weaknesses you have. Most people score high totals in one temperament, with a second temperament also showing a relatively high total. These two temperaments make up your personality blend and cause you to respond to circumstances as you do. Let's meet the four temperaments.

SANGUINES-Life is for living.

"Life is a play. It's not the length,
but the performance that counts."

Sanguines are warm, outgoing, and demonstrative, and feel that they must entertain others. They are emotional, make work into fun, and love to be with people. Feelings, rather than rational thoughts, are used to form the Sanguine's decisions. They're so outgoing, they're usually considered superextroverts. Sanguines have an unusual capacity for enjoying themselves and usually pass on their fun-loving spirit to everyone present. Their motto: "If it's not fun anymore, I don't want to do it," dominates throughout their lives. They're fascinating storytellers. The Sanguine's warmth and vivid recreations help others to relive the experience as he tells it.

Sanguines may not have more talent or opportunity than other temperaments, but they always seem to have more fun. Their bubbly personalities and natural charisma draw people to them. As they grow up they continue to draw friends. They have leads in plays, are voted most likely to succeed, and become cheerleaders. At work, Sanguines are the ones who plan the office party or volunteer to decorate for Christmas.

They tend to be very talkative, sometimes talking endlessly from the time they get up in the morning to the time they go to bed at night. One of their favorite habits is to hold on to their listeners as they speak. This grasping is done because the Sanguines are afraid the listener will leave before they finish saying what they have to say. They touch, hug, pat, kiss and stroke their friends. They get so excited, they finish sentences for others. In traffic, I can often spot a Sanguine. Instead of watching where they're going, they're looking over at the person in the car with them and talking a mile a minute. If there's no one in the car with them, they're looking over in the next car to see if they recognize someone inside.

Sanguines are not good with detail. They have trouble remembering names, dates, places and facts. They volunteer for projects, but don't always follow through. Their closets are a mess. If they need clothes, they just reach in and pull out the first thing they get their hands on. Sanguines prefer loud colors and will always remember the colors of the clothing people wore, instead of remembering names and topics of conversation. They call people Honey, Sweetie, Baby; names of others are not important to them, but their own name is.

They love to be noticed. Sanguines like center stage and do well in careers as greeters, hosts, receptionists, masters of ceremonies and club presidents. They never want to miss anything. At parties, if one is involved in one conversation and hears his name mentioned across the room, he will stop midsentence and turn to the new voice. They want to know everything; they even go as far as trying to find out the details about their own surprise birthday parties.

As babies, they coo and laugh at anything. They're happy to be picked up by just about anybody and love to play Patty-cake, Patty-cake. As they grow up, Sanguines keep their child-like qualities. While other temperaments desire to leave childhood behind, the Sanguine's wide-eyed innocence follows them well into old age.

They bounce on the tips of their toes as they walk because of their abundance of energy and enthusiasm. Their mannerisms are extremely large, far away from their bodies, and the animation in their faces, while speaking, can wear their viewers out. Sanguines like to charm others and do so, by talking excitedly to everyone they meet. They can't help themselves; it's almost like a sickness.

I'm a Sanguine and can relate to this description. I was making copies of documents recently and noticed two women at the copy machine next to me, also making copies. For no reason at all, I said to them, "You girls look real busy." Neither of them answered. I thought to myself they probably didn't hear me and again said, "You ladies look as though you really have a lot of copying to do."

One of the women glared at me and said, "We're glad you said *Ladies*, because we certainly don't see any *Girls* here!"

You'd think I would have learned my lesson, but I just keep talking and talking to everyone I see. I tell you, it's a sickness.

CHOLERICS - Life is for doing.

"Life consists not in holding good cards,
but in playing those cards you hold well."

This extroverted, opinionated personality thrives on activity. Cholerics take pride in accomplishing activities that others think are impossible. In every case, their stubborn determination allows them to succeed where others have failed.

Cholerics are natural born leaders, and like the Sanguine, are outgoing and optimistic. But, while the Sanguine is talking, the Choleric is doing. They're the easiest temperament to understand and get along with, as long as you live by their golden rule: "You're going to do it my way NOW!" As they're relating their motto to others, they usually point a 50 foot finger at their listener's face.

The Choleric likes to take charge and begins to do so at a very young age. As early as three, a mother says to a Choleric baby, "We'll go eat pizza tonight."

The baby says, "HAMBURGER, Mama."

The mother says, "No, baby, we'll eat pizza."

The baby yells back, "HAMBURGER, Mama, HAMBURGER."

The mom then says, "OK, I guess it's hamburger we'll have." Cholerics learn at a very young age that they can control others by directly demanding what they want.

Cholerics can run anything. They solve problems, save time and decide on issues instantly. They have the innate ability to rise to the top and take over. They're more concerned with reaching goals, though, than with pleasing people. They have the answers, they know what to do, they can make quick decisions, they bail others out, but they are rarely popular with people because their assertiveness and confidence make others feel insecure. Their ability to lead and not care what others think makes them appear bossy. They frequently become loners, not by intent, but because no one can keep up with them.

Have you ever spoken to someone for a while and any subject you chose to speak on, they always seemed to know it better? They had been there, done that, experienced it. These people are probably Choleric. They always think they know better than the rest of us and that tends to tic us off. But, know what, they usually do know better than the rest of us. Cholerics are very resourceful. They research, they read, they have the correct answers.

They're determined. It is visible in their walk and in the way they drive their cars. They hit the floor, heel first, then toe, heel, toe, with so much intensity in each step that the jowls on their faces jiggle. This hard, fast, determination is also demonstrated by the death-grip in which they hold their steering wheels and their floor-boarded feet on car accelerators.

Since the Choleric is so anxious to keep tight control on others, he also is in control of himself at all times. He does not sympathize easily with others, nor does he cry in the presence of others. He is often embarrassed or disgusted by the tears of others and regards these as weaknesses in people. This unemotional quality makes the Choleric able to excel in emergencies. They don't get upset; they take charge. They notify the fire department, tell everyone the best exit routes, and then begin using the fire extinguisher to help calm the flames. (Of course they've had CPR training. They know everything.)

Cholerics make excellent entrepreneurs, military service personnel, sports figures, and teachers. Remember your teacher saying to you, "You'll do it until you do it right!" Cholerics want to make everything that is wrong, right. They straighten your crooked pictures when visiting, tell you what lane to drive in on the highway, assign your seat when entering a restaurant, and pull lint off your suits. Even if they don't have the right cards, Cholerics will scold you for playing the wrong card when you're their bridge partner.

MELANCHOLIES - Life is for learning.

"If it's worth doing, it's worth doing right."

Do you know anyone who makes lists and lists and lists? Someone who goes to bed at night, realizes that something that needs to be completed from the list is not, and gets up to complete the chore? Then, after it's done, finds his list and scratches the completed item? If you do, then you've met a schedule-oriented, organized Melancholy. Not only do they complete tasks, Melancholies complete each task with perfection and commitment.

Their motto, "If it's worth doing, it's worth doing right," is present in all of their endeavors. They think through every situation, analyze the pros and cons, then proceed with their plans.

The Melancholy is the richest of all the temperaments. They are analytical, gifted perfectionists with a very sensitive emotional nature. Without the Melancholy, we would have very little poetry, art, literature, philosophy or symphonies. They bring to us culture, refinement, taste and talent. The Melancholies are the deepest thinkers of all the personalities. They evaluate everything. If you mention to a Melancholy that you like his shirt, he thinks to himself, "Did she really like my shirt, or is she making fun of my shirt?" While the Sanguine is talking and the Choleric is doing, the Melancholy is analyzing, planning, creating and inventing.

They are very patient and stick to an assignment until it is accomplished. They sit through piano lessons, enjoy writing research papers, and enthusiastically tackle difficult math problems. Unlike the Sanguine's boisterous, spontaneous speech, Melancholies communicate with softly spoken, well thought out messages. Their mannerisms are very close to their bodies and little expression can be seen in their faces as they talk. Since they are somewhat insecure, they tend to lean against walls or tables as they speak and stand with their weight on one leg. Melancholies tend to drag one foot as they walk. You can always tell one, because the heel of one shoe will be worn down.

The Melancholy's determination to understand things has labeled them as the smartest of all the personalities. Aristotle said, "All men of Genius are of Melancholy temperament." It is believed that Einstein and Michelangelo were Melancholies. It took Michelangelo four years, lying on his back, to paint the scene on the ceiling of the Sistine Chapel at the Vatican in Rome. Melancholies are completers. Can you imagine what would happen if a Sanguine were assigned to paint that same picture? He'd paint for a half hour, and when it was no longer fun, he'd feel he had painted enough and get up and leave.

Quality, rather than quantity, is always more important to the Melancholy. It's never a matter of how fast something can get done, but how well it can get done. If a Melancholy is in charge of a project, you can bet that it will be done correctly and on time. They read directions before putting bicycles together, write grocery lists before going shopping, and love to find a bargain.

Melancholies make excellent counselors because they are willing to listen to people's problems, analyze them, and come up with workable solutions. They believe that reason and logic can solve everything. Melancholies are looking for perfection in every part of their lives. For this reason, they usually marry late in life. Since their goal is to find the ideal mate, and we know that no one is perfect, Melancholies have a hard time finding someone that they'd like to spend their organized, purposeful, analytical lives with.

Melancholies are deep, faithful and devoted. They will never tell you that they love you first, but when they do fall in love with you and are certain of your love for them, Melancholies will love you for a lifetime. They make deep commitments. Their memories are so superb that they never forget names or hurt feelings. The classmate who remembers everyone's name at the twenty year class reunion surely is a Melancholy.

Their desks at the office will usually contain objects that can be taken apart and put back together again. Because Melancholies are so analytical, they need to figure out how things work. Since they're such perfectionists, they don't drive their cars in the slow lane, nor the fast lane. They drive in the next to slow lane, follow the speed limit, and can't understand why the Sanguines and Cholerics are speeding by them at eighty miles an hour.

As children, Melancholies drift to the parent that is the most organized. They're fussy, eat on time, sleep on time, and play at designated times, and hate to be passed from hip to hip while being carried. At young ages, Melancholies neatly pick up all their toys before taking a nap.

Because of their need for accuracy and orderliness, many Melancholies become accountants, inventors, engineers or scientists. Certainly it was a Melancholy, after careful analysis and deliberation, who determined the scientific theory concerning Saturn: "The scientific theory that I like best is that the rings around Saturn are composed entirely of lost airline luggage." Who else would even care?

PHLEGMATICS - Life is for peace.

Rule 1: "Don't sweat the small stuff."
Rule 2: "It's all small stuff."

The peace loving Phlegmatic is God's gift to the other crazy personalities. They're never in a hurry and usually don't get disturbed over situations that bother the rest of us. Their motto, "Peace, no matter what," follows them through life. Phlegmatics don't offend, avoid conflicts and decisions, and quietly do what is expected of them without looking for credit. (Veronica Mannequin Hargrave is a Phlegmatic). They're the easiest type of person to get along with and the most likeable of all the temperaments.

Phlegmatics are easy to spot. If you ask someone where he wants to have dinner and he responds, "Anywhere you want." Then you say again, "But really, where would you like to have dinner," and he again responds, "Anywhere you want," he is Phlegmatic. To Phlegmatics, anywhere you take them is fine. They don't like to make decisions. If they must make a decision, it's never a spontaneous one. They'll usually contemplate for a while and then say, "Let me think about it and I'll get back to you."

Phlegmatics are the one temperament that remains consistent every time you see them. Beneath their cool, almost timid personality lies someone who is dependable, respectful and supportive. One of the most admirable traits of the Phlegmatic is his ability to stay calm at all costs. Emotion doesn't overwhelm him. He backs up, waits a minute, then moves quietly in the right direction. Phlegmatics also take this same approach when driving. They come to a full stop at a stop sign, look around, press on the accelerator, go up a bit, then hit the brakes again. They stop, start, stop, then start again. They can't decide whether they need to drive through the sign or not.

In business, Phlegmatics prove to be competent, steady workers who get along with everyone. They follow orders, work patiently through the ranks, and never need to have their own way.

Because of his kindness and gentleness, the Phlegmatic has loads of friends. If a friend visits, the Phlegmatic will drop everything, sit down and relax. They're the best listeners. Have you ever spoken to someone for a long time and as you walked away said to yourself? "That's the nicest person I ever met." Of course he was nice; he listened to everything you said. Phlegmatics always get the prettiest boyfriends and girlfriends because of their intense listening skills. They enjoy parties because they can sit back, watch, and be entertained by others.

Even though their voices are soft and their mannerisms are small, the Phlegmatic has a funny streak and a quite will of iron. Their idea of humor is in cutting, sly remarks, and although they're hard to upset, once they've had enough, they'll let you know and then the incident will never be mentioned again.

Phlegmatics stand with their hands in their pockets and constantly play with their change. They shift all their weight on one foot, place the other foot in front and stand there with an expressionless look on their faces. As they walk, they tend to turn their toes and hips out in an unhurried Charlie Chaplin shuffle. This unhurried shuffle of the Phlegmatic is his cool, calm manner for never breaking a sweat. Phlegmatics don't sweat the small stuff, and even realize it's all small stuff.

GETTING ALONG WITH A DIFFERENT COMMUNICATION STYLE

Now that you have analyzed your personality style, and understand temperments, let's examine how to get along with people that are different from you.

SANGUINES

1. Give them credit or applause upon completion of a job.
2. Recognize their difficulty in accomplishing tasks.
3. Don't expect them to remember appointments or be on time.
4. Support their dreams and intuitions.
5. Remember that their emotions go up and down, depending on the circumstances around them.
6. Motivate decision making by offering incentives.
7. Realize that they mean well.

8. Remember that they love presents (childlike qualities).

Choleric

1. Give them results.
2. Indicate how valuable their time is.
3. Recognize that they are born leaders.
4. Be efficient, but insist on two-way communication.
5. Support their conclusions and actions.
6. Know that they don't mean any harm; they just speak straight out.
7. Motivate decision making by giving them options and probabilities.
8. Realize that they are not passionate.

Melancholy

1. Give them statistical findings.
2. They need a climate that provides details.
3. Follow schedules. Be accurate, use charts, grafts.
4. Know that they are very sensitive and get hurt easily.
5. Support their principles and thinking.
6. Compliment them sincerely and lovingly.
7. Motivate decision making by giving them evidence and service.
8. Accept that they like it quiet sometimes.

Phlegmatic

1. Give them attention.
2. They need a climate that suggests.
3. Support their feelings (motivate them), help them set goals.
4. Motivate decision making by giving them guarantees and assurances.
5. Don't expect enthusiasm.
6. Encourage them to accept responsibilities.

Laugh with the Sanguines, work with the Cholerics, analyze with the Melancholies, and relax with the Phlegmatics. Enjoy others for their differences, rather than disliking them for their disparities.

Reviewing the wonderful qualities of all the various personalities makes me think how dull life would be if any one of them were missing. It doesn't matter which way we each look at life or how we behave. What matters is that we each make an impact in this life, that through our differences we add excitement and balance to what might otherwise become a monotonous existence.

CHAPTER 4

Love Signs:
Nonverbal Communication
Courtship Gestures

XXXXXXXXXX, Take a long, slow, deep breath; relax your entire body; close your eyes. Prepare yourself for a pleasant journey; you are returning to your past. You are with that special someone who made your knees weak, your heart pound, your stomach churn. You have longed for his lips upon yours; at last you are alone. Now submerge yourself in the feeling of your first stolen kiss. Imagine lifting your face to his and experiencing the excitement of your first long, lingering, wet, passionate, kiss; feel the sharp pangs of sorrow that accompanied the farewell kiss; it's such a simple thing, but that decision to kiss for the first time is a crucial one in any love story.

When I was in high school, nice girls didn't go all the way, but man, did we kiss! We kissed for hours in the busted-up front seat of a borrowed Chevy; we kissed extravagantly on the swing of a back porch; we kissed delicately, in timid explorations. We kissed torridly, with lips not wanting to part; we kissed elaborately, as if we were inventing kisses for the first time; we kissed articles of clothing or objects belonging to our boyfriends; we kissed our hands when we blew our boyfriends kisses across the street. We kissed shamelessly, with all the robust sappiness of youth; we kissed as if kissing could save us from ourselves.

A kiss may seem only the movement of the lips, yet it can capture deep, wild emotions. Many theories exist about how this delightful activity began. Some believe it evolved from the act of smelling, inhaling a face out of friendship or love in order to measure mood and well-being. In some cultures today people still greet one another by putting heads together and inhaling each other's essence. Some sniff each other's hands. Because the membranes of the lips are exquisitely sensitive, we often use the mouth to savor texture. The sensory receptors in the nose add to this pleasureable experience by adding flavor. It seems very likely that we may have really started kissing as a way to taste-and-smell someone.

We don't just kiss romantically, of course; we also kiss dice before we roll them, kiss our own hurt finger or that of a loved one, kiss a religious symbol or statue, kiss the flag of our homeland or the ground itself after we return home from a long journey, kiss a good-luck charm, kiss a photograph, kiss the bishop's ring and kiss our own fingers to signal farewell to someone.

Hershey sells small foil-wrapped candy "kisses;" in America, we "kiss off" someone when we dump them, and then yell "kiss my _____," when we're angry. Some of us press lipsticked mouths to the back of envelopes being mailed to our sweethearts; we even refer to pool balls as "kissing" when they touch delicately and then move away from each other.

Drawing a row of XXXXX's at the bottom of a letter to represent kisses began in the Middle Ages, when some were illiterate and a cross was acceptable as a signature on a legal document. To pledge their sincerity, they would kiss their signature. In time, the "X" became associated, though, with the kiss alone.

Perhaps the most famous nonverbal kiss message in the world is Rodin's sculpture *The Kiss*, in which two lovers, sitting on a rocky ledge, embrace tenderly, and kiss forever. Her left hand is wrapped around his neck and he rests his open right hand on her thigh, seemingly ready to play her leg as if it were a musical instrument. They are glued together by touch at the shoulder, hand, leg, hip, chests, and mouths. Touching in only a few places, they seem to be touching in every cell. Ecstasy pours from every inch of them. The greatness of Rodin is his ability to "fill his sculptures with life," capture desire, emotion, tenderness and love in an object that did not even move.

Desire, emotion, tenderness and love are feelings that can be communicated by gestures and body movements without words being spoken. While some courtship signals are studied and deliberate, other are given unconsciously.

He loves me, he loves me not; he loves me, he loves me not. Sound familiar to you? I bet it does. We've all wondered just how much someone loves us, or if they love us at all. Therefore, we'll begin at the beginning.

Silent language has been used for years to woo someone we find attractive. We see it in the sexual posturing of the body; we feel it in the heated, direct or indirect glances; we are very aware of what is going on, and it is our choice to answer or not. Shall I call this "flirting?"

Usually, females make the first move in attracting attention, using one of fifty-two different kinds of behavior. A key fact concerning love signs is that "you have to give in order to receive." You must be approachable, if you want to be approached.

Men and women's courtship signals fall into three main categories: movements of the face or head, gestures, and posture changes. Psychologists studying dating among Americans have identified what they call a "courtship dance" that leads from that initial first meeting to a loving relationship. For the courting to be successful, the man must wait for an appropriate signal from his partner before moving to the next step of the dance. When the male holds the female's hand, for example, he must wait until she presses his hand, before attempting the next step, which is entwining his fingers with hers.

My mind drifts back to the words of a poem I read years ago that reawakens the "courtship dance" in my mind. The poem compared loving relationships to dancing, I will translate it to you in my own words. "If you hold me too tightly, you'll smother me and surely I'll run away; but if you hold me too loosely, I know again, I'll stray. Let's make it a back and forth motion, swaying your way sometimes, and sometimes swaying mine . . .."

Men and women label one another "slow" or "fast" depending on how they move through this dance. Those who skip a few steps are considered "fast". It is a step by step process. Remember the song....."If you touch my calf, you're going to want to touch my thigh, and if you touch my thigh, you're going to want to touch my waist, and if you touch my waist, you're going to want to touch my breast, and on and on."

It is almost as though there is a dance/courtship protocol that we subconsciously all follow.

MALE COURTSHIP SIGNALS:

The first step in courtship for a male is to attract attention to himself so that eye-contact can be made. There are various ways of doing this. Most involve a form of self-grooming, such as adjusting the tie, fiddling with the collar, rearranging cuff links or smoothing hair. Another way to attract positive attention is to carry an interesting object (book, Wall Street Journal, etc.) that could be used if someone noticed it and wanted to start a conversation. It is much easier to talk about something, rather than to someone, when the two parties do not know each other.

Once attention has been caught, the next step in successful courtship is the correct use of eye contact and facial expression. Long stares and lingering looks at this stage are not favorable in the "dance" protocol. An initial gaze of around three seconds is appropriate, and you should not smile immediately upon making eye contact. The message that is conveyed by the delayed smile is, "I was only being polite at first, but now that I've taken a good look, WOW!"

Initial eye contact should last about two seconds. It should be broken by looking downward, either right or left. Gaze should then be immediately re-established, with a high-intensity simple smile and perhaps an eyebrow flash can even accompany it. You should continue to smile and gaze for a few more seconds before making an approach.

If you want to convey a more macho image, the eye contact should be longer and the smile either made less intense or avoided entirely. Posture should be less relaxed and more dominant. One way in which a man can signal dominance is to "take possession" of part of the room or furniture; to spread out; meaning his arms or belongings.

Once the preening has occurred, men then go into a variety of more serious courtship signals. Let's progress from the simple to the complex:

1. Three things that are done with the jacket that buttons or zips are crucial signs in courtship. Men begin by slowly buttoning and unbuttoning, or zipping and unzipping the jacket, indicating slight nervousness. They then open the jacket at the waist with both hands and hold it open in this position for a few minutes; indicating further discomfort and nervousness. The third and most crucial step is when they take the jacket off after having completed steps

one and two. Taking the jacket off means, you have them hook, line and sinker.

2. Men show interest in women by playing with circular objects in the presence of the woman. He may squeeze, then let go of, a Coca Cola can or a glass, then squeeze and let go again. What he is actually implying is: "I'd like to squeeze you, Baby."

3. Glancing at a woman's body, and letting her see him do it is also a courtship gesture made by males.

4. My favorite male courtship gesture, that seems to happen daily all over the world is the sock-pulling gesture. When uncomfortable or nervous, in the presence of a woman, men tend to pull their socks up.

5. Lightly stroking either the outer or, less often, the inner thigh is an indication of sexual interest.

6. When seated in a chair or leaning against a wall, he may sometimes spread his legs to give a crotch display.

7. To accentuate physical size and show readiness to be involved with a female, men will often stand with their hands on their hips.

8. The most aggressive sexual display a man can make is the aggressive thumbs-in-belt, "cowpoke" stance. This is accomplished when one or both thumbs are hooked into the belt of the pants with the downwardpointing fingers framing the groin area.

9. Partly unbuttoned shirts, masculine-smelling colognes, softness of winter sweaters, sleekness of combed-back hair, and flashy sports cars are all used by men when courting.

10. Men in a courtship situation usually tend to have high muscle tone, that is, body sagging seems to disappear, stomachs are tucked in a little tighter and chests tend to protrude a little more. It seems that the body assumes a more erect posture than usual.

11. Sly winks, accidental touches beneath a business table, gentle rubbing of the back and moving in closer are also all considered courtship gestures.

12. Excited interest can be seen by a flushed appearance in the cheeks and pupil dilation.

FEMALE COURTSHIP SIGNALS:

As dancer Martha Graham once stated, "Nothing is more revealing than movement," and women have, at times deliberately, at times unconsciously, and at times unfortunately, used movement in some form or another to get courtship messages across.

Women have a far greater and more subtle repertoire of courtship signals than men do. The redness of our lips, the softness of our skin and even the height of our heels all convey courtship. From the tip of our heads to the soles of our feet, we can use every inch of ourselves in a silent message that says, "I'm available."

1. Women toss their hair, whether long or short, briskly from side to side, over a shoulder, or away from the face to indicate preening.

2. Sometimes with partially dropped eyelids, the woman holds the man's gaze just long enough for him to notice, then she quickly looks away. This has the tantalizing feeling of peeping or being peeped at, and can light the fires of most normal men.

3. Women also use the sideways glance to show interest. This glance involves looking at the man through partially closed eyelids, but dropping the gaze a moment after it has been noticed.

4. Licking the lips, slightly pouting the mouth, or applying cosmetics to moisten or redden the lips all are indicators of a courtship invitation.

5. Slight exposure of the shoulder from a partially fallen blouse is again an example of "flirting." Rae Dawn Chong said it best: "You can seduce a man without taking anything off ... without even touching him." This revealed shoulder is one example.

6.   When women massage their necks or head with one hand, it has the effect of raising the breast on one side of the body and intensifying cleavage. It also exposes the armpit, which, even when shaved, has an erotic significance.

7.   A female interested in making a subtle courtship gesture might gradually expose the smooth, soft skin of her wrists. The wrist area has long been considered one of the highly erotic areas of the body. In this position, the palms of a woman are also made visible to the male.

8.   Playing with any cylindrical object such as a pencil, pen, stem of wineglass or finger is often a reflection of subconscious desires.

9.   Sometimes women will even accentuate the roll in their hips when walking in front of a male they want to attract.

10. When a woman sits with one leg tucked under the other and points the folded leg toward the person whom she wants to attract, the message communicated is, "I feel very comfortable with you. I'd like to get to know you better."

11. Women tend to stand with their legs apart with weight on one foot, when displaying a sign of openness or availability.

12. Slowly crossing and uncrossing the legs while being watched by an interested male is a strong attraction signal, especially if the woman is simultaneously slightly stroking her thigh.

13. Women entwine their legs to draw attention. Most men agree that the leg twine, (one leg is pressed firmly against the other to give the appearance of high muscle tone) is the most appealing sitting position a woman can take.

14. Once the legs are crossed, sometimes a woman begins to slightly kick her top leg back and forth. This kicking or thrusting, again, displays a courting signal.

15. Dangling one shoe while seated in a relaxed position, with one leg crossed over the other at the knee, is one of the most intense courtship signals women use to indicate interest in a male.

16. Even when a woman keeps time to music with her head or hands, leans forward towards a male, or even sometimes brushes the male's body with her hand or breast, she is still conveying effective courtship gestures.

Now that we have gone over the signals that attract, let's examine the steps taken once the couple gets together.

1. Eyeing the eyes. As intimacy increases so does the amount of mutual eye contact, resulting in those long, soulful, longing looks so beautifully described by romantic poets.

2. Hand touches hand. This hand contact is usually light, but lingering. Sometimes it is disguised by some apparently innocent action; placing one hand beneath your partner's elbow to guide him or her through a crowded restaurant, helping to put on a coat, or even touching his chest pretending to admire his muscles. Even handing someone a paper or a pen is a way we "reach" others when we are too afraid to touch.

3. Hand touches shoulder. This gesture, too, can be hidden by some socially acceptable gesture. This is the point at which either party can withdraw from the encounter without either suffering too much loss of pride. Both can pretend that no advance was made. The next step, though, involves a definite commitment.

4. Arm encircles waist. This movement signals a desire for greater intimacy. If this is accepted and continu-

ously invited, then the couple moves quickly to the next step. Once couples feel fairly comfortable with each other, more intimate steps are taken.

5.   Mouth touches mouth. The intense kiss is a uniquely human nonverbal signal that lets the partners know that each cares for the other.

6.   Hand caresses head, hair and face. This is especially significant because it indicates great trust between the couple. Because our heads are extremely vulnerable, only those we feel close to and at ease with, can touch them without our protest.

7.   Hand touches body. The couple begin to explore each other's bodies through clothing or probing beneath them. By step 7 the couple has "eyes only for each other," and the proximity is so close that they often close their eyes. They can even seem to be able to eliminate useless and distracting noises, (Sometimes asking each other: "Is there anyone else in here besides us?") allowing them to concentrate more fully on their delicate senses of temperature, smell and touch.

The temperature of a normal, healthy human is 98.4 degrees Fahrenheit, but skin temperature is always lower than this and varies according to our emotional state. When we are anxious or afraid, our temperature drops as blood is sent back to the muscles. If we are relaxed or in the state of courtship, the blood flows back from the muscles to the capillaries in the skin, therefore increasing our temperature. When a man or woman is described as "hot stuff" or we speak of a "warm embrace," it may well be literally true.

We have long used the sense of smell to attract and squire others. It is known that three centuries before the birth of Christ, Aristotle noted that the Romans took fragrant baths and massages with sweet-smelling oils before going out to court. In fact, the first gift to the Christ Child was incense.

What part does smell play in courtship? I am certain that, blindfolded, you could recognize by smell any man that you have known intimately. When a lover goes away or a husband dies, an anguished woman goes to his closet and takes out a bathrobe or shirt, presses it to her face, and is overwhelmed by tenderness for him. Few men report similar incidents, but women, in general, have a stronger sense of smell. In the movie "Scent of a Woman," Al Pacino demonstrates how, since his blindness, he is quite capable of using his sense of smell to describe the details of a woman sitting at the table next to him. Research done by Robert Henkin, from the Center for Sensory Disorders at Georgetown University, suggests that a quarter of the people with smell disorders find that their sex drive disappears.

Nothing is more memorable than a smell. One momentary, fleeting scent can conjure up a childhood memory of summers at the lake, blueberry bushes, first-grade glue, or your grandmother's house. Yet another unexpected scent can stir up memories of hours of passion on a moonlight beach or a family dinner of pot roast and sweet potatoes.

Smells lie softly in our memories like land mines, hidden under years of experiences, but one quick, scent can make the memories explode and the vision comes to life. Cover your eyes and you will stop seeing, cover your ears and you will stop hearing, but if you cover your nose and try to stop smelling, you will die. Breaths come in pairs, inhaling and exhaling; except at two times in our lives—the beginning and the end. At birth, we inhale for the first time; at death, we exhale for the last time. In fact, per day, we breathe approximately 23,040 times.

Smell is the most direct of all of our senses. Unlike the other senses, smell needs no interpreter. Hold a violet to your nose and inhale, the effect is immediate and no translation is needed by language or thought. The perfume industry has capitalized on this fact and bombards us with smells everywhere to catch our attention. It has even been noted that when we give perfume to someone, we seemingly are giving them liquid memory. Chanel No. 5, which was created in 1922, has remained the classic for sensual femininity. Once, when asked by a reporter what she wore to bed, Marilyn Monroe flirtatiously replied, "Chanel No. 5."

All this brings to mind the story of the beautiful young princess, who, having danced for a long time and feeling slightly overcome by the heat of the ballroom, went into a dressing room where one of the Queen's maids helped her to change into a clean chemise. The Royal Duke, who came by chance into the room after the young princess had left, picked up the discarded chemise and used it to wipe his face. "From that moment on," noted a contemporary writer, "the Duke conceived the most violent passion for her."

This story, fictitious or not, is reminiscent of the gentleman who offers a woman a crisp, white handkerchief to wipe her face after slightly perspiring during a walk in the park, or for that matter, the finely sculptured body builder who offers his large towel to a woman in the gym. It's something to think about; it kind of makes you want to go "uhmmmmmmm!"

Since the delicate sense of touch is also so important in non-verbal courtship gestures, it is only fitting that we examine it more fully. Our skin, weighing from six to ten pounds, is the largest organ we have on our bodies. It longs, needs, desires to be touched and is the key organ of sexual attraction. Our skin is what stands between us and the world; it is waterproof, washable and elastic, but most of all it houses our sense of touch.

Some parts of the body are ticklish, and others respond when we itch, shiver, or get goosebumps. Feeling doesn't take place in the topmost layer of skin, but in the second layer. The top layer of skin sloughs off easily. This is why safecrackers sometimes sandpaper their fingertips; it makes the top layer of the skin thinner and more sensitive to touch.

We remember the feel of a loved one's hand, how his body curves, the texture of his hair. Touch allows us to find our way even in darkness. Sometimes we use our hands as though we were brailling another. Think of the ways we use our hands to calm our selves. We hide our faces in our open palms, we wrap our hands around our shoulders and rock as if we were a mother comforting a child, or we press an open palm to a cheek when startled. Touch is so important in emotional situations that sometimes we touch ourselves in the way we'd like someone else to comfort us. Hands are messengers of emotions.

When we are distressed, we wring our hands and caress them as if they were separate people. At the outset of a romance, the feel of the first shared touch can last a life time, and holding the hand of someone ill or elderly soothes them and gives them an emotional lifeline.

The more we are affectionately cuddled and caressed as babies, the better adjusted we grow up to be. Nurtured babies are more active, alert, and responsive, more aware of their surroundings, better able to tolerate noise, and cry less. Children who are difficult to raise get abused more often, and people who aren't touched much as children, don't touch much as adults. So the cycle continues.

Research has even shown that children returning library books will continuously go back to the librarian who slightly brushes their little hands when they are returning a book. In yet another experiment, a researcher leaves money in a phone booth, only to return when she sees the next person pocket the money. She then casually asks if they've found what she has lost. If the researcher insignificantly touches the person while asking for his/her help, the likelihood that the money will be returned rises from 63 to 96 percent.

PUT-OFFS TO COME-ONS:

In its earliest stage, the ritual of courtship is performed through silent speech. At any point, either partner may decide to stop the "dance" and change partners. This may be done by refusing eye contact, turning away or even sending out positively discouraging messages by frowning or glaring.

Both men and women send out two types of put-off messages when wishing to discourage further nonverbal advances: blocks and barriers.

1. Body blocks. These are attempts to shut out the unwelcome message by putting some physical object between yourself and the other person. In restaurants or on busses, when we do not want to start up or continue a conversation with a stranger, we tend to raise our newspaper or book, keep dark glasses on, or even lift a large wine glass to our lips. Although blocking often marks the end of an exchange, there are occasions when it is actually a come-on rather than a put-off. This happens when a young woman pretends to be coy and hard to get. She tends to wiggle in mock embarrassment, partly cover her eyes and then turn away. These pseudo-blocks are easily identified by their brief duration and by the fact that all the other body signals are positive and welcoming.
    An "end of the road" block will involve the blocking gestures accompanied by tense posture, a

hostile expression and little body movement. It is a red light warning you to go no further.

2.   Barriers. These are usually less defensive than blocks. They translate into spoken language as, "convince me that you're interesting." The most widely used barriers involve folding the arms or crossing the legs. Let us examine the variations of these crossings.

   a.   Standard fold: One arm across the other, at chest level, with fingers displayed, communicates a defensive, negative attitude and reveals uncertainty and insecurity.

When used as a response in a courtship encounter, it represents a challenge, but not an insurmountable obstacle to success. The best approach is to slow down, and maybe even take a few steps back.

   b.   Fist fold: One arm across the other, at chest level, with hands clinched tightly is a stronger message. The person is not only defensive, he is aggressive also. You will have to work much harder to break down this type of barrier.

   c.   Arm clasp: One arm across the other, at chest level, with hands gripping arms above the elbow represents extreme anxiety or great anger over the situation.

The quickest way to try to break any type of arm fold in a social situation is to offer the person a glass, something to eat, a cup of coffee, a document, or even a pen. As soon as the barrier is down, seize your opportunity to remove the cause of negative feelings.

Men will sometimes turn a chair around and straddle it, putting each leg on the sides and using the inside of the chair against his chest as a protective shield toward the conversation he is engaged in.

3.   Partial blocks. One arm across the chest area holding onto the other arm which hangs to the person's

side signals, not so much rejection, as a lack of confidence.

This gesture has a comforting effect on insecure people because it echoes the experience of having a hand held as a child.

When this signal is seen in a courtship dance, the most effective counter-response is to reduce the amount of self-confidence you are communicating. People feel more comfortable in exchanges with those whose level of self-esteem matches their own.

4. Leg barriers. Crossing the knees, one leg over the other, or folding the top leg and laying the ankle of it on the knee of the other leg in many situations, does not indicate a negative attitude. If, however, the person shifts to this position after you have started to send out come-on signals, and combines this with other silent messages of displeasure, you will need to change your strategies.

5. Hand-locked legs. Hands gripping the folded leg near the calf and drawing the leg into the body represents an extremely defensive and negative attitude. Your message is not being well received at all and the best advise is probably to quit wasting your time and find a more receptive partner.

6. Standing leg cross. Standing upright with legs crossed at ankles is a typical posture when people are introduced to a group for the first time and are uncertain how to proceed. If you see it in response to your come-on signals, you are certainly proceeding too fast. Back off for a while. One method for breaking someone from this position is to suggest that you both move to another part of the room, or move to chairs in the room.

Sensitivity to the many signals used during courtship pays big dividends. These love-signs of silent speech are often far more important than words in developing intimacy. We all desire. Remember that famous quote: "Actions speak louder than words."

Courtship is a complex dance of silent signals which people find difficult to read. Whether the dance is a waltz, a jitterbug, the swing or the rumba, the couple that reads each other's signals right can make beautiful music together.

Learn, practice, and watch the movements of your loved one. Begin to understand their need for love and intimacy by studying their desires, their passions and their emotions expressed by body movements. Romance, trust, honesty, and communication are the prescriptions for true love, for love that lasts, love that heals, and love that brings us insurmountable joy.

We all need romance in our lives; it is the champagne, the frosted glasses of love, the magic that gives love a melody to dance to, a fragrance to remember, and deep passion to our very existence.

Didn't we start this with a kiss? Perhaps we should end it with one. Kisses are the food of love. They make us feel desirable, beautiful, sensual, joyful, happy, carefree, invincible, and LOVED. Shower each other with kisses, and to you I say. "This chapter is S. W. A. K. "(sealed with a kiss)

LOVE LINES:

Look for someone who makes you happy. Love isn't supposed to hurt.

Relationships that don't end peacefully, don't end at all.

Talk is cheap! The true proof of love is in actions, not in words.

The loneliest I've ever been was at a party surrounded by joyous people and you weren't there.

Love is a choice, not an obsession.

Just as the most beautiful of flowers soon withers unless it is firmly rooted in nutritious soil, love unnurtured dies. If this happens, you must bury it, mourn for it, and then move on.

A relationship is two people coming together to live, to work, to play, to laugh, to grieve, to rejoice, to make love. Love just is.

He said he'd call soon, but soon's all gone now.

The distance between any two people is only the length of their arms.

CHAPTER 5

Winning Through Hugging: Don't Tell Me That You Love Me, Show Me

ELisa Dolittle's message in MY FAIR LADY was: "Don't tell me that you love me, show me." There are 1,000 different ways in which we can show someone that we love them without really speaking the words, "I love you!" We nonverbally communicate caring feelings with smiles, with winks, with laughter, with hugs and with kisses. Go ahead, wink at me; try it again. Makes you feel good, doesn't it? Now spread your arms; I'm running to you!

Research indicates that men who kiss and hug their wives every morning upon leaving for work:

1. Live an average of 5 years longer.
2. Are involved in fewer automobile accidents.
3. Earn 20 percent to 30 percent more money than men who do not kiss their wives.

AT&T urges us to "Reach Out and Touch Someone." By making good use of the telephone, they are appealing to us to reach others. To reach out to another sometimes involves risk. However, if we don't risk showing others that we actually care, we are the losers. Most unhappiness stems from unexpressed love. Are we actually afraid of telling others how we feel? Take the risk; go with your heart. You won't regret it.

It bothers me that as we grow older, we become more guarded, almost afraid of taking chances. Keeping our "childlike qualities" of risk and trust would make this world a better place to live. As children, we risked trying to get out of our play pens; we risked learning how to ride a bicycle, learning how to swim, even learning how to walk. We eagerly tried. We failed, but we tried again and again until we got it right. As children, we truly trusted others.

83

Picture two small children on a playground meeting for the first time. If they feel it's right (and with small children it's almost never wrong), in five minutes they will be relating to each other as adults relate only to lifelong friends.

These children trust each other completely from the beginning, and even if one turns out to be a little pushy, the other just accepts that fact and quickly learns to "forget it". We need to compare this with our own approach toward new people we meet. How long is your period of "initial shyness?" Or, are your glorious, precious, childlike qualities still with you?

The risk that I am asking each of you to take is the risk of reaching out and touching others who seem to need it. My mother once told me: "You can believe something when you can touch it." I know she couldn't be all wrong; it's been good advice and I've been touching and enjoying it ever since.

Scientific research supports the theory that stimulation by touch is absolutely necessary for our physical, and emotional well-being. Hugging and comforting touches are used to relieve pain, depression, anxiety; to boost a patient's will to live and to help premature babies grow and thrive. In fact, therapeutic touch, which is recognized as an essential tool for healing, is now part of nurses' training in several large medical centers.

Research has proven that touch can make us feel better about ourselves and our surroundings and have a positive effect on children's language development and I.Q.

If hugging is going to make us smarter and strengthen our level of self-esteem, can we take the chance to tire of it or not indulge in it at all?

The legendary qualities of "Famous Huggers" has survived throughout the centuries. You almost can't think of Fred Astaire without thinking of Ginger Rogers and their exquisite dance steps to sentimental melodies. What is that tune from the early sixty's I'm hearing? Is it Unchained Melodies?

> Oh, my love my darling
> I've hungered for your touch
> a long lonely time.
> Time, goes by, so slowly,
> and time can do such much
> Are you still mine?
> I need your love
> I need your love

God speed your love
to me.

Recognize these huggers? Can you identify their partners?

1. Romeo   _____

2. Cleopatra   _____

3. Minnie Mouse   _____

4. Barbie   _____

5. Adam   _____

6. Donald Duck   _____

7. Beauty   _____

8. Dick Tracy   _____

9. Rhett Butler   _____

10. Snow White   _____

11. Sampson   _____

12. Lucy   _____

13. Miss Piggy   _____

14. Superman   _____

15. Cinderella   _____

16. Jack   _____

17. Ozzie   _____

18. Laurel   _____

19. John Smith   _____

20. Tweedledum   _____

(Answers are at the end of the chapter.)

I embarked several years ago on my Hug Crusade to prepare myself for my role as a Hug Therapist. It is a title I treasure. Hour after hour, I studied people hugging and caressing in airports, movie theaters, amusement parks, cars, weddings, funerals and even supermarkets. I witnessed hugs of joy, hugs of sadness, hugs of passion, hugs of fright, and hugs of utter delight. I made drawings, listened for sounds, watched eyes close and identified specific needs for each type of hug. The squeals from audiences across the country as I present these findings are my reassurances that the study was needed. Get your arms ready!

The benefits of hugging:

1.   Feels good
2.   Eases tension
3.   Keeps arms and shoulder muscles in condition
4.   Provides stretching exercises if you are short
5.   Provides stooping exercises if you are tall
6.   Is portable
7.   Makes happy days happier
8.   Makes impossible days possible.

Although we move around in a world of many languages, the nonverbal language of hugging is universal. Now you will know another language, and when someone asks how many languages you can speak, list your basic ones and add, Hug Language; i.e. "I speak five languages: English, French, Spanish, Cajun, and Hug."

Hugging involves our sixth sense: intuition. We know when it feels right and we know when it's needed. We hug from our hearts. Our lives are so packed with reason and technology that we are in danger of losing touch with our senses. When we hold each other in a spirit of compassion, we come back to our instincts and reaffirm our trust in ourselves and in others.

In difficult times, we may not know the correct words to say, but we do know when we hug in a time of joy or sorrow, a genuine message is conveyed. A hug can say:

"It's good to see you!"

"I feel your pain."

"I like you soooo much!"

"I was so lonesome, it feels good to hold you."

"I could squeeze the daylights out of you; I missed you so much!"

An embrace from the heart often cannot be translated into words; it is something that is felt through and through. When asked what I would carry with me if I were stranded on an island for two months, I replied, "Give me someone of wisdom, intelligence and warmth, with two strong arms, and together we can exist for a lifetime." The very best thing to have around us as we travel the crooked roads of life is Arms!!! Arms of mothers, arms of fathers, arms of friends, arms of lovers, arms of teachers, arms of children; let's really stretch our arms out and reach those who need us.

I would like to prepare you to become a Hug Therapist. The qualifications are simple:

1. Understand that Hug Therapist hugs are done out of compassion, not passion.
2. Sincerely believe that hugging is a healing process.
3. Spread the message of hugging as you go through life.
4. Know and be able to demonstrate the sixteen basic hugs at any time.

A word of warning. Be certain you have permission before giving a hug. Sweethearts or close friends will probably welcome hugs almost any time. Others will sometimes let you know through nonverbal communication that they need one.

Also, be sure to ask permission when you need a hug. Huggers must sometimes be huggees. As we become more aware of what the language of touch can say about affirmation and support, we will discover that hugging is healthy communication that enriches our lives. As hugging becomes more acceptable as a "second language," the fees for risking will lessen accordingly.

VOCABULARY OF HUGS:

1. *A-FRAME HUG.*

    Position: Stand facing each other, wrapping arms

around shoulders, sides of heads pressed together and bodies leaning forward, but not touching below shoulder level.

Purpose: Somewhat formal. It is used for new acquaintances, professional colleagues, great aunts, former teachers or any situation that requires a degree of formality.

Message: "It's good to see you; how have you been!"

2   *ANKLE HUG.*

Position: Very small person, usually a small child, stands behind a parent and encircles one of the parent's ankles, with both his/her little arms.

Purpose: The child needs attention at this time; usually wants to be picked up or given a security hug by the adult.

Message: "Mama, Mama; notice me!"

3.   BACK-TO-FRONT HUG.

Position: The huggee's back is facing the hugger. The hugger places both his arms around the waist of the huggee.

Purpose: Playful. The hugger wants the huggee to know that he's conscious that she's around and just wants a playful touch at this time.

Message: "Hey, Sweetheart, how's it going?" "Just wanted to say, 'I love you.'"

4.   *BEAR HUG.*

Position: Hugger (much larger than huggee) completely engulfs the huggee with his arms and his head; in fact, head is bent over the huggee.

Purpose: Powerful. Hugger wants huggee to feel secure at the moment of the hug.

Message: "Everything is going to be all right; I have you!"

5. CHEEK-TO-CHEEK HUG.

Position: Hugger stands behind huggee, who is sitting. Hugger gently places one of his hands on the huggee's cheek and presses one of his cheeks to the huggee's other cheek.

Purpose: Tender, loving. Lightly given, it can have a spiritual quality.

Message: "It's alright, I'm here now." or "Hi ya, Baby!"

6. CUSTOM-TAILORED HUG.

Position: Any hug that fits your needs at a particular time. Whether it's when you hug your pillow, hug your teddy bear, or hug yourself.

Purpose: To make you feel better.

Message: "I feel insecure right now, but this makes me feel better."

7. FACE-HOLDING HUG.

Position: Stand or sit facing each other. Hugger gently holds the face of the huggee with both hands.

Purpose: Loving, caring, playful.

Message: "I like you sooooooo much!"

8. GRABBER-SQUEEZER HUG.

Position: Stand facing each other. Hugger wraps arms around the waist, hips or back of huggee; gives a quick hug and squeezes the part of huggee's anatomy where his hands are hugging.

Purpose: Playful, affectionate.

Message: "Heyyyyyy, Baby!"

9. GRANNY HUG.

Position: Hugger wraps right arm around the waist of someone feeble, while holding huggee's left hand with his left hand.

Purpose: To help a feeble person walk.

Message: "Here, let me help you."

10.   GROUP HUG.

Position: Group (3 or more) stands in a circle, facing each other. In this position, each holds the one at each side of them at the waist or shoulders.

Purpose: To share joyful feelings after completing a project or winning a game.

Message: "Hooray! We did it!"

11.   GUESS-WHO HUG.

Position: Hugger comes from behind and places both hands over the eyes of the huggee.

Purpose: A prank hug for longtime friends.

Message: "Guess Who!"

12.   HEART-CENTERED HUG.

Position: Bodies are facing each other, touching the entire length. Arms are wrapped around waists or shoulders of each other. Eyes are usually closed in this hug and it can last as long as needed. Gentle pats are common by the hugger and the huggee.

Purpose: To convey genuine feelings between two people who love each other. It is called heart-centered hug because the hearts of the two people are almost at the same level, and feelings are flowing from one heart to the other heart.

Message: "I deeply care for you."

13.   I-GOT-YOU-HUG.

Position: Hugger stands upright, and encircles one arm around the neck of the huggee, and usually gently and lovingly "pulls" huggee in the direction he is walking.

Purpose: To display ownership or possession of huggee.

Message: "I got you, Babe!"

14. LOVER'S-KNEE HUG.

Position: Hugger is in a beginning waltz stance (one arm around huggee's waist and the other hand is holding the huggee's hand) and gently swings huggee backwards. (Looks like a backward lunge.)

Purpose: Ending gesture of a wonderful dance together.

Message: Huggee exclaims: "Yyyyes!"

15. SANDWICH HUG.

Position: Two huggers hug one huggee.

Purpose: To give a complete feeling of security to the huggee.

Message: "We'll protect you; no matter what!"

16. SIDE-BY-SIDE HUG.

Position: Two huggers, both facing the front, side-by-side, hug each other at the waist.

Purpose: A playful hug that is often used while strolling together.

Message: "Being with you makes me feel good."

All of us need hugs and other kinds of supportive touching. A validating back pat can sometimes be a more sensitive way than words to communicate support to a friend. We playfully rub heads or give relaxing neck massages to let others know how much we care. As you go through life you will discover more hugs and hopefully your Hug Vocabulary will grow.

I believe more must be done to break down the emotional barriers that prevent us from experiencing the healthy nourishment of touching and hugging. My contribution to solving this issue is the presentation of The Hug Card that follows.

Becoming a Certified Hug Therapist means that you are able to demonstrate any of the 16 hugs at a moment's notice and can state, from memory, the three components of a Hug Therapist. Hugs are powerful. Use them to communicate your feelings to others. Carry your card with you at all times. The motto of the Certified Hug Therapist, "Hug Often. Hug Well," should be wished to others after you have hugged them.

INSTITUTE OF HUG THERAPY
CERTIFICATE OF MEMBERSHIP
THIS IS TO CERTIFY THAT

_____
NAME

HAS COMPLETED THE COURSE OF STUDY OFFERED
BY JAN HARGRAVE'S HUG THERAPY LECTURE AND
IS NOW A PRACTICING HUG THERAPIST DEDICATED
TO THE FURTHERANCE OF HUGGING FOR HEALTH
AND WELL BEING ON AN INTERNATIONAL SCALE.

Chap. 5, Fig. 2

Congratulations on your new title! Hopefully this certification will aid you in communicating your feelings to others. Don't let a relationship sour because "we never communicated." Practice caring looks, interested looks, enthusiastic looks, even sympathetic looks. Practice, practice, practice. Smile at people. Get into the habit of greeting people, even if it is just visually acknowledging them with a nod of your head. As you begin to make contact with the world at large, new avenues begin to open for you. In your life, how many times have you discovered that someone you had been interested in had also been interested in you, yet you both had done nothing about it? How many times have you found yourself wishing: If only I knew then what I know now? Next time, begin at the beginning with body language that expresses your positive feelings. Smiles, nods and casual greetings lead to courtship and marriage.

Small talk must come first. It is an invitation that can lead to a successful relationship. This art form is sometimes considered shallow and phony, but it has a purpose. How else can you get to the heavy, meaningful dialogue? I doubt that you would think me very interesting, or sane, if I approached you on a park bench and asked if you thought the Baldridge Approach to Quality was the best model to use when measuring customer focus and satisfaction. You'd think I had flipped my lid. But if we first talked about, say, the weather, the economy, or a famous person in the news, you might then understand my intended meaning.

Whether it is through small talk or intimate questions, successful relationships are dependent on a couple's willingness to share their thoughts and feelings. Several intimate questions intended to improve communication and understanding between two people contemplating a relationship follow.

I hope you have fun. The questions, meant to provoke warm feelings between you and your love, should be asked with gentleness in your voice, softness in your eyes and sincerity in your heart. Answer them alone or with your mate. Every question is intended to reveal information couples need to know to bring them closer to each other.

1. What words do you like to hear whispered in your ear over and over again?
2. What did you learn from your mother? your father?
3. Using three adjectives, how would you describe yourself?
4. Past or present, what five people would you like to borrow some brains from?
5. What is the best way to end an argument?
6. How many people have you loved?
7. Would you wipe my tears away with your kisses if I cry?
8. Did you ever feel that your broken heart would never mend?
9. If you could tell me that you love me in a song, what song would it be?
10. When you wish on a star, what do you wish?
11. When my hair has turned to silver, will you still call me sweetheart?
12. What is it about love that makes you afraid?
13. When we're apart, do you wonder how often I think about you?
14. How much absence should there be in a relationship to keep the heart growing fonder?
15. What is your favorite type of kiss?
16. If you carved a love message in the bark of a tree, what would it say?
17. When you say your prayers, what do you pray for?
18. If you wrote me a love letter, what would it say?

Whether you're dating, engaged or married, your mate's answers can give you a better understanding of his/her fantasies, desires, priorities and values. Communicate with those you love; it is the primary means of beginning and establishing friendships and relationships.

Sometimes words spoken or written to us touch us so deeply that they have all the wonderful qualities of a hug. As I composed this chapter, I received a beautiful love letter that illustrates this point perfectly. Let me share these Hug Lines with you:

Jan

I gotta see you
Smile big at you
Buy you crazy stuff
At Victoria's Secret
Talk sexy to you
Be terrific to you
Hold your hand
Kiss your face
Your ears
Make you laugh and
Scream with pleasure
Give you butterflies
Walk slow with you
Run wild with you
Learn you, teach you, warm you, chill you
Hug you
Chug-a-lug you
Dunk you in fun
Fill you up
Touch inside you
Make you
Like me
Want me
Ache for me
Buzz with me
Squeeze me
Wring me out
Play with me
Stay with me
Undress with me
Mess with me
Crush on me
Gush on me
Love with me
Come with me
The Palm
ASAP

Answers to "Famous Huggers"

1.	Juliet	11.	Delilah
2.	Mark Anthony	12.	Desi
3.	Mickey Mouse	13.	Kermit
4.	Ken	14.	Lois Lane
5.	Eve	15.	Prince Charming
6.	Daisy Duck	16.	Jill
7.	Beast	17.	Harriet
8.	Breathless Mahoney	18.	Hardy
9.	Scarlette O'Hara	19.	Pocahontas
10.	Seven Dwarfs	20.	Tweedledee

CHAPTER 6

Write the Right Stuff: Nonverbal Clues That Are Revealed in Your Handwriting

How many times were you reminded to mind your "p's" and "q's"? Well, when it comes to handwriting, that's not a bad idea. Handwriting unveils the mysteries of the soul. You can tell just about anything you want to know about a person from the symbols in his handwriting.

Your handwriting reveals how passionately you kiss, which traffic lane you drive in, what kind of greeting cards you send, how you behave in long grocery store lines and how often you call your mother. Professionally, your handwriting can pinpoint perfect career choices, reveal your creative potential, indicate whether or not you will be willing to work overtime on Saturdays, and even if you are honest or dishonest in business dealings.

Three thousand European firms and 85 percent of businesses in the United States are now using handwriting analysis in the job application process. The connection between personality and handwriting has been known for centuries. Twenty-five hundred years ago, Confucius warned us to beware of people "whose writing is like a reed in the wind."

Each of us learned the same letter formations in grade school, but not one of us writes exactly the same as anyone else today. Graphology is the true interpretation of the popular philosophy, "different strokes for different folks." There is only one chance in 64 trillion that your handwriting would be exactly like anyone else's. Handwriting is a mental process. The brain sends the order through the nervous system to the arm, hand and fingers. The intent to write forms deep within the creative processes of the mind and makes writing an expressive gesture representing the mind behind the pen.

Writing is such a mental process, that if one lost the use of his hands and had to write with his teeth, feet or toes, his teethwriting would be exactly the same as his handwriting is now. A perfect example of this is when we write our names in the sand with our toes; that writing is made up of the very same strokes that we use when writing with our dominant hand.

The best part is, although professional graphologists must undergo rigorous training, it's a cinch to learn the basics. You'd be surprised at how much you already know.

Test your knowledge with these simple examples:

1.   Which of these writers is happier?

A.   *My birthday is in January*

B.   *where's the party?*

Answer: A   (Explanations are at end of chapter.)

2.   Who's smarter?

A.   *The hill is very high.*

B.   *Jane's climbing faster than Jill.*

Answer: A

3.   Who's more emotional?

A.   *I saw her crying.*

B.   *Her laughter was contagious.*

Answer: B

4. Which of these writers is lying?

A. My watch cost $300.

B. My jewelry is always gold.

Answer: A

5. Who's more easy-going?

A. Let's get together.

B. Let's get together.

Answer: B

6. Who hides his feelings?

A. Playground rules are awful.
B. Let's play ball in the park.

Answer: A

7. Who wrote faster?

A. I love oranges.

B. I love apples.

Answer: A

8.   Can you tell who's more secretive?

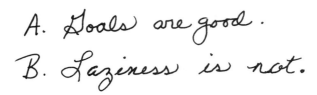

A. Goals are good.
B. Laziness is not.

Answer: A

Handwriting analysis is best learned when you analyze your own handwriting. Therefore, follow these steps:

1.   Use white, unlined paper with no margins.
2.   Use a ballpoint pen.
3.   Place the writing paper directly on the surface of a table (do not put books or other papers under your writing paper).
4.   Use cursive or printed writing; whichever is your usual handwriting.
5.   Write the following paragraph:

"Now is the time for all good men to come to the aid of their country. Don't worry, be happy! Whenever I think of the person I love, it always seems to make me smile." Sign your name below the paragraph in your normal handwriting. Then, as teeny, tiny as you can, write: "A stroke is a stroke." Below this, even smaller, write again, "A stroke is a stroke." Now for a third time, even smaller, write, "A stroke is a stroke."

I am hoping that you noticed, the smaller you wrote, the more tense your body became. Point number one; the smaller the writing, the more up-tight, tense or sub-conscious the writer. Larger writing indicates that the writer is extroverted and out-going.

Next, notice the spacing between words and letters in your handwriting sample. Spacing between words and letters is indicative of how the writer relates, on a personal level, to other people. If he is cautious or introverted, the letters and words will be crowded close to each other, showing that the writer is craving contact. The combination of narrow spacing between letters and words and wide spaces between them, is indicative of a person who appears to be very outgoing, but is inwardly up-tight and cautious with his feelings.

Lay your paper face down and feel the back side. Can you feel your writing through to the back of your paper? Writing that can be felt through the backside is an indication of anxiety, worry or stress in the writer.

As we examine the letters in the words you wrote, let's consider how you formed your "a's" and "o's." Are these letters closed tightly or are they left with an open area? You may say, "I have some open and I have some closed." Count the number of open "a's" and "o's" as opposed to the number of closed "a's" and "o's." Whichever is larger, that is your target. Information concerning a person's willingness to tell all about himself and talk endlessly can be seen in open "a's" and "o's." The tight-lipped, shy, less talkative person has tightly closed "a's" and "o's" in his handwriting sample.

Our interest now shifts to how you moved your pen up and down as you wrote your way across the page. This is your slant of writing. It reflects your underlying, inner emotional responses; how you react to all the people and events in your life.

Slant ranges from extreme left to extreme right. Generally speaking, leftward slants signify suppressed emotional feelings, while the rightward slants indicate unrestrained enthusiasm.

The more letters lean to the right, the more future-oriented, aggressive, courageous, expressive and reactive the writer is. The farther writing leans to the left, the more passive, past-oriented, introverted, repressed and cautious the writer is. Vertical writing shows independence, self-reliance, emotional control and a balance between extroversion and introversion.

There are seven basic slants in handwriting. A handwriting sample will usually contain two slant positions; a variation of three or more slants in one sample is considered unstable. The larger the number of variations, the more unstable the writer is emotionally.

When the slant never varies at all, it can be determined that there is some emotional rigidity or stubbornness being expressed by the writer. Use the following chart to determine your slant.

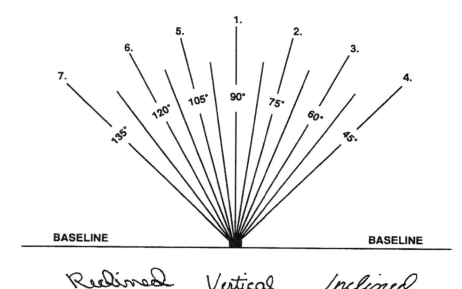

1. *Vertical:* This non-slant indicates that the writer keeps his emotional expressions under control. His head rules over his heart. He is undemonstrative, independent, detached and even indifferent. Once this type of writer loses his emotional control, it can quickly be regained. This person functions well in emergencies, has a great deal of personal magnetism, and tends to posses a dry wit. NOTE: If you are ever in a wreck, make certain it is with someone that writes this way. He won't get upset or panic. He'll know to call the ambulance, the police department, and calmly notify your mother. The vertical writer makes an excellent poker player; never showing excitement over a good hand, he remains poker-faced.

For identification purposes, we'll call these writers *Thinkers*. Thinkers have emotions, but seldom will they get passionate about them. They feel more comfortable being aloof and logical.

Thinker mates: Once you've captured the heart of a Thinker, you're in for a relationship unlike any other you've had before. Thinkers are not going to fight you and they're not going to tell you when they're angry with you. The reason they're this way is that they see no purpose in challenging something in you that you probably won't change. Thinkers tend to be romantically passive, they're usually loyal and faithful lovers and maintain friendships from nursery to grave. They are not likely to change old habits, so you'll probably just have to learn to live with them. Thinkers make some of the best mates because they're loving, slow to anger and adore their children.

2. *Inclined:* This slant is considered the "normal" one. The writer is normally sensitive and emotionally healthy. He is logical, but can express sympathy and compassion when needed. His range of expression, though, is seldom over-demonstrative. People who write this way make excellent judges; they are logical, yet can empathize with others. This juggling of logic and emotions helps us to identify these writers as: *Jugglers*.

    Juggler mates: Jugglers can be sane and rational in love, but they are highly emotional. For example, if Jugglers break up with a lover, they decide the relationship didn't really matter anyway. They then run to the nearest distraction, but their inner sense of loss eventually catches up with them and they get moody and irritable because they're playing games with themselves. Jugglers want to be loyal, but when they see what they think are "greener pastures," they often jump the fence. They may regret their decisions later and feel guilty, but that still won't stop them from straying. Jugglers may fake passion, but they don't really want to.

They say all the right words, but if they're not as intensely involved as they pretend, they don't feel good about it. They will only settle down when THEY are ready to settle down. Since they often try to juggle a career and a family, they are more likely to become more stable as lovers when they are in their late thirties and tired of running around.

3. *Very inclined:* These writers cry and laugh easily. They freely express emotions, are very affectionate, sensitive, impulsive, and loving, but can also yell, blow up, or break down emotionally within seconds. They tend to want to please others and will sympathize quickly with others. If they see you cry, they usually begin to cry. These Pleaser writers make excellent actors, politicians, ministers, teachers, nurses, secretaries or psychotherapists.

Pleaser mates: Pleasers need to be one-half of a couple to feel good about themselves. These heart-centered pleasers are deeply concerned with being loved, and they live to express themselves. They believe they can't do enough for the ones they love and are likely to feel guilty if they suspect they could have done more. They are impulsive and likely to enter into relationships without considering the pitfalls. They believe that their love is so powerful that they can convince themselves they can make an alcoholic stop drinking or a kleptomaniac stop stealing, simply because they love them.

4. *Extremely inclined:* These writers are a volcano of emotional reactions. They are extremely passionate, jealous, easily offended, very demonstrative, and even capable of hysteria. These Reactors tend to have very high highs and very low lows; they almost wear themselves out. The extremely inclined writer plunges into relationships and causes.

Reactor mates: These mates are extraordinarily emotional and passionate. They'll respond so intensely to things that you'll think they're exaggerating or faking their excitement, but their enthusiasm is genuine and they will expect you to join them in their inspired state. They fall hard, give everything, and even can't seem to separate your problems from their own. They are the most devoted of all mates. They use enormous amounts of energy just to exist, and at times they may seem like a roller coaster. Reactors are highly impressionable and tend to believe what other people tell them without ever checking things out for themselves. They want so desperately to be good and for you to love them that they quickly feel rejected when they don't get the approval they seek. Because they react so strongly, be extremely careful when breaking off a romance with one of them.

5. *Reclined:* This type of writer represses his feelings. He does not acknowledge his fears and anxieties and tends to "cover up" most of his feelings. Often there is found in this type of writer an immature attachment to the values of his mother figure who has usually played a dominant role in shaping his social personality. In most cases of reclined (*Bender*) writers, the father has played a weak or negative role. These writers have a desire to make everything bad, good. They tiptoe along life's path and try diligently to be perfect. They need approval in order to feel okay, but it's very difficult to convince them that they are indeed acceptable people.

Bender mates: As their writing bends to the left, they are known for bending over backwards to make sure everything is wonderful for you (outer personality), but inside (inner personality) they find it difficult to receive the same affection they show to others. They feel they don't deserve it. Being timid, Benders won't be extremely passionate. They think, "If people don't see how much I care, they won't know where to aim the arrows when they get mad at me." Benders are attracted to people that need them. Keeping a relationship going with a bender may cost you social freedom because they tend to get jealous of your outside friendships.

6. *Very reclined:* This type of writing (Rebel) indicates that the writer has complete self-interest. He is independent and hard to get along with. This writer usually acts friendly, but keeps you at "arms length." They rarely show true feelings or desires, are past-oriented and strongly influenced by the values of their mothers. This leftward writing suggests that the writer acts contrary to the norm and habitually does things in an unconventional way, whether out of defiance, fear or pride. Teenagers frequently adopt this slant, reflecting a time of emotional uncertainty. When a person is able to work out of his self-imposed shell, his handwriting takes on a more forward direction.
Rebel mates: The "rebel without a cause" writers keep you in a state of uncertainty. Just when you think you have them all figured out, you're in for a big surprise. They are incredibly difficult people to understand, let alone love. They have their own idea of what reality is, and that isn't easy for others to understand. They must be accepted by their own terms or not at all, and because they are so erratic, their terms may change on a daily basis. They can be affectionate one moment and hostile the next. The only way to get along with them is to be super flexible and independent. They are quite a handful, and it takes strength to work things out with them. Most of the time, you'll develop that strength quickly or abandon the relationship.

7. *Extremely reclined:* This slant (*Blocker*) is very rare; it has all the above characteristics amplified and suggests that the writer is "out of touch" with his environment. This type of writer usually lives in the past, and has such a strong "Mother identification" that his individual development is blocked. On the outside, these writers can still show charming personalities, but repress emotions

out of an unconscious fear and a strong need for security.

Blocker mates: There is such a strong need for security in the Blocker that they rarely last in relationships. All love and attention must be on them, but they cannot give love and attention to others. It seems as though it's just never enough. They tend to say, "If only you would . . .," or "If you had told me . . .." They need to be totally cared for, sometimes reflecting personalities of young children at an age when they are very dependent on their mothers.

Fold your paper from the bottom up, until you are directly beneath the "N" of "Now" in your handwriting sample. Does your line of writing rise or fall? This invisible line along your writing paper is your baseline. Baselines are indicators of the mood, morals, temperament and disposition of the writer. When the line is naturally straight, it shows a mood that is composed, orderly stable, and dependable. If it is overly rigid, the writer appears inhibited and void of any spontaneity in his actions. Baselines that tend to slant upward show spirit, ambition, and optimism in the writer as opposed to baselines that slant downward, displaying depression, fatigue, disappointment or discouragement in the writer.

When specific "personal" words in a handwriting sample rise above the other words, there is an indication to believe that a positive emphasis or feeling was present when the writer wrote that particular word. Check the word "person" or "love" in your handwriting sample to see if they rise or fall in comparison to the other words in the sentence. If specific words fall below the others in a sentence, it indicates that the writer felt negative or uneasy feelings when writing that particular word.

What is the shape of your handwriting? Look at the general appearance of your letters and the connections between them. There are four basic shapes of handwriting: Garland, Arcade, Angular and Thready. Each one reveals a different personality, the public image that others see. Find your writing shape on the following chart.

Does your writing look like a row of umbrellas—round "m's" and "n's"?

Is it very rounded, composed soley of curved lines?

Does it form little cups along the baseline?

Is it angular and notched—like dandelion leaves?

Chap. 6, Fig. 4

1. *Garland.* Garland handwriting gently curves as it contacts the baseline; it is considered the quickest and most natural writing stroke. These writers tend to be gentle, soft and loving. They usually don't have an aggressive bone in their bodies and generally take the path of least resistance because they are so emotional and sensitive. Because of their passiveness, compassion, and kindness, it is likely that their friends choose them more often than they choose their friends. In the yin-yang principle, the garland is seen as the feminine yin, representing receptive, maternal instincts.

2. *Arcade.* The arcade stroke forms the upper part (umbrella) of a circle. Its shape is convex, like an arch or a roof, and provides support and structure. Arcade writers are guarded, secretive, protective and proud. This shape represents the masculine counterpart to the yin-yang principle, (protective

and paternal). Imagine a turtle. The outside convex shape of the turtle shell is hard and protective,
and from the outside turtles look very tough.
However, without its shell it is very fragile.

These writers have a good memory, but do not
absorb information quickly. They resist major
change. In fact, they're probably the most stubborn
and conservative of all the writing shapes.

3. *Angular.* Angular writing is comprised of two
   movements. For this reason, it is slower to write
   with angles than with garlands or arcades. It is an
   abrupt, precise stroke (almost a strike) that is
   indicative of a writer that is analytical and logical.
   They see the world in terms of black and white,
   right or wrong. Since nothing is neutral, they
   prefer argument to compromise, and will try to
   impose their beliefs on others.

   They work long hours, are impatient, love a
   challenge, and demand much of themselves and
   others. They like to figure things out and make
   excellent mechanics, engineers, electricians and
   scientists.

4. *Thready.* Threaded movement isn't entirely straight
   or curved, but a little of each. The writing is
   formless, like an unravelling ball of yarn. This
   formless shape evades commitment, control and
   direction, and shows writers that are creative,
   broadminded, undisciplined, highly impressionable
   and unpredictable. They take a broad view of the
   world and want to see and know everything.
   Threaders have a love for all the arts and want
   freedom to follow their own talents. They won't
   be pinned down, thus making them hard to
   understand.

   The thread formation sometimes appears as a
   result of speed. The mind is rushing along while
   the hand struggles to keep up. This speedy thread

is identified with high intelligence, possibly even genius. Albert Einstein, a fast-flowing thread writer, proved that Threaders are mentally ahead of their own time and capable of developing original theories.

The stroke which ends a word is called an ending or terminal stroke. This ending stroke on words is the indicator used to tell the graphoanalyst if the writer is a completer of tasks. If one takes time to complete his letters, he will take time to complete his tasks. These completed strokes tell others that the writer is generous, considerate and extravagant. This is the indicator used by employers to determine if a job applicant would be willing to work overtime, work late on Saturdays, or "go the extra mile" on projects.

The stroke which begins the first letter of a word is called a lead-in stroke. These strokes, or the absence of them, give clues to the manner in which a writer relates to authority. The presence of these lead-in strokes shows that the writer continues to look to authority figures and institutions for guidance; a pattern of behavior learned in childhood. The omission of these lead-ins is an indication of maturity. These people take a direct route to problem-solving, and are quick and decisive.

LETTER SPECIFICS:

Most handwriting analysts consider the letter "t" by far the most graphologically important letter of the alphabet. In order to cross the "t," the writer must interrupt his normal up, down, and circular movements and produce a separate and direct line. How and where the writer draws this bar tells how will power, goals, and personal drive are expressed in his life. The most common "t-bar" crossings follow:

Low, Medium, and High on stem indicate low, medium, and high goal setting on the part of the writer.

High above stem shows that goals are not realistic (head in clouds); too high to ever achieve.

Crossed over means the writer is persistent, will keep going, no matter what.

Descending crosses express stubbornness and an argumentative nature.

Ascending crosses show optimism, enthusiasm and ambition.

Leftward return strokes show a desire to protect self, lack of confidence, and jealousy.

Whip shaped cross shows that the writer is a practical joker.

Crossing to the left of the stem indicates procrastination or indecisiveness in setting goals.

Crossing to the right of the stem shows impulsiveness, enthusiasm and sometimes nervous energy.

No crossing is a sign of carelessness, absentmindedness, and haste.

Dotting the "i" is also an interruption of the forward movement of writing. Its placement shows preciseness, conscientiousness, good memory and concentration.

Round and placed directly over the stem shows order, method and precision.

Dots placed behind the stem indicate impatience and impulsiveness.

Dots placed before the stem mean procrastination and caution.

A sharp accent above the stem is an indication of a lively wit and a sharp mind.

Circle I-dots indicate an interest in feminine hobbies; fashion, dancing, cosmetics or hair styling.

Omitted dots show carelessness or absent-mindedness on the part of the writer.

The personal pronoun "I" is symbolic of the writer himself. The formation of this letter reveals the person's ego, that is, his self image and his sense of his own worth. Studying the pronoun "I" also gives you clues concerning the degree and quality of influence that the mother and father figures have had in shaping the writer's personality.

The larger the letter "I" is written, the larger the writer's ego; a shrinking letter "I" indicates a crushed or totally immature ego. When the letter "I" is written as we learned to write it in grade school, a larger upper portion indicates that the writer was heavily influenced by his father, and a larger lower portion indicates that the writer's mother strongly influenced his life. "I's" that are printed or written as single straight lines show that the writer can "stand alone" and doesn't possess immature ties to either parent figure or that he doesn't need any emotional support concerning self-image from others.

 = Father influence.

 = Mother influence.

 Printed or stick figure "I's" show that the writer stands alone without ties to either parent; he/she is very independent and desires to stand out.

 Using the number two shape as an "I," indicates that the writer has felt second-class, either physically or emotionally.

 (dollar sign) Shows that the writer's ego level is based on money as a source of personal value. (Possibly "bought off" as a child.)

 Xing to form the "I" indicates strong fears and dependency on the part of the writer.

 A lower case letter in the place of a capital "I" shows that the writer has either a crushed or totally immature ego.

The lower case "y" gives away information about the writer's sexual personality. Sharp, unkind angles, domineering t-bars, and letters jammed together seeking closeness gives us clues to the writer's attitude toward physical intimacy.

A normal lower zone with an upward ending stroke on the "y" is indicative of a warm and receptive nature, free of fear and inhibition.

Long, heavy plunges indicate defensiveness and determination.

Unfinished loops are signs that the writer has courtship expectations that are unfulfilled.

Downward ending loops show anger toward the writer's current sexual partner.

Tics leftward or rightward are indicative of sexual frustration in the writer.

Large, long loops that are tied off, indicate that the writer is very materialistic (money bags) when it comes to picking a partner.

Long, full, round heavy loops indicate that the writer gets emotionally involved in all relationships.

Lying and secretiveness can be seen in a person's writing by observing cramped letters, extremely coiled ovals, counterclockwise strokes, or first letters of a word being very clear with later letters indistinguishable or omitted. Pathological liars tend to make very tall capitals and extremely high t-bars. They have a flamboyant signature, use a highly ornamented writing style, and write with very light pressure on the page.

Aggression, hostility and stubbornness are evident if there is very heavy pressure in the writing sample. Heavy pressure can be seen when lower-zone letters are clubbed (circles are darkened) or certain letters have been "gone over" more than once.

A person's signature is very hard to decipher since a signature is not our true writing style. People will practice their signature until they get it to their liking. Remember when we wrote the words, "Mrs. Tom Brown, Mrs. Tom Brown," over and over again until we got it just perfect.

Some indicators of personality, though, can be seen in signatures. Overscoring or underscoring (Ben Franklin and Charles Dickins) indicate that the writer has an extremely high level of self-confidence. Large capital letters in a signature (Jacqueline Kennedy, John Wayne) indicate that the writer has an extreme pride and wants to achieve a prominent place in life. People who encircle their signatures (Meadowlark Lemon) indicate a desire to enclose or shelter themselves from others. Dots (periods) that follow signatures (Charles DeGaulle) indicate that the writer always wants to have the last word.

Like facial expressions and body language, handwriting analysis expresses personal characteristics. Since it reflects the thoughts, feelings and habits of the writer, use your knowledge of the subject to better understand the relationships in your life. If you're involved with someone, you're concerned that their beliefs be in harmony with yours. The Compatibility Test that follows, through comparison with your writing, will help you determine the potential of any relationship.

Have someone that you are interested in write a paragraph. Scan the writing sample for a few minutes before writing anything down. Keep your mind open and try not to focus on any particular formation. How do you react to the writing? Once you have received an overall impression of the writing, begin to look for extremes, such as very small or very large writing, closed or open letters, baselines or slants. Make a note of these. The importance of the first impressions can't be overemphasized; often they are amazingly accurate.

HANDWRITING COMPATIBILITY TEST

1. Determine the person's slant:
   - If the slant is the same as yours, score 60 points.
   - If it's the slant next to yours (either side), score 40 points.
   - If the slant is two away from yours, score 20 points.
   - If it's more than two slants away, score 10 points.

2. Is the basic handwriting shape Garland, Arcade, Angular or Thready?
   - If it matches yours, score 50 points.
   - If you're a Garlander and he's an Arcade, or vice versa, score 40 points.
   - Garlander and Angular, score 10 points.
   - Garlander and Thready, score 20 points.
   - Arcaders and Angulars, score 0 points.
   - Arcaders and Threadies, score 20 points.
   - Angulars and Threadies, score 0 points.

3. What is the spacing type: crowded, loose or balanced?
   - If the spacing matches yours, score 50 points.
   - If it's balanced and yours isn't, score 40 points.
   - If it's crowded and yours is loose, score 0 points.
   - If it's loose and yours is crowded, score 0 points.

4. What kind of lower loops does the writer make most often?
   - If they match yours, score 35 points.
   - If they're large and locked, score 30 points.
   - If they drop down, unfinished, score 25 points.
   - If they're small and locked, score 10 points.
   - If they are highly angular, score 0 points.

5. Determine the person's base line:
   - If it tends to rise, score 40 points.
   - If it is very rigid, score 10 points.
   - If it tends to fall, score 10 points.
   - If it is erratic, score 10 points.

6. Is the writing large or small?
   - If they're both large, score 50 points.
   - If it is small and tight, and yours is fluid and large, score 10 points.

- If it is fluid and large, and yours is tight and small, score 20 points.
- If they're both small, score 0 points.

7. Determine if the ovals (a's and o's) are tight or loose.
    - If yours are open (loose) and theirs are tight, score 30 points.
    - If yours are tight and theirs are loose, score 20 points.
    - If both yours and theirs are loose, score 50 points.
    - If both yours and theirs are tight, score 10 points.

8. Observe lead-in strokes.
    - If both of you have lead-in strokes, score 50 points.
    - If theirs has no lead-in strokes, and yours does, score 20 points.
    - If theirs has lead-in strokes, and yours doesn't, score 30 points.

9. Look for coiled ovals and counter-clockwise strokes.
    - If either sample has any, deduct 10 points for each.

10. Look at the personal pronoun "I."
    - If the writer is female and inflates the bottom portion of the I, score 50 points.
    - If the writer is male and inflates the top portion of the I, score 50 points.
    - If the writer is female and inflates the top portion of the I, score 30 points.
    - If the writer is male and inflates the bottom portion of the I, score 30 points.
    - If the "I" is printed in cursive writing, score 20 points.
    - If the "I" is printed in printed writing, score 10 points.

Add up the score. If you scored from 390 to 435, you've found a rare relationship, perhaps even a soul mate.

If you scored 280 to 390, you have differences to work out, but it's a good match. In the score is 200 points and below, you'll need to do a lot to make this relationship work.

Your goal is to see handwriting as a portrait of the personality. You'll know you're on the right track if you can determine more about people from their handwriting than you could from actually becoming acquainted with them. Get lots of practice. Every time you see a few lines of writing, think about what you already know from the slant, the letter formations and the baseline.

Let's test your accuracy, here's a sample of my writing.

I believe in the soul, crying when you feel like it, anywhere, anytime, for any reason. I believe in long, slow, deep, soft kisses that last three days, and I believe that movie stars and teachers should swap salaries. I believe in opening your presents Christmas morning rather than Christmas eve and I believe we need to be gentle with ourselves. The tasks of living, loving, learning and growing are difficult; don't be afraid to make a mistake!

Chap. 6, Fig. 6

Explanations for handwriting examples quiz:

1. A Notice the positive outlook shown by the upward slant in general, and the upward stroke on the ending of words.
2. A Generally, smaller letters mean a higher I.Q. They usually show that the writer has greater concentration and is more focused.
3. B The rightward slant indicates emotion in a writer.
4. A Coiled ovals and cramped writing are indicative of writers that lie.
5. B The larger and more relaxed the writing is, the more relaxed the writer is.
6. A An introvert's handwriting usually slants to the left.
7. A It is not as rigid as B. When writing slows down, it is a clue that the writer has lost his natural expression and has started to carefully think out his responses.
8. A Locked, tight ovals indicate a tight-lipped person. Circle letters that are left open indicate that the writer is talkative and very willing to share his ideas.

Section II

PROFESSIONAL

CHAPTER 7

How to Turn a Job Interview Into a Job: Using Body Language to Get Hired

Happy birthday to you,

Happy birthday to you,

You can use this chapter

To make your dreams come true.

I've gathered all your beautifully wrapped birthday presents in a pile and I'd like you to open first the package that most appeals to you.

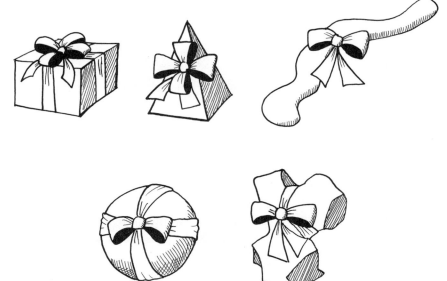

Chap. 7, Fig. 2

If your favorite package shape was the , then you

are a person whose strongest quality is leadership; if you selected

the , then you are considered an outgoing people person;

if you selected the , then you are one who will make a

very successful business executive; if you selected the

then you seem to be very indecisive about situations in your

life; and if you selected the , it is an indication that you

are perverted or wild.

No matter what package shape you selected, each is filled with the uniqueness of you, with many inner qualities and strengths. Let us note, also, that these unparalleled qualities and strengths, along with the uniqueness of a person's attitudes and emotions, can cause their package shape selection to change daily.

Job hunting success depends 70% on packaging yourself and interviewing, and 30% on background and ability.

The interview is the single most important step in winning the employment game. The interview is your chance to determine if you would like to work for an employer and the employer's chance to determine your suitability for a job. Too many interviews are psychological games; think of the interview as a negotiation where the basic issues are: What do I want? What does he/she want?

Interviewing should be considered nothing more than packaging yourself for sale. The only difference between selling yourself and selling something else is that you are both the goods and the salesperson. You determine the package color and design, the size of the ribbons, and whether the box is rectangular, circular or square in shape. In packaging yourself, you need to remember that body language counts. Speaking confidently and frankly are a must. Letting your natural personality come through is essential, and projecting positiveness and enthusiasm are as vital to your success as a neat and complete resume is to getting that initial interview.

Before we begin our research, let's check your knowledge concerning some important aspects of the interview. Answer true or false to the following questions:

1. People who have confidence in their personal worth seem to be magnets for success and happiness.
2. A relaxed manner is one of the most effective means of projecting an image of self-confidence.
3. People like to hire people that are like themselves.
4. The "bone crusher" handshake is best to use in an interview when you want to make a positive, strong impression.
5. The most effective place for your chair, if you are across the desk, is directly in front of the interviewer.
6. Interviewers that analyze every question they ask are likely to have a very cluttered, disorderly desk with two phones on it.
7. When the interviewer has his feet on his desk during the interview, it is a nonverbal gesture indicating that he is suspicious of your answers.

8. When the interviewer throws his glasses on his desk and begins to point a finger at you, he is expressing a sign of confidence.
9. Pinching the bridge of the nose with closed eyes is a sign of honesty during the job interview.
10. Upper-lip pulling by the interviewer is a sign that he is very bored by what you are saying.

Research indicates that the people who interview successfully (package themselves successfully) are the people who are promoted faster, have more self-esteem, and bounce back from the ravages of corporate life faster and higher than anyone else.

"Know thyself," said Socrates. A healthy self image is the basis for a healthy professional attitude and an enticing package. Each of us carries with us a mental blueprint of ourselves that expresses itself to others in the way we carry out our duties, handle others, and reach decisions on the job.

Everything begins with self-esteem. Everything! A fantastic job, excellent health, a great marriage, and a happy family life. When all these factors are complete in a person's life, the result is a total package. If you think nothing of yourself, you will never aspire to obtain anything of worth for yourself. Many people have more respect for Rembrandts and Picassos than for themselves. But we human beings are the real masterpieces, the real prizes. Pope John Paul II once said, "The value of a man isn't measured by what he has, but by what he is." When a person has self-esteem, he or she can build outward into the world and create works of art, just as Rembrandt and Picasso did. Believe in your own possibilities and strive to make your dreams come true. You're worth it.

Most of us hold within us the unspoken word and perhaps even unacknowledged notion that we do not deserve *all* the things we want. How absurd! Of course we're worthy; actually, we are meant to have everything our hearts desire; all the presents we want.

People who have confidence in their personal worth seem to be magnets for success and happiness. Good things drop into their laps regularly, their relationships are long-lasting, and their projects are always carried to completion.

In direct opposition, some people seem to be magnets for failure and unhappiness. Their plans go awry, they disown potential success, and nothing seems to work out for them.

The following questionnaire is designed to measure your level of self esteem, your packaging level, how you see yourself. It is not a test, so there are no right or wrong answers. Answer each item as carefully and accurately as you can by placing a number by each one of the following:

    0 = None of the time
    2 = Rarely happens
    4 = A little of the time
    6 = Some of the time
    8 = A good part of the time
  10 = Most or all of the time

_____ 1. I feel that people would like me if they really knew me well.

_____ 2. When I am with other people I feel they are glad that I am with them.

_____ 3. I feel that I am a very competent person.

_____ 4. I feel that if I could be more like other people I would have it made.

_____ 5. I feel that I get pushed around more than others.

_____ 6. I am afraid I will appear foolish to others.

_____ 7. My friends think very highly of me.

_____ 8. I think I make a good impression on others.

_____ 9. When I am with strangers I am very nervous.

_____10. I feel that I am a likeable person.

SCORING: Total the scores for a grand total. This gives a range of 0 to 100 with high scores giving more evidence of the presence of a high level of self-esteem. High scores on 1, 2, 3, 7, 8, and 10 indicate high self esteem, whereas high scores on 4, 5, 6, and 9 indicate low self-esteem.

Anyone can change his self-perception; his package. A person with low self-image is not doomed to a life of unhappiness and failure. It is possible to get rid of negative attitudes and gain the healthy confidence needed to realize one's dream. Here's how:

1. *Develop a positive attitude.* (You control the thoughts in your head.)
2. *Focus on your potential; not your limitations.* (There is only one you with limitless talents and abilities.)
3. *See yourself as successful.* (Visualize the result you want.)
4. *Build a network of supportive relationships.* (Associate with people who are optimistic and enthusiastic about life and you will soon pick up their optimism.)
5. *Dress the part.* (Although outward appearance cannot substitute for inner qualities, a positive change in outward appearance is often the beginning of a change in inner image.)
6. *Devote yourself to something you do well.* (There is nothing so common as unsuccessful people with talent.)

If you feel unsure of yourself going into an interview, the anxiety will reduce your effectiveness, make it difficult to think on your feet, and inhibit your ability to speak in a relaxed, confident manner. Your feelings will be easily detected by most interviewers and will likely be interpreted as reflecting a lack of self-confidence.

The result of a high level of self-esteem is an increased investment in self because you finally firmly believe you're worth it. Remember, you choose how you see yourself; you choose what kind of package you present to the world. There is only one you, and you are full of endless potential and talents; believe in your greatness and achieve life's rewards every day.

Once you are willing to identify and develop the uniqueness of your talents and abilities, you can identify your marketable assets, develop an action plan for getting the right interviews, prepare all the documents needed for your job search, and research organizations you want to contact.

Assuming that you have researched the interviewing company, prepared your resume and made an appointment for an interview, let us prepare for the interview itself.

For every interview you go on, there are likely to be many people under consideration. Therefore, it is important for you to come across with more "going for you" than others.

A relaxed manner is one of the most effective means of projecting an image of self-confidence when you first walk into the interview. When you appear at ease, the interviewer will feel more comfortable (remember, many interviewers may be as anxious as you are) and hence you will make a better impression. In fact, assuming you are technically qualified through experience or know-how for the position you are seeking, the degree to which the interviewer feels comfortable with you is probably the single most important determinant of your acceptability as a candidate. So let's examine some ways to help keep your anxiety level at a comfortable point.

1. Be prepared. It's obvious. The better prepared you are, the more confident you will feel.
2. Get there early. Allow yourself plenty of time to find the office.
3. Organize your materials. Have all your papers neatly organized to hand to your interviewer. It would also be helpful to have a small notebook. Sometimes during the interview, the interviewer may mention a name or telephone number that is important to remember.
4. Reduce tension. Feelings of tension can be diminished by simple relaxation exercises. (Try this one.)
   a. Take 3 deep breaths through your nose and slowly release each through your mouth.

The first key to becoming great at interviewing is to know how to build personal chemistry. When you arrange or confirm an appointment, never allow yourself to come across as flat or lacking in personality. Be sure you use the opportunity to gather more information. This will help you to be able to build better chemistry in your interview.

Can you guess what percentage of executives say their secretaries' opinions influence them? What do you think? One-third? Half? Well, about two-thirds of them do. Therefore, please be attentive to the secretary and others who work up front. You can do more than make friends; engage in a conversation that gives you helpful information for the interview. If you have to wait and the secretary is too busy to talk, give the impression that you can put the waiting time to good use.

Psychologists tell us that the way we expect to be treated has a lot to do with the way we are treated. Therefore build positive expectations and picture a friendly interviewer.

People react to the image you project, to your posture and to your body language. They react to the things you say and the way you say them. The image you project reveals your attitude, your enthusiasm and your outlook on life.

The initial greeting with the interviewer is particularly critical, since this is when the seeds that stereotype you are planted. Professional interviewers unconsciously form rigid first impressions because of the large volume of contacts they make. Stereotyping, like insisting on resumes, becomes a matter of survival.

The initial greeting should consist of the following ingredients:

1. Erect posture and a walk that shows some vigor
2. A smile
3. Direct eye contact
4. The words, "Hello, I'm (first name) (last name). It's a pleasure to meet you."
5. The interviewer's name locked in your memory and used during the interview
6. A firm but gentle handshake

Enthusiasm in the handshake properly sets the tempo of the interview. This does not mean to use a "bone crusher," to which interviewers are subjected to approximately one-third of the time. Another third will be subjected to the "dead fish" handshake. One type is painful, the other is cold, but both create a negative impression.

Once the initial impression is completed, the interviewer should motion to the interviewee to have a seat. Seating arrangement can also play a large part on the outcome of the interview.

As the interviewee enters the office he is confronted by the authority figure usually seated behind an imposing desk. A highback chair increases the feeling of authority; the two seats immediately in front of the desk are less powerful. The desk acts as a barrier separating the more authoritative from the less authoritative. Sitting in one of these chairs with the interviewer remaining behind the desk leaves you under the control of the interviewer.

Many executives, especially in job interviews, test prospective employees to see if they will attempt to control this type of situation; they may well be on the lookout for someone who can command some authority. Others go out of their way to meet you on an equal plane, seating themselves on the sofa or in one of the chairs in front of the desk.

If you're seated across the desk from the interviewer, be careful not to line the chairs up directly parallel to each other. This position can create antagonism and intimidation. If at all possible, try to get at right angles with the interviewer. Asking him to review a brochure or other written piece of information that you've brought with you allows you to move in close to him. Be on guard, however, that you don't offend the authority figure.

If you're sitting on the sofa and the other person is not, you're at a further disadvantage; the sofa swallows you up, especially if you're small. If there is a chair in front of the sofa and the discussion is a less formal one in which closer contact is needed, the sofa and chair combination is less intimidating.

Small tables in offices work especially well for meeting clients. The authority figure can still retain authority by sitting at one end of the table, while the client/interviewee is seated on either side of the table. Seating at angles from each other allows ease of conversational flow and eye contact between two people.

Once the interviewer and interviewee are comfortable in their seating positions, conversation begins. The interviewer is trying to find out, "Can you do the job?" and "What are your assets?" "Will you fit in?" and "What are your weaknesses?" Does that seem shocking? Look at it this way. The interviewer would not be talking with you unless you already had met most of the company's requirements for the job.

Again, what all this comes down to is that you need to sell yourself. For most people, being relaxed and being yourself will help gain acceptance from interviewers.

A big part of selling yourself rests on your ability to "read" your interviewers so that you respond in ways that will make the interviewer feel comfortable. This means that you "talk their language." You communicate and express yourself in a manner similar to the way the interviewer thinks and expresses himself. People like people that are like themselves.

This is not as hard to do as you might think, once you understand communication styles. Every interviewer has a communication style. It is based upon the way the individual thinks and organizes his or her thoughts.

There are four basic communication styles. Just as there are four basic temperament styles (Chapter 3), there are four interviewer styles with each one communicating differently. When someone is interviewing you whose communication style is similar to yours, the probability of hitting it off is good; you both speak the same language. When the styles vary in great depth, difficulties in relating are likely to occur.

The Four Basic Styles

1. Feelers/Sanguines. Feelers rely on gut reactions. They are perceptive to the needs of others, often sensing the right thing to say or do. They are people-oriented. They usually want to become your friend before they begin talking about the job at hand. Feelers are often attracted to jobs in areas such as sales, human resources and customer service.

   DESK. Their desk contains personal memorabilia such as family photos and mementos from previous jobs (paper weights, pen set).

   OFFICE. Their office is informal, often personalized with pictures of family, company golf outings, diplomas, certificates, or famous quotes.

   DRESS. Their clothes more casual than normal for the office. For instance, a male may wear a sport jacket with dress pants, when the more acceptable dress mode is a suit. Feelers are not afraid of color; bright dresses or ties are common.

   QUESTIONS. They are likely to spend significant time in small talk. They will probably ask questions about your relationships with others—boss, subordinates, even family. They are also likely to show in their questions an interest in you as a person, rather than simply exploring your educational or work experiences.

ANSWERS. Let the interviewer indulge in extensive small talk. If he asks about your family, you can ask about his. Emphasize your skills in working with others and the satisfactions you derive from such activities. Sharing a common family or community interest will be very appropriate.

2. Activators/Cholerics. Activators are those people with a "do-it-now" mentality. They are the doers in our world. They are concerned with end results and what is practical and tangible. They tend to be bossy and like to be in charge of the situation. Activators are often attracted to jobs in production, professional athletics, or fast-paced work environments.

DESK. Their desk is cluttered and disorderly. It is likely to be filled with piles of papers and possibly two phones.

OFFICE. Their office usually appears disorganized; piles of papers everywhere. Wall hangings are strictly business (picture of company's product); if paintings are present, they are likely to be highly action-oriented.

DRESS. They are most inclined toward simplicity. Men Activators are likely to have jackets off and sleeve cuffs rolled up. Female Activators usually dress casually.

QUESTIONS. Questions will focus on results accomplished—what did you do, how did you do it, how much did it contribute to profits? Questions are likely to be brief and to the point.

ANSWERS. Keep your answers short and to the point. Above all, don't ramble. Expect to be interrupted by phone calls. Try to include factual achievements and end results as you discuss your background. Emphasize your ability to get things done.

3. Analyzers/Melancholies. Analyzers are those that are logical, systematic, orderly, and structured. They are fact-oriented. They have a tendency to weigh everything very carefully that is said in the job interview, therefore, pay careful attention to your answers to questions. Analyzers are often attracted

to jobs in accounting, engineering, and data processing.

DESK. Their desk is always neat and orderly, sometimes almost bare, except for a calculator or computer.

OFFICE. Their surroundings are businesslike. No frills. Charts and grafts are important giveaways of the Analyzer. Their office will always be neat and tidy.

DRESS. Analyzers usually dress conservatively. Whatever they wear will look neat, tidy, and well pressed. Male Analyzers will often wear ties that are plain or have neat geometric designs.

QUESTIONS. The Analyzer will ask for many facts and figures—what was your grade point average? Your salary in each of your jobs? How much did your efforts contribute to profits? Their questions are likely to appear businesslike and perhaps even curt.

ANSWERS. The interviewee should try to describe his background in a complete and chronological manner. The Analyzer likes information presented in an organized, logical, and systematic way. The interviewee should avoid ambiguous expressions such as "approximately" or "really did well" and also avoid excessive expressions of emotion.

4. Conceptualizer/Phlegmatics. Conceptualizers are the most diplomatic, easy going interviewers. They are concerned with future events, are creative and innovative. They are the best listeners and very easy to talk to, but as you talk, they are weighing all your answers. Conceptualizers make good structural engineers, draftsmen, statisticians and because of their meticulous patience, are drawn to the field of education.

DESK. Their desks are piled with books. Often two piles of reports, side by side, being studied for trends.

OFFICE. The interviewee should look for bookcases filled with technical literature. The room may also include intellectual toys (Rubik's cube, three-dimensional tic-tac-toe, kaleidoscope) and abstract paintings.

DRESS. There are two possibilities of dress for the Conceptualizer. If he is fashion-conscious, his dress will be trendy or avant-guard. If the Conceptualizer is not concerned with fashion (more typical), dress may appear like stereotypical absent-minded professor—things may not quite match.

QUESTIONS. The Conceptualizer's questions will center about your ideas and concepts--particularly about the future. Conceptualizers do not focus on the here-and-now issues. Typical questions will begin with, "What do you think about . . .?"

ANSWERS. The interviewee should avoid dwelling on the past and talk about future goals. Whenever possible, the interviewee should mention new or innovative ideas that he developed. The Conceptualizer sometimes goes off on tangents; therefore, the interviewee should contribute his ideas and follow along.

If you would like practice in tailoring your way of thinking and communicating to that of your interviewers, turn to the end of this Chapter and complete the Commonly Asked Interview Questions (This test lists the most often asked questions during interviews and asks the test taker to answer each one as if it were asked from a Feeler, an Activator, an Analyzer and a Conceptualizer.) and the Communication Styles Questions. You will probably find these exercises both fun and informative.

Knowing that interviewers have different communication styles gives you an advantage for responding to questions in ways that will gain acceptance. A key ingredient to a successful interview is to enable the person across the desk to feel comfortable with you. This is most easily achieved using responses that match the interviewer's pattern of thinking.

Another nonverbal message that the interviewee can use to gain acceptance by the interviewer is to learn to read the interviewer's body language. His gestures, body signals, and how he uses the space around him all convey a message.

One can learn to use and incorporate gestures and body movements into everyday situations to reflect a sincere and confident self and to "read" others more effectively. People use their natural instincts to observe others and are thrown off by nonverbal signals that contradict a spoken message. Because body signals encompass so much information, we will focus on several gestures commonly seen in the job interview process by both the interviewer and interviewee.

Next are the eight basic categories of nonverbal expressions that are visible during the job interview. Keep in mind that no single gesture or position means a specific emotion or attitude. However, a number of signals from the same category will clue you in on others or on your own feelings.

1. *Dominance, Superiority, Power*
   This first category is often exhibited by someone who is very high in the corporate structure. He usually lets others know who is the boss. Power signals include:

   long pause before answering the door knock
   large desk with owner's chair larger and higher
        than guests
   hands on hips
   fingers hooked in belt
   steepling (finger tips touching)
   hands behind neck
   leg over chair
   sitting astride chair
   exaggerated leaning over table or desk
   piercing eye contact
   standing while other is seated
   palm-down handshake
   feet on desk

   Usually it is easy to see their need for control. Don't let them intimidate you, but don't start a power struggle either. Never use these gestures yourself in a job interview.

2. *Submission, Apprehension, Nervousness*
   People who use these signals usually need reassurance. These signs are visible in those who feel insecure about making decisions. Perhaps they have

just been promoted and they don't want to make any mistakes. Submission signals include:

palm-up handshake
hand-wringing
fidgeting
fingers clasped
hands to face, groin, hair
head down
minimum of eye contact
rubbing back of neck (disgusted)
briefcase guarding body
constant blinking
unnecessary throat clearing
twitching
whistling

People who are unsure of themselves and their ability to make good decisions will show their nervousness. Don't mirror their behaviors or come on too strong. Again, don't use these gestures yourself.

3. *Disagreement, Anger, Skepticism*
   These signals are usually reactions to what you have said. Most people begin indicating their feelings of disagreement, anger, or skepticism in very subtle ways. If you don't acknowledge these messages, they will become increasingly agitated, sometimes to the point of violence. They may even throw things or pound on their desk. Beware of:

   redness of skin
   crossed arms, legs
   hands gripping edge of desk or table
   throwing glasses on desk
   fist in sight
   finger-pointing
   pursed lips
   squinting eyes
   frown
   turn body away
   finger under the collar (hot under the collar)

People may be hesitant to verbally shout at you, but their body language will warn you that they're unhappy. Don't copy their gestures and never exhibit any of these extremely negative behaviors.

4. *Boredom, Disinterest*
These messages reflect a person's reaction to your overall answers. Your job is to regain their attention before disinterest turns to dissatisfaction.

dead fish handshake
shuffle papers
clean fingernails
lack of eye contact
look at watch, door, out of window, at ceiling
play with objects on desk
pick at clothes
doodle
drum table, tap feet
head in palm of hand
pen-clicking

Interviewer may be listening to you out of politeness rather than interest. If you notice any of these signals, stop what you are doing or saying and use some attention-getting tactics.

5. *Suspicion, Secretiveness, Dishonesty*
These messages are just as important in interviews as they are to law enforcement agencies. When one party suspects that the other is lying or concealing information, it brings open communication to a halt. Watch for:

left-hand nose touching while speaking
left-hand ear tugging while speaking
left-hand eye rubbing while speaking
covering mouth while speaking
consistent avoidance of eye contact
move body away from you
peering over glasses
crossed arms and legs with body forward
squint eyes
fingers crossed

Almost everyone displays nonverbal clues when lying, so watch yourself.

6. *Uncertainty, Indecision, Time Stalls*
    When people exhibit these signs, it usually means that they need a break from your presentation. More information is not always helpful when people cannot make up their minds. Others will appreciate your sensitivity to their needs when you slow down or pause for a few moments. Note these signs:

    pinch bridge of nose with closed eyes
    tug at pants while sitting
    pace back and forth
    pencil to mouth
    clean glasses
    bite lip
    scratch head
    shift eyes to right and left
    neck-pulling
    putting objects in mouth (pen, pencil)
    jingling money in pockets

    When people have questions that keep them from making a decision or need time to think, they display the above signs. Give them some time to gather their thoughts and formulate their questions before probing.

7. *Evaluation*
    These signals are important because they indicate whether a person is listening to what another is saying. They are indicators to tell us whether to go on with our conversation or not. Look for signs like:

    hand stroking chin with index finger, middle finger
        and thumb pointing upward
    bent index finger and thumb gripping chin
    head tilted slightly
    index finger to lips
    touch tips of temple bars of glasses to lips
    upper-lip pulling

good eye contact
nodding
ear turned toward speaker

When someone is evaluating what you are saying, these gestures are present. Positive evaluation gestures on your part show others that you are interested in what they are saying.

8. *Confidence, Honesty, Cooperation*
These signals should be given out by everyone when trying to reach others. They signify people that are relaxed, happy, open and friendly. These positive signs are:

palms toward other person, open hands
lean forward in seat
sit far up in chair
good eye contact
legs uncrossed
jacket open
hands to chest
mirror speaker's positive movements
vertical handshake
smile

As an interviewee, you should concentrate on using the signals in this list as often as possible, regardless of other's negative signals.

In sales, the saying, "Know when the sale is over and then leave," is often used to remind us of the conclusion of an event. This same principle applies equally well to employment interviews. The interviewer will almost always give an indication when the interview is about to end. It's extremely important to be alert for these subtle nonverbal clues. An interviewer is clearly letting you know something if he:

1. Peeks at his watch or wall clock
2. Begins shuffling papers on his desk
3. Glances at his appointment calendar

Whatever the clues, it is very important not to ignore them. The more straightforward they are, the more essential it is to react to them.

Once you assume that the interview is over and you've said all that you wanted to say, it is important to remember to stress these points in your closing.

1. Your strong interest in the position
2. Your excitement and enthusiasm about the job/company
3. Your confidence in your ability to do the job

You want to leave the interviewer reassured that his decision to make you an offer is the right one. This means that it is as important to pay attention to your exit as it is to your entrance. Folding up and quietly slipping away at the end can easily undermine a good impression made during your interview. For this reason it is a good idea to plan and rehearse a strong basic exit statement and procedure.

When it comes to getting the job you want, successful interviews are absolutely essential and nonverbal communication is a vital part of that success. Dr. Albert Mehrabian, professor of psychology at UCLA, put things into perspective when he found that our feelings and attitudes are communicated only 7 percent with words, 38 percent with tone of voice, and 55 percent nonverbally.

No matter how solid and impressive your background may be, the way you are perceived during your interview, how well you can convince the interviewer that you are the kind of person that he wants in the job, and how many presents (positive qualities) you can bring to the table, will determine what will happen next—job offer or job turndown.

Keep in mind that to get hired for a particular job all you need to do is PRESENT yourself as a perfect solution to the interviewer's problem. Make certain that your ENTIRE PACKAGE is perfect.

Answers to Quiz at beginning of Chapter:

1.	T	6.	F
2.	T	7.	F
3.	T	8.	F
4.	F	9.	F
5.	F	10.	F

COMMONLY ASKED INTERVIEW QUESTIONS
(ADAPTING YOUR INTERVIEW COMMENTS)

This exercise will help you adapt your interview comments to match the communication style of your interviewer (after you have discovered that his style is different from yours).

In each example, imagine you are faced with an interviewer who prefers the communication styles given. Write out a possible response.

1. "Tell me about yourself."

   Activator: _____

   _____

   Feeler: _____

   _____

2. "What are your strengths?"

   Analyzer: _____

   _____

   Feeler: _____

   _____

3. "What are your major weaknesses or limitations?"

   Conceptualizer: _____

   _____

   Analyzer:_____

   _____

4. "What are your financial requirements?"

   Conceptualizer: _____

   _____

   Feeler: _____

   _____

5. "Why are you leaving (or did you leave) your present position?"

   Activator: _____

   _____

   Analyzer: _____

   _____

6. "What are your career goals for the next five years?"

   Feeler: _____

   _____

   Analyzer: _____

   _____

7. "What kind of a position are you looking for?"

   Activator: _____

   _____

   Conceptualizer: _____

   _____

8. "What was your most significant accomplishment in your last position?"

   Analyzer: _____

   _____

   Activator: _____

   _____

9. "Have you ever been fired?"

   Feeler: _____

   _____

   Analyzer: _____

   _____

10. "What was the last book you read?"

   Activator: _____

   _____

   Conceptualizer: _____

   _____

COMMUNICATION STYLES QUESTIONS

Which of the four basic communication style interviewers (Feelers, Activators, Analyzers, or Conceptualizers) would more than likely ask each of the following questions?

_____ 1. How were your high school/college grades and rank?

_____ 2. Have you managed people before?

_____ 3. What major challenges have you faced?

_____ 4. Describe a typical day in your job?

_____ 5. What do you think of your ex-boss?

_____ 6. Can you fit into an unstructured environment?

_____ 7. How have you helped reduce costs?

_____ 8. How effective are you as a motivator?

_____ 9. How do you handle confrontation?

_____10. What full- or part-time job did you hold while in school?

_____11. What activities were your involved in during high school or college?

_____12. How did you finance your education?

_____13. How often have you had raises?

_____14. What do you think you are worth?

_____15. Who are your closest friends? What do they do?

_____16. How often have you been absent from work?

_____17. Have you ever been arrested or convicted?

_____18. Are you interested in sports?

_____19. How much debt do you have?

_____20. In what areas can you improve?

_____21. Who do you admire?

_____22. Why should we hire you?

_____23. What work environment are you looking for?

_____24. How old are you?

_____25. What subjects did you enjoy most? Least?

CHAPTER 8

Business as Usual: Cultural Diversity at Work in Nonverbal Communication

Bon jour! Buenos dias! Olla! Hallo! Ciao!

Remember the movie, *Around the World in 80 Days?* Well, fasten your seat belts. We're going around the world in 80 minutes!

Did you know that you shouldn't show the soles of your feet in Saudi Arabia, talk business at lunch in Paris, be long-winded in London, or short spoken in Japan.

These are a few of the reasons why, if you plan to do business abroad or with different cultures, you should thoroughly investigate the following information. As Americans landing in another country, we're easy to spot. The moment we step off the airplane there seems to be a mark on our forehead that says, "Made in USA, by Americans." We feel unique and special, and often desire preferential treatment.

As a point of reference, I will use the term "American" to apply solely to citizens of the United States. I have chosen this mode since people from the other Americas typically call themselves Canadian, Brazilian, Venezuelan, Mexican, and so on, *not* American. "Foreigner" is the word I have chosen to use when referring to people of other cultures. To an American, a foreigner is any non-American; the word "foreigner" is not meant to have any discriminatory connotation.

Americans who have the greatest success in doing business abroad are those who have learned how to strike a balance between capitalizing upon the strengths and advantages they enjoy as Americans and showing a credible appreciation and understanding of the social and business customs of other cultures.

147

The global marketplace has become highly competitive. The United States is losing out not only to Japan but to South Korea, Taiwan, Brazil, Mexico, and a host of other nations.

We are innocents abroad, because fewer than 10 percent of U.S. colleges and universities require knowledge of a foreign language for entrance. In fact, only a few years ago, 40 percent of high school seniors in a national poll thought Israel was an Arab nation.

Americans are critically deficient in skills required for international business, whereas other countries and foreign businesses send representatives to the United States for the purpose of gathering information about rival companies and trying to understand Americans.

We must also look on the other side of the coin. American business practices are respected around the world. We have excellence to be proud of and an inescapable cultural influence in the world. Coca-Cola is requested in over eighty languages and is served several million times a day. We can even hear a Japanese child in San Francisco exclaiming, "Daddy, they have McDonald's in America, too!"

The American way of doing things is quite distinct from the way business is done in every other country. It is made up of the ways Americans behave at work and the way they do their jobs. Certain behaviors that are expected and rewarded here are considered unprofessional and counter-productive by other cultures.

People around the world feel as strongly about their culture as we do about ours. It is pointless to argue whether a culture is "good" or "bad"; every nationality thinks its culture is the best.

Test your knowledge of other cultures by completing the following "Are You Internationable?" quiz:

1. The Sabbath is observed on Friday in :
    a. Germany
    b. South America
    c. Saudi Arabia

2. Confucianism is the predominant religion in:
    a. Spain
    b. Hong Kong
    c. France

3. The proper way to address Miss Li Win Son is:
   a. Madame Son
   b. Madame Li
   c. Madame Win

4. "Triple play" kisses (one cheek, the other cheek, and then back to the first cheek again) is common in:
   a. Japan
   b. France
   c. Germany

5. In Japan, which number is equivalent to our unlucky number 13?
   a. 4
   b. 5
   c. 15

6. The color for mourning in Mexico is:
   a. Purple
   b. White
   c. Yellow

7. Invitations sent out in this country usually tell you to arrive at "American" or "airport" time. The country is:
   a. Brazil
   b. Germany
   c. Japan

8. Business cards should be accepted with both hands in:
   a. India
   b. Africa
   c. Japan

9. With regards to space, which of the following people require the least space in a two-party conversation?
   a. Germans
   b. Australians
   c. French

10. In Japan, when referring to a person who is a bragger, the Japanese will:
    a. place a fist to their nose
    b. point to their nose
    c. pinch their nose

11. "Thumbs up" is equivalent to raising the middle finger in America, in:
    a. France
    b. Australia
    c. Africa

12. "San" is always added to the surname of a person in:
    a. Japan
    b. South Africa
    c. Germany

13. What country believes that the left hand is dirty and should be reserved for toilet paper, nothing else?
    a. Hong Kong
    b. Saudi Arabia
    c. Germany

14. Making a circle with the thumb and index finger:
    a. means "money" in Japan
    b. is vulgar in Brazil
    c. is considered impolite in Russia and Greece
    d. all of the above

15. "Ramadan," the month-long fast, is celebrated in:
    a. Sweden
    b. Saudi Arabia
    c. Greece

16. In this formal culture, people are always addressed with Herr, Frau, or Fraulein placed before their last name. The country is:
    a. Australia
    b. Spain
    c. Germany

17. Which of the following people use the expression, "sitting near the window," to refer to employees who are being retired?
    a. Arabs
    b. Japanese
    c. Spaniards

(Answers to "Are You Internationable?" are found at the end of this chapter.)

Cultures have their own logic. Anthropologists point out that cultures are different because various peoples had to deal with diverse circumstances to meet their common human needs: different climates, different resources, different terrain. Just as animal species evolved differently to adapt to different conditions, mankind also evolved diverse solutions to life's problems. Over the years, the complex array of solutions to problems (many of which disappeared long ago) created the patterns in cultural behaviors. One can only begin to understand the customs of a nation by analyzing and considering the different past, present and future of that nation.

The first step to understanding another culture is understanding your own. What follows are the most outstanding differences that seem to separate Americans from the rest of the world. The outstanding differences that cause American problems are:

Problems of pace: Time is money. To many foreigners, we seem to always be in a hurry, rarely stopping to enjoy the present. We come across as harried and jittery, slaves to the clock. In other countries, clocks walk; in America, clocks run. Foreigners have observed that we treat time as a valuable, tangible and limited resource. Like money, we save time, waste time, give time, take time, make time, spend time, and even run out of time.

We even use time as a form of nonverbal communication that is understood loud and clear within our own culture. On a typical appointment in America, one would be on time. To arrive early, though, could suggest anxiousness or over-eagerness to the client.

A client in America will be kept waiting only briefly. A longer wait communicates disrespect or an extreme inequality in status. Presidents can keep janitors waiting, but subordinates cannot keep supervisors waiting.

Once the meeting begins in America, both parties expect that the business can be conducted within twenty, thirty, or sixty minutes and they both move unhesitantly toward the final objective. If the meeting is interrupted by phone calls or other distractions, the client will resent the loss of time, and if the objective of the meeting is not accomplished near the end of the appointment, panic may set in. If the meeting proceeds on schedule, however, a conclusion will be reached and all involved will feel a sense of accomplishment.

Meetings are likely to progress in a like manner in Australia, Israel, Germany, Switzerland, or Scandinavia. But in many parts of the world, time is not the issue. People come late to appointments or don't show up at all. In many countries, meetings begin with long socializing over many cups of coffee or tea. This socializing does not mean five or ten minutes, it may mean hours, perhaps even several meetings during which the business objective is not even mentioned. Note that, Americans consider coffee breaks and social visiting as doing nothing, whereas Arabs consider drinking coffee and chatting as doing something. Americans who resent this "waste of time," need to know that during these apparently aimless conversations, important progress is being made toward establishing credibility and rapport, which are fundamental to the conducting of future business.

Americans are also frustrated by how meetings progress once they start. The visitor to Saudi Arabia is likely to find that the appointment is not a private affair. Many people may be in the room at the same time (including competitors) and the Saudi may "do the rounds," circulating around the room, stopping to chat with each of the visitors. An American asking the question, "Could we speak privately?" during a business meeting is accommodated simply by the Arab leaning closer to him/her.

Americans work by schedules and deadlines. We rush to beat the clock. Deadlines elsewhere, though, may produce opposite results. An Arab may take a deadline as an insult. In Japan, a delay means something quite different. Japanese invest much research and analysis in a decision, but once a decision is made, it is carried out much quicker than a decision made in the United States because of the preparation that went into the decision.

In Mexico, tactfully asking if the meeting is to be held on "Mexican time" or "American time," can help to clarify the beginning time for a meeting. Saudi clients might have an American flown in to some major city or exotic resort for a meeting, only to delay for days. The American sometimes spends one to five days waiting in his/her hotel until the Saudi is ready to see him/her. Of course, he/she is well compensated for his/her time and expenses.

Problems of conduct: Form over substance. Years ago, Japanese were required to behave in precisely prescribed ways: wearing permitted clothing, walking only a certain way, sleeping with their heads pointed in a certain direction, and even with their legs arranged a certain way. Many work tasks, such as eating, greeting, gesturing with hands and opening doors had to be done in an assigned way without deviation. This unspoken code of conduct became a measure of morality and virtue.

Other societies, too, have a prescribed form and manner for every familiar situation that might arise. Throughout East Asia, actions are judged by the manner in which they are performed. The question of how someone went about trying to complete a task is more important than the accomplishment of the task itself. Questions like, "Did he act sincerely?" and "Was this done in good faith?" are often asked during the completion of the task. Americans are more goal-oriented than method-conscious.

The aspect of "saving face" is another aspect of form that is important in Japan, China, Asia, Arabia and South America. What an American might see as a little honest and constructive criticism, the foreigner may take as a devastating blow to pride and dignity. For some countries, just about anything can be taken personally. Even not taking your shoes off in a mosque or complaining about the heat can seriously insult a foreigner.

Environmental concerns are also very important in some countries. In Japan a woman would wear a soft pastel dress to a flower show so as not to take away from the beauty of the flowers. In countries where people believe in reincarnation, they are careful about any and all forms of life. In India, for example, people are careful not to swallow gnats or step on ants; one might be a relative.

Whereas Americans exchange business cards only when they need to pass on information about addresses and telephone numbers, business persons in other countries use them to establish rank and status and exchange cards before doing any business. The cards themselves must be treated with respect, not scribbled on or stuffed into a back pocket and sat upon. Business cards should have the English translated into the language of the hosts, either on the back of the card or immediately below each line on the front. Business cards that are to be used in foreign countries should not have any abbreviations on them. In most of Southeast Asia, Africa, and the Middle East, it is not proper to present the card with your left hand. In Japan, one should accept the card with both hands, making sure the type is facing the recipient and is right-side-up.

Before visiting a country, it is wise to find out what the major holidays are and what the days of the week represent to that culture. Arabs observe Friday as their Sabbath; some businesses even close early on Thursdays in preparation for Friday. During Ramadan, the Moslem month-long fast season, not much business is done at all.

In Israel, the Sabbath is observed on Saturday, and many Catholic countries have a carnival season just before Lent (like Mardi Gras in New Orleans). It is called *Fasching* in Germany, and *Carnival* in South America.

In China and elsewhere in Asia, the New Year celebration, also call the Spring Festival, is held in the winter and lasts two weeks. The Japanese have many holidays, including the New Year holidays, which last for five to ten days beginning December 28. Many firms also close from April 20 to May 5.

In Europe many people go on vacation the entire month of August, closing their shops, restaurants and business offices.

Not only are holidays in other countries celebrated on different days than Americans celebrate them, but some countries even have different manners in which they consume their food.

In some countries, people eat with their hands; in others with chopsticks, and in others with knives and forks. Arabs eat using the right hand only. Europeans eat with knives and forks, but don't switch them from hand to hand the way Americans do. They use the right hand for holding the knife and cutting and the left hand for holding the fork and eating.

Meal times vary too. The main meal may be at midday, followed by a siesta. In Spain and Latin countries, the evening meal is hardly ever eaten before 10 p.m.

Problems of communication: What is truth and does it mat-

ter? In America we tend to be direct, open, to the point, and are uncomfortable with silence. Americans who use this style for negotiating may not be particularly effective in countries that consider directness abrupt and demanding, or intrusive. A direct person may be seen as untrustworthy. Giving details and specifics may insult one's intelligence. Written contracts, to some, imply that a person's word is not good.

1. *Be careful how you express emotion.* The kiss, for example, is not always associated with romance or love. Some cultures see kissing as unsanitary or crude, and certainly not something to be done in public. Americans sometimes suspect marital problems if a couple does not kiss or hug at the airport, but, in Japan it would seem odd to embrace when getting off a plane. Men and women do not touch in public in Japan. While the British and Scandinavians are reserved when demonstrating affection, a kiss on both cheeks (and in some countries a "triple play," one cheek, the other cheek, and then back to the first cheek again) is common in France and other French-speaking countries. Brazilians also kiss enthusiastically in public, and in Russia men often kiss squarely on the mouth.

    Arabs first shake hands, then put their right hand on your left shoulder and kiss you on both cheeks. You are not supposed to shake hands with Arab women.

    Men, though, are free to weep, shout and gesture wildly in the Arab world. To Arabs, loudness (decibel levels that are obnoxious by American standards) is a sign of strength and sincerity, while soft tones imply weakness or deviousness.

    In the less expressive countries of China and Asia, the people are inclined to giggle or smile when embarrassed or when told bad news; they also laugh at the sad parts in movies. There is a difference, though, in their smiles of pleasure and their courtesy smiles meant to suppress emotion; it can plainly be seen in their eyes.

2. *Silence is a form of speech; don't interrupt it.* Americans feel uncomfortable with too much silence; we talk when we should wait patiently.

Some cultures use silence as their "communication spaces;" time to formulate their next move. Scandinavians are flustered by the American tendency to interrupt or finish sentences. Africans are offended by our tendency to talk at them and to interrupt. Even our agreement phrase of, "I know, I know," is taken as a putdown. It is far better to listen quietly and not interrupt.

3. *Learn to speak body language.* In America, we are sometimes more careful about what we say than how we say it. Abroad, 90 percent of communication is accomplished without words.

As travelers, we believe that if we do not know the language, we will be able to use gestures to get our message across. Gestures, though, have quite different meanings in different parts of the world; body language is not universal.

Thumbs up is considered vulgar in Australia, Iran and Ghana, and is equivalent to raising the middle finger in the United States. (Former President Bush learned this lesson on a visit to Australia.) In Yugoslavia, people shake their heads from side to side for yes; appearing to us to be saying no.

Making a circle with the thumb and index finger, a sign for "okay" in America, is a vulgar sign in Brazil, is considered impolite in Russia and Greece, means "money" in Japan, and "zero" or "worthless" in southern France.

Generally Americans expect a firm handshake at greeting and at parting. This is not the case in Arab countries. The Arab handshake is limp and light and done several times a day, often after only a brief separation. Arab handshaking follows a protocol based on rank. You must shake hands with the most important person first, then move on down the line. The rank order can be identified by focusing on the person who sits in the middle of the room, surrounded by other guests who pay obvious honor to him.

Looking someone in the eye is disrespectful in many parts of the world. Americans are more likely to trust and like someone who looks them straight in the eyes, rather than someone who looks away. However, in Japan a person who looks a subordinate in the eye is felt to be judgmental and degrading, while someone who looks his superior in the eye is assumed to be hostile or slightly insane.

Arabs like eye contact, while the British try to keep your attention by looking away while they talk. When their eyes return to yours, it signals they have finished speaking and it is your turn to talk.

The way a person walks or sits also produces a large impact on his nonverbal message. In America, we often slouch and tend to relax in business meetings. This reclined position in northern Europe, however, reveals that your parents didn't teach you proper posture. To make a good impression in Japan or Korea, you must sit with your feet squarely placed on the ground. This position indicates good breeding and maturity.

Even though it is not advisable to wear the costume of the country you are visiting, dressing properly in specific countries is important.

In Europe, coats and ties are required for business. Even in the hottest months, coats stay on in offices and restaurants. Women never wear pants to a dressy restaurant and sometimes a striped tie in England can be mistaken for a regimental tie worn only by those who have been members of certain military regiments.

Women visiting strict Moslem countries should wear dresses and skirts well below the knee, keep elbows covered, and necklines high.

4. *Be aware of other nonverbal messages.* In some countries, colors are ranked, just as we rank gold or silver. Depending on the occasion, the color of clothing, gifts or gift wrapping can cause great embarrassment.

Green, America's color for freshness and good health, is often associated with disease in countries with dense green jungles. Black is not universal for mourning; in many Asian countries it is white, in Brazil it is purple, yellow in Mexico, and dark red in the Ivory Coast. Americans think of blue as the most masculine color, but red is more manly in the United Kingdom or France. While pink is the most feminine color in America, yellow is more feminine in most of the world. Red suggests good fortune in China, but death in Turkey.

Symbols, too, have different meanings in different countries. The lemon scent in the United States suggests freshness, but in the Philippines, it is associated with illness. In Japan, the number 4 is like our number 13; and 7 is unlucky for Ghana, Kenya and Singapore. The stork symbolizes maternal death in Singapore, and the owl is bad luck in India, just like our black cat is here in America.

"No" is said nonverbally in the Middle East by an arrogant, backwards jerk of the head, a sudden raising of the eyebrows, or a clicking of the tongue.

Japanese beckon by fluttering the fingers palm down, the way we Americans say good-bye. When referring to themselves, Japanese point to their noses. Pinching the nose indicates a dislike for a person and a fist to the nose indicates a bragger.

A crocked index finger conveys dishonesty. Japanese grind their fists in the palm of their hand as a sign of flattery.

Problems of work attitudes: If there's a will, there's a way. Underlying much of American enterprise is the conviction that individuals and organizations can substantially influence the future, that we are the masters of our destiny. This is not so in many other countries.

In Moslem countries from Libya and Turkey to Indonesia, the will of Allah influences every detail of life and many feel it is irreligious to plan for the future. Even though many Moslem executives do think in terms of strategy and plans, they will regard their efforts in the context of what God wills.

Americans take pride in their work; we take work home, we conduct business at social functions, and other people find us to be "workaholics." Very few other cultures have such a devotion to work as the Americans. In some countries, work is generally something that must be done out of necessity, not an all-consuming drive.

America is dominant in world enterprise, but our direct, efficient and materialistic standards clash with ethical and aesthetic values in many parts of the world. In South America, business is done among friends in a leisurely and sympathetic way. Hiring of relatives is widely practiced around the world. Here in America, we call it nepotism. Perhaps, though, it is wise to hire family members that will be loyal to you, rather than strangers who feel no family obligations. Cooperation, rather than competition, is Japan's mode of conduct. Workers are encouraged to work in teams and are highly embarrassed if singled out either for praise or criticism.

Money is not an incentive everywhere; honor, dignity and family are sometimes more important.

Problems of relationships: Individualism versus the group. In America, great value is attached to "doing your own thing." We tend to admire independence in a person. However, in other countries, American self-reliance and independence are seen as a curse to family and community responsibility. In many countries, friends, family, tribes, or even employers are not to be taken lightly. Dependence on these institutions is considered social insurance.

Abroad, a business partner is more desirable if he is well connected to a respectable family or network of friends. They feel that one who is connected to others of any status is better than one who is a loner. Perhaps it would be wise if Americans traveling would realize this and not be afraid to tell someone of their lives and backgrounds.

Problems of space: My space or yours? Space speaks. Americans treat space similarly to the way they treat time. The larger the space, the more status. Americans who are moved to smaller offices or who are crowded together worry about their status in an organization. While window offices are high-status in the United States, the Japanese expression, "sitting near the window" refers to employees who are being retired.

The French are likely to place a supervisor at the center, where workers can be kept under control. In Japan, everything is open and crowded. Supervisors sit at one end of a room, maybe at the head of a giant table where they can view everything that is going on in the room. A Japanese room typically has most of the furniture in the middle of the room, whereas we place furniture and room decorations around the walls of a room.

Personal space varies among nationalities also. Americans usually stand just a little over an arm's length apart. Next time you are talking to an American, you will probably be able to stretch out your arm and find your thumb pointing into his/her ear. (Try it!) Arabs or South Americans are comfortable much closer, so close that an American may become extremely uncomfortable. In general, the following nationalities can be characterized as preferring a closer or more distant space on the first meeting:

Preferred distances	Nationalities
Close	Arabs
	Japanese
	South Americans
	French
	Greeks
	Black North Americans
	Hispanics
	Italians
	Spaniards

Moderate   British
                             Swedish
                             Swiss
                             Germans
                             Austrians

Far   White North
                                Americans
                             Australians
                             New Zealanders

From the above facts, it is easy to see that people around the world just do not see and do things the same way; our ways of thinking are at odds with the rest of the world. Let's examine the following question and see how various nationalities deal with it.

You are traveling on a sea voyage with your wife, your child and your mother. The ship begins to have problems and starts to sink. You are the only one in your family who can swim and you can save only one other individual. Whom do you save? In Western countries, 60 percent of those responding would save the child, 40 percent would save the wife. None saves the mother. In Eastern countries, 100 percent would save the mother. The Eastern rationale is that you can always re-marry and have more children, but you can never have another mother. Are Easterners sending a nonverbal message to their spouses?

Nonverbal symbols and messages cause a great deal of misunderstanding in intercultural communications; therefore, the remainder of this chapter clarifies the sensitivities, forms of address, courtesies, business do's and don'ts, entertainment re-quirements, languages and religious beliefs of a few select countries that are main trading partners of the United States.

A GLIMPSE AT AUSTRALIA:

Sensitivities: Do not give any unsolicited advice or comment. Avoid any artificial behavior that would be adopted to impress others.

Forms of Address: First names are widely and quickly used, but wait to use first names until invited to do so.

Courtesies: Shake hands at the beginning and end of meetings. People here are generally more informal; don't be too stiff.

Business Do's: At the beginning of meetings, try to make brief preliminary comments (sports, cultural events, Australian sights), then get quickly down to business. Communicate directly, with confidence and good humor.

Business Don'ts: Do not use social occasions to talk business; recreation and eating are for relaxation.

Entertainment: Dinner is usually about six o'clock. Please be on time, never late. Guests sometimes bring flowers, wine or beer, not usually gifts. A "thank you" upon leaving is all that is expected.

Language: English

Religion: 80 percent Christian (about evenly Anglican, Roman Catholic, and Protestant); 15 percent uncommitted.

A GLIMPSE AT BRAZIL:

Sensitivities: Brazil is very different and proudly independent from the rest of South America. Use Portuguese (not Spanish) and do not refer to Brazilians as Latin Americans.

Forms of Address: Brazilians are quick to use first names, but wait to be asked. Last names are often a combination of both the mother's and father's last names. Most often, people are addressed by their first name with a title, as in Senhor Paulo or Dona Maria.

Courtesies: When entering or leaving a party, go around to each person and say the appropriate, "good evening" or "goodbye." The broad "hi everybody," is insulting to the Brazilian.

Business Do's: Conduct business in person as much as possible, and try to maintain a continuous working relationship. It is a good idea to use business cards.

Business Don'ts: Don't speak Spanish; use English or an interpreter. Do not rush your visits and do not get directly down to business.

Entertainment: Invitations will usually tell you to come "American" or "airport" time, which means on time; otherwise be a bit late so as not to embarrass your hosts by arriving before they are ready. Candy, champagne or a basket of fruit would be appreciated. Flowers should be sent the next day.

Language: Portuguese, not Spanish.

Religion: Predominately Roman Catholic.

A GLIMPSE AT CANADA:

Sensitivities: Many Canadians feel snubbed by Americans; they hate being "talked down to" by Americans. Recognizing that Canada is one of our major trading partners as well as a good neighbor is greatly appreciated.

Forms of Address: Use first names after being invited to do so.

Courtesies: Canadians are generally more reserved and more attentive to etiquette than most Americans.

Business Do's: Business should be conducted with directness, clarity and thoroughness. Canadians like to hear that you are familiar with their geography, political system and current events.

Business Don'ts: Don't come on too strong or too slick.

Entertainment: Dinner is sometimes served as early as five o'clock, or after seven. Plan to stay two or three hours and a "thank you" upon leaving is sufficient.

Language: Canada is officially bilingual (English and French), except in Quebec, where the official language is French.

Religion: Christian. The Roman Catholic Church predominates in French Canada; Catholics, Anglicans and Baptists predominate in Atlantic Canada, and United Church predominates in Western Canada.

A GLIMPSE AT THE PEOPLE'S REPUBLIC OF CHINA:

Sensitivities: Avoid remarks about politics or Chinese leaders. Foreign currency is forbidden. Gifts are risky, and tipping is officially discouraged. Keep a record of every transaction, and bring out of the country everything you take in with you, or you will be suspected of bribery.

Forms of Address: The family name is always mentioned first, so that Son Wu is Mr. Son, or Li Win is Madame Li.

Courtesies: A nod or slight bow from the shoulders (not the Japanese bow) is customary, but shaking hands is acceptable. Using proper introductions and following proper banquet etiquette is important.

Business Do's: Business cards in Chinese and English are essential. Pay strict attention to rank and hierarchy. Go to meetings thoroughly prepared and bring a team of experts; the Chinese expect you to know every detail about your own (and competitors') products.

Business Don'ts: Business is not usually discussed at meals. Do not give gifts except ceremoniously at banquets; avoid any suggestion of a bribe.

Entertainment: Most entertaining will be at banquets. Each guest may be seated and served by the host; do not serve yourself. Eat sparingly, because there are many courses. Always make a toast so that others will join you; never drink alone. The host will signal the end of the meal, and you should depart promptly.

Language: Chinese; but there are hundreds of dialects. Interpreters are essential.

Religion: Communist; officially, atheism is endorsed.

A GLIMPSE AT FRANCE:

Sensitivities: Avoid talking about politics, money and personal matters.

Forms of Address: First names alone are seldom used, even among colleagues. Once you are allowed to use a person's first name, address them as either Monsieur, Madame or Mademoiselle without adding the surname. When introducing one's wife, it is incorrect to refer to Madame Smith, but rather, "my wife."

Courtesies: A single, quick jerk of the hand, with light pressure in the grip, is the proper handshake. During meals, good, cultured conversation is a must. One should present a business card whenever making a call.

Business Do's: For success, a local representative, joint ventures, or branch offices may be needed. Allow plenty of time; decisions are made only after much deliberation.

Business Don'ts: Avoid personal questions; the French are very offended by our prying. Don't talk business over lunch.

Entertainment: Dinner begins around eight or later and you can comfortably arrive ten minutes late. Unless you know your wines, bring flowers, pastries, candies or even a plant. A "thank you" note is expected.

Language: French

Religion: The majority are Catholic.

A GLIMPSE AT GERMANY:

Sensitivities: Refer to the country as the Federal Republic of Germany, not West Germany. Politics and World War II may be sensitive subjects.

Forms of Address: Never use a first name unless specifically invited to do so. Always address the person as Herr, Frau or Fraulein with the last name; anyone with a doctorate degree (such as lawyer) is addressed Herr Doktor X, and a professor is Herr Professor X. It is important to know a person's proper title.

Courtesies: Germans are formal and reserved and may seem unfriendly in first meetings. A firm handshake is a must when meeting and leaving. Be punctual.

Business Do's: Make appointments well in advance; always dress neatly; maintain formal manners, and conduct business with great attention to order and detail.

Business Don'ts: Avoid surprises and hard sell; don't give spontaneous presentations.

Entertainment: The evening meal is generally simple. Always keep both hands above the table. Candy, wine or flowers may be brought or sent afterward. A "thank you" note is expected.

Language: German

Religion: About evenly Protestant and Catholic; but Germany is a secular society.

A GLIMPSE AT HONG KONG:

Sensitivities: Always show respect. Saving face is important.

Forms of Address: Like China, the family name is mentioned first.

Courtesies: A nod or slight bow from the shoulders (not the Japanese bow) is customary; shaking hands is also acceptable. Introductions are formal, and proper banquet etiquette is essential.

Business Do's: Hong Kong Chinese are more experienced in working with Westerners, so business is easier. Still, it is wise to work through an agent or commissioned importer.

Business Don'ts: Never embarrass a Chinese, thus causing loss of face.

Entertainment: Chinese businessmen usually entertain in restaurants where eight- to twelve-course meals are common. If entertaining is conducted in the home, guests are expected to arrive on time, gifts are often brought for the children, or fruit for the home. At a restaurant, the guest of honor usually ends the meal by rising and thanking the host on everyone's behalf.

Language: English and Chinese.

Religion: Confucianism is predominant. Many also practice Buddhism, Taoism or Christianity.

A GLIMPSE AT ITALY:

Sensitives: Avoid discussion of taxes or Italian politics.

Forms of Address: Only close friends use first names. Use titles, and when in doubt, address someone as "Dottore."

Courtesies: Shake hands on meeting and leaving.

Business Do's: Get an Italian agent or local attorney. Business cards are a must. Get right down to business after a few minutes of casual conversation. Be well prepared for your presentation; have a solid knowledge of your products.

Business Don'ts: At social events, don't talk business. Talk, instead, about family, sports, or international events. Italians do not like joking at purely business meetings.

Entertainment: Except in Milan, business entertaining is not popular. Dinner is usually from eight to ten. Gifts or flowers may be sent afterward, but not chrysanthemums, which are used for funerals and grave sites. Hands are always kept above the table during dinner. When having dinner at their home, compliments on the meal and home are appreciated.

Language: Italian; most businessmen speak French.

Religion: Catholic

A GLIMPSE AT JAPAN:

Sensitivities: Japanese are highly status-conscious. Always show respect. Loudness of any kind is offensive. Never single an individual out of a group, either for criticism or praise.

Forms of Address: People are addressed by their surname and the suffix *san*, as in Brooks-san. Never use first names.

Courtesies: Japanese usually bow to each other, but handshaking is common in business. If you bow to a peer, bow as low and long as the Japanese. If you are visiting a Japanese home, remove your shoes before stepping inside. The Japanese are formal but warm, and strive to create "wa;" good feeling and harmony.

Business Do's: Travel with hundreds of business cards and give them to everyone present in the room. Proper introductions are essential. Allow time for the Japanese to get to know and trust you. Be ready to give gifts in a number of situations. Participate in their evening entertainment over sake; it serves as a superb time to communicate freely with your Japanese associates.

Business Don'ts: Don't rush and don't always assume that "yes" means agreement or understanding.

Entertainment: Although most entertaining is done in restaurants, if someone invites you into his/her home, bring a small gift and present it with both hands to the host. Sake is served before dinner, and it is polite to fill each other's cups. Try to use the chopsticks and send a note of thanks.

Language: Japanese
Religion: Buddhism and Shinto

A GLIMPSE AT KOREA (SOUTH):

Sensitivities: Great respect is paid to age and position. Rituals of courtesy and preserving face and harmony are important. Avoid discussion of socialism, Communism or Korean politics.

Forms of Address: Address business associates by their titles and the one-syllable family name. The family name always comes first. Hence, Lee Song-Win, is Mr. Lee.

Courtesies: Men bow slightly and shake hands; women do not shake hands. Business cards are expected whenever introductions are made. A sweet coffee, tea, or soft drink is usually offered at meetings; drink it without comment.

Business Do's: Stay formal until a relationship has been established. Travel with plenty of business cards. Commenting on the country's tremendous economic growth is always appreciated.

Business Don'ts: Never criticize, openly disagree, behave abruptly, or appear to be excessively proud of your accomplishments with Koreans.

Entertainment: Entertainment plays a major part in business; it develops rapport. When entering a Korean home, remove your shoes and wait to be invited inside. Bring a small gift or flowers. Conversation takes place after, not during, the meal. Wives are rarely included in invitations to a restaurant or bar.

Language: Korean
Religion: Buddhist, with strong Confucian tradition.

A GLIMPSE AT MEXICO:

Sensitivities: Mexicans are proud of their independence from the United States and will be sensitive to any hints of condescension or comparison.

Forms of Address: First names are not used unless you know a person very well and are on friendly terms. "Senor," "Senora," or "Senorita," are used for Mr., Mrs., and Miss. When in doubt about a woman's marital status, refer to her as "Senorita."

Courtesies: Shake hands each time you meet someone and when introduced for the first time. When meeting a Mexican woman, bow slightly, and shake hands only if she offers hers.

Business Do's: Take time to establish rapport and always be warm and friendly. Get agreements confirmed in writing, since verbal agreement may be reached out of politeness, only to be reversed later by mail.

Business Don'ts: Don't push, don't rush. Don't injure an individual's pride or dignity.

Entertainment: The main meal is served in the afternoon between two and five o'clock. For a first visit to the home, flowers for the hostess are usual. Dinner is around eight-thirty or nine. Never come early. "Thanks" at the door and a telephone call later is sufficient.

Language: Spanish
Religion: Mainly Roman Catholic.

A GLIMPSE AT SAUDI ARABIA:

Sensitivities: Do not eat or smoke in public in the daytime during Ramadan; alcohol is against the law. Women's dress must not expose arms, legs, or shape. Refer to the Gulf as the Arab Gulf, not the Persian Gulf. Avoid discussions about women, politics or religion.

Forms of Address: Use the titles Mr., Sheik (pronounced "shake," not "sheek"), Excellency (for ministers) or Your Highness (for members of the royal family) with the first name until you are accepted as a friend or a business associate. For example, Sheik Ahmed Abdel Wahab is Sheik Ahmed and Prince Mohamed

Ibn Feisal is Your Highness Prince Mohamed.

Courtesies: Do not inquire about the women in a man's family. Accept endless cups of coffee or tea. Use business cards, and shake hands with everyone present when arriving or leaving. Sit without exposing the soles of your shoes (This is considered an insult since the feet are the lowest part of the body and touch the dirty ground.) and avoid using your left hand. The left hand is reserved for toilet paper, nothing else. If you're left handed and forced to write before an Arab, apologize so that it's clear you meant no insult. Do not admire an object or the Saudi will feel obligated to give it to you.

Business Do's: Work with a Saudi agent. Make frequent visits to cement the business relationship. Begin each meeting with social conversation and tolerate frequent diversions and waiting.

Business Don'ts: Allow time for deliberation; don't press for immediate answers. Don't say "no religion" on your passport.

Entertainment: Entertaining is usually done in restaurants and hotels. Women are generally not included and in the home, they will dine in a separate room. Be prepared to eat with your hand (the right one). Leave immediately after eating.

Language: Arabic

Religion: Islam

A GLIMPSE AT SOUTH AFRICA:

Sensitivities: Racial tensions simmer. You may be distrusted both by whites who tire of the outsider's disapproval and by blacks who think you are not doing enough to change the status quo. Black Americans face harder scrutiny and expectation than White Americans. There are even some animosities between the Afrikaners and the whites of British decent.

Forms of Address: Until invited to do otherwise, address people by using Mr., Mrs., or Miss. First names, though, are increasingly the custom.

Courtesies: Greetings should not consist of a mere, "Hello." One should ask about family or make other social conversation. Shaking hands is customary on meeting and leaving and in some parts of the country, blacks may shake hands, clench thumbs and shake hands again.

Business Do's: Be punctual and somewhat more formal than in the United States, but be prepared for bureaucratic complexities and delays.

Business Don'ts: Don't be loud or boisterous; both British and Afrikaners are more reserved.

Entertainment: Dinner may be as early as five o'clock. Arrive on time and bring a gift. The fork is used in the left hand and guests do not ask for anything to be passed at the table. Plan to stay for several hours after the meal.

Language: Afrikaans (derivative of Dutch) and English are official. There are also nine widely spoken African languages in the country.

Religion: Christian. White Afrikaans-speaking people are predominately members of the Dutch Reformed Church.

Around the world in eighty minutes? Well, almost! Welcome back, and thanks for coming with me on our partial journey of the various countries. I hope you enjoyed learning how international customs and protocol differ among our neighbors. These differences are to be treated with respect and honor. Whether home or abroad our image should reflect us as ambassadors of goodwill. Happy trails to you!

Adios!

Asti Lavista!

Sayonara!

Ciao!

Au Revoir!

Answers to: ARE YOU INTERNATIONABLE?

1. c		10.	a
2. b		11.	b
3. b		12.	a
4. b		13.	b
5. a		14.	d
6. c		15.	b
7. a		16.	c
8. c		17.	b
9. c			

Negotiating Successfully with Nonverbal Communication Skills: Getting Someone to Say Yes When They Really Want to Say No

Our lives are very similar to trees. Above the ground, each appears different, branching out, changing colors with the seasons, weathering the storms alone. Each grows with the warmth of the sun, existing in spite of adversity. Yet their roots, like ours, tangle in the darkness underground, seeking the source that makes us one.

People are more alike than they are different. If everyone understood that idea, negotiation and cooperation would be an easy task. Culture, language, nationality, and beliefs make us different on the exterior, but understanding the concept that all people cry, laugh, eat, worry and die brings the act of understanding others and negotiating into a new perspective.

Negotiation depends on communication; it takes place between human beings, not computers. Since it occurs inside ourselves or between individuals, a knowledge of human behavior is essential to any negotiator.

In spite of its seeming complexity, human behavior is predictable and understandable. If we understand ourselves, it is easier to understand others.

When human behavior is mentioned, one always thinks of Professor Abraham H. Maslow's hierachy of needs. These needs provide a useful framework for studying needs in relation to negotiation, since needs govern behavior. We are all trying to satisfy our basic needs, and whether that need is ending hunger or developing self-esteem, people are most able to proceed once their needs have been met. When a person has a need, it involves his whole person. We have never heard someone complain, "My stomach is hungry." Instead, we hear, "I'm hungry." Needs involve one's total being. When basic needs, like hunger and safety are not met, a person's perception changes, his memory is affected, and his emotions are usually tense. However, negative responses subside when basic needs are met.

After dominant needs (physiological, safety, love, belonging) have been adequately satisfied, one tends to progress to the higher levels. These higher levels (esteem, self-actualization, and needs to know and understand) are the primary needs that an individual values in negotiations.

Needs and their satisfaction are the common denominator in negotiation. If people had no unsatisfied needs, they would have no reason to negotiate.

Broadly defined, negotiation is the back-and-forth communication process between two or more people in which they consider alternatives to arrive at mutually beneficial and agreeable results.

We all negotiate every day. Much of our time is spent trying to reach agreement with others and within ourselves. Think for a moment of how you make important decisions in your life . . . you negotiate within yourself.

On a typical day:

You negotiate with yourself on what time to get up, what to wear, what to eat for breakfast. You get in your car and negotiate with traffic: Will I let this car get in line before me; will I pass through this yellow caution light, etc. At the office we negotiate all day: we won't purchase from someone until they give us a discount; we get in line to use the copy machine or at lunch we try to return a defective appliance. When we return home at the end of the day, we negotiate whether we must stop off at the grocery store, what we will fix for dinner, even how we can use the phone when our teenager has been on it for an hour.

When we can't talk with others, we talk with ourselves. We rationalize. We react. We try to remain calm, and sometimes we give-in.

Before we begin our study of negotiation, let's examine how familiar we are with the following negotiation terms.

Define these to the best of your knowledge. Each will be explained in detail as you progress through the chapter.

1. Paraphrase
2. Breakthrough Strategy
3. Stonewall
4. Gotcha
5. Dodge
6. Scrooge
7. Mother-May-I
8. Ransom of Red Chief
9. Mirroring
10. Strikeback

Negotiation is, first of all, a civilized method of conflict resolution. You are already successful in negotiating. If you could remember all of the negotiations you've made in your lifetime, you would have to say you've had more successes than failures. Since all of us would like to increase our successes and minimize our failures, let us examine the methods used in effective negotiating.

In our study we will evaluate styles that range from total compromise to blatant inflexibility, made famous through the persona of Ebenezer Scrooge. Scrooge's method is favored by negotiators who do not want to concede in the least while trying to reach a compromise. They take pride in forcing the other person to give in first, manipulating them into giving up more and settling for less.

Ebenezer Scrooge, in fact, with his miserly, very tight-fisted ways, is considered by some would-be negotiators to be the patron saint of negotiation. Getting a dime out of Scrooge was like trying to wring liquid from a stone.

Speaking of being tight with money, did I ever tell you the one about the Cajun who held on to his money, even his change, so tightly that the Buffalos lost their humps, the Lincolns gasped for breaths, and the torch was extinguished on the back of every dime?

Well, this tight Cajun was in a bus station in Opelousas, Louisiana, and needed to use the rest room. When he entered the rest room, he noticed that he had to use one of his precious dimes to get the door open and enter the toilet section. Now, he had that dime. In fact, he had it in his hand, but he was so tight, he figured he'd wait until someone exited the stall, then jump in while the door was still open and get on with his business.

The door opened and he got so excited about trying to get in that he rushed, held the door with his hand, slipped, and oooops, his dime fell into the toilet, which, by the way, the previous user forgot to flush. As he looked at that dime in disgust, he contemplated whether to stick his hand down there or not.

After much contemplation, he stuck his hand in his pocket, pulled out two quarters, and tossed them into the toilet with the dime. He then exclaimed, "For a dime, NO; for sixty cents, YES!"

What situations tend to precipitate negotiations? The key here is conflict, and this Cajun was full of conflict. Any situation where there is real or perceived conflict within ourselves or between two or more people is ripe for negotiation.

Examine the following situations, and check the items in the list that you feel are negotiable:

_____ Price of a wallet in a retail store.
_____ An insurance settlement.
_____ Schedule for completing a construction project.
_____ Assignment due for a teacher.
_____ Your child's weekly allowance.
_____ The allocation of household chores.
_____ Peace treaties.
_____ Real estate salesperson's commission.
_____ Prices on items at a garage sale.
_____ Vacation schedule at work.
_____ The purchase of an automobile.
_____ Terms of a lease agreement.

As you can see, any situation where there is conflict can be appropriate for negotiation. Whenever people meet to draw contracts, make buying or selling transactions, settle differences, or develop working relationships, the name of the game is negotiation. Everything is negotiable!

How effectively you negotiate depends on how well you understand two basic concepts:

Concept 1: To negotiate effectively, you must be able to read people and relate to them.

No matter what's happening at the bargaining table, the real pros at negotiating always focus on the people involved. When you focus on people, you build a sense of trust among the people involved in the negotiation. Learn to focus on others by employing the following skills:

A. *Learn to read people.* Being able to identify a person's real personality by studying the face he or she presents to the public world is a valuable skill in negotiation. When you understand what motivates an individual, you can predict his or her reactions to your words and actions.

You can get additional clues about the type of information your negotiating partner wants to hear by listening to his choice of words. Most people lean toward one of the three major modes of communicating.

I. Visual-oriented language
Those who prefer visual-oriented language use phrases like, "I *see* what you mean." "Can you *show* me that again?" "Let me *look* at this closely." This type of communicator likes to see charts, brochures, and the product if one is involved in the negotiation. When negotiating with this type of individual, use similar phrases.

II. Auditory-oriented language
Individuals who prefer auditory-oriented information use sound words like, "That doesn't *sound* quite right to me." "Yeah, that seems to *ring* a bell." "I don't think I *heard* what you said." Anything that makes a noise will interest this type of individual. They are especially tuned into your tone of voice, so concentrate on making it as pleasant as possible.

III. Action-oriented language
People who desire action-oriented information use physical phrases like, "I don't think I get a

good *feel* for this." "Let's *start over* from scratch." "Let me *kick* that idea around with the boss." These are the people who love demonstrations in which they can try out a product; they want to touch it, do it, and hold on to it. Emphasize action words in your own speech when negotiating with this type of person.

To continue with people reading, let's examine the body language of the person you are negotiating with to see signals of acceptance of your offer, signals doubting your offer, and signals that indicate severe defensiveness concerning your offer.

Acceptance Signals: Body leaning toward you
Face is friendly, smiling, enthusiastic
Arms are relaxed, open
Hands are relaxed, open
Legs are uncrossed, or crossed towards you

Doubting Signals: Body leaning away from you
Face is tense, displeased, guarded, frustrated
Arms are crossed, tense
Hands are clasped, tense, fidgeting with objects or clothes
Legs are crossed away from you

Defensiveness Signals: Leaning far back and away from you, or thrust toward you
Face is angry, tense, tight
Legs crossed away from you, or straddling chair with person facing back of chair
Arms are tightly crossed, hands gripping arm just above elbows
Hands are tightly clinched in fists
Finger is pointed (at you)
Eyes looking at watch (stop)
Fists hitting on desk (time to go)

While one would chose only positive responses to deal with a person exhibiting acceptance signals, acknowledgment of a person's doubts or hesitations and putting him or her at ease is the best way to deal with caution signals.

Mirroring (imitation) of any positive signal is also an excellent method of "winning over" doubters. Intense negative/defensive reactions are clear signals that the negotiation may not happen. The only manner in which you can salvage this type of situation is to try to retrieve the other's trust. This can be done by:

- Conveying understanding and letting them see and hear that you are aware of their negative reaction.
- Redirecting your approach to a discussion on the main advantages of whatever it is you are trying to negotiate.
- Expressing only positive nonverbal signals of openness with palms facing upward.

Let's test your own powers of observation. For each nonverbal communication item described, write in your interpretation. Let's assume that you are in a negotiation session and are observing these reactions.

1. Staring in silence _____

_____

2. Leaning forward across the table _____

_____

3. Blushing _____

4. Tapping a pencil on the table _____

_____

5. Looking out of the window _____

_____

6. Maintaining a blank expression, or poker face

_____

7. Clenching jaw _____

_____

8. Gesturing or moving hands excessively ____

_____

9. Maintaining eye contact with you when you

speak _____

10. Getting up from the table and moving around

the room _____

11. Blinking very frequently _____

Check your answers:

1. Anger or agitation
2. Interest, commitment, or curiosity
3. Embarrassment, anger, or aggression
4. Nervousness, anxiety, or impatience
5. Boredom, disenchantment, disinterest, or lack of concentration
6. An emotional reaction that is intentionally stifled
7. Aggravation, irritation, or impatience
8. Agitation, tension, or nervousness
9. Interest, candor, or agreement
10. Agitation, entrapment, tension, or frustration
11. Anger, excitement, or frustration

B. *Develop double vision.* Put yourself in the other person's shoes and try to see the negotiation from his side. Learn to put him at ease from the very beginning by:

- Sincere smile (shows confidence and enthusiasm)
- Unbuttoned jacket (conveys a friendly, open attitude)
- Solid stance (weight evenly distributed on both feet)
- Vertical position handshake
- Best possible seating arrangement
- Positive eye contact
- Positive gestures

In negotiation, listen . . . and listen well . . . with your ears and with your eyes. God gave us two ears and one mouth; therefore, he must have wanted us to do a lot more listening than talking. This is difficult, though, for the proven fact is that people speak at a rate of 125 to 135 words per minute, and we are capable of listening and understanding information at a rate of 400 to 600 words per minute.

Taking into consideration this differential between rates of speaking and listening, it is easy to understand why people sometimes "tune out" others as they are speaking with them. Frequently we hear, but do not really listen. Concentration is essential to both listening and reading with the basic difference that if you cannot concentrate on what you are reading, you can always return to it at a later time.

As we listen to others, we spend a lot of time thinking about the next words that *we* want to say. Research tells us that we only hear about 25 percent of what is said, and after two months, we only remember one-half of that. Even though we always think that children "never listen," research also indicates that in first grade we heard 90 percent of what was said to us, in second grade we heard 80 percent, in seventh grade 43 percent, and by ninth grade only 25 percent. If this information is true, we are really in trouble.

Let's check your listening skills. Try these three listening exercises before we continue:

Exercise 1:

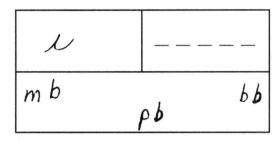

Chap. 9, Fig. 2

Using the above rectangle, please listen (read) and follow these directions:

1. In the top left square, place a dot on the i.
2. In the top right square, write the word *XEROX* in the blank spaces.
3. As I was driving down the road, in a field I spotted a (mb) mama bull, a (pb) papa bull, and a (bb) baby bull. I would like you to circle the kind of bull that doesn't belong in this rectangle.

Exercise 2:

Henry's mother Mabel had four children and that was all.

The first was named Spring and the second was named Fall.

Winter was the third, and then there were no more,

Can you give me the name of the last child she bore????

Exercise 3:

You are driving a bus that contains 40 passengers. At the first stop ten people get off and three get on. The next stop, seven get off and two get on. At the next stop a mother and her two children get on. The bus breaks down at the next stop, and eight passengers get crosstown transfers and leave. The bus starts up again and proceeds to the next stop, and breaks down again. The remaining passengers ask for transfers and leave the bus.

1. How many passengers got transfers at the final stop?
2. How many stops did the bus make?
3. What was the bus driver's name?

(Answers are at the end of the chapter.)

How did you score? Is your listening as good as it should be? Let's examine the types of listeners we find in society today:

PSEUDO LISTENER: One who *pretends* to be listening, but really isn't. Often this type of listener is preoccupied with issues he feels are more important to him than the speaker's remarks. At other times this type of listener thinks he has "heard it all before," and therefore tunes the speaker out.

STAGE HOG LISTENER: This person is only interested in expressing his ideas and doesn't care what anyone else has to say. This type of listener usually interrupts the speaker.

AMBUSHER LISTENER: This person will listen carefully, but only because he is collecting information that he will use to counterattack what the speaker says.

INSULATED LISTENER: This is a person who hears only what he wants to and ignores anything that is unpleasant. When you remind him about a problem you share (an unfinished job, poor grades, etc.), he will usually just nod or answer you with a "yeah" and then promptly forget what you've said.

DEFENSIVE LISTENER: Defensive listeners take practically everything the speaker says as a personal attack.

ABSORBED LISTENER: These listeners are absorbed in their own little worlds. They tend to daydream or become preoccupied and their thoughts seem to wander after a fairly short period of attention.

Tips on how to be a better listener include:

LOOK THE PART: You should show the speaker that he is the most important person to you right then. Leaning forward, smiling, nodding approval, establishing eye contact and asking relevant questions are all definite indicators of an active listener. It was once said that the secret of conversing is to pretend that you're passing a marble back and forth as you talked. The trick is to put the marble in the other person's hand and try to keep it there.

BE SILENT BEFORE REPLYING: You should make sure that the speaker is completely through with his message. You should even try to decode the message for key points.

TAKE NOTES: When listening to a speaker and remembering what was said are important to you, you should take notes during the talk and afterwards sort out your ideas and opinions.

SENSE HOW THE SPEAKER IS FEELING: Put yourself in the speaker's shoes when you are listening to him. To get the complete message, it is important to sift out the feelings being conveyed. You must determine what he is *not* saying.

BE AVAILABLE: You should get from behind your desk and papers and totally concentrate on the speaker. Never look around the room or at the ceiling or get up and do something else while pretending to listen. Avoid drumming fingers on a desk or table or answering a phone call in the middle of a conversation. This shows disrespect.

PARAPHRASE: Good listeners restate messages they hear without judgement or evaluation. This type of listening encourages a speaker to share more information.

Encourage others to listen to what you are saying by:

LOWERING YOUR VOICE VOLUME: Make the other person *have* to listen.

PRESENTING THE INFORMATION IN AN INTERESTING MANNER: Encourage others to participate by bringing them into the conversation. Address people by name whenever possible.

C. *Get to know the people you are negotiating with.* What is important to you as an individual in terms of types of information you wish to send and are willing to hear may not be important to the person you are communicating with. He or she may have a different set of preferences in choosing how to receive information. For this reason, it is important that we study the various communication and personality styles and understand the various preferences of others when sending or receiving information.

The more information you have on the communication style of the person with whom you are negotiating, the easier it will be to "bridge the gap" that occurs as a result of differences in styles or informational preferences.

Each different behavioral style exhibits different predominant characteristics. Learning the characteristics of each style will help you communicate effectively with people.

In psychology, and in Chapter 3 of this book, the four personalities are called Sanguine, Choleric, Melancholy and Phlegmatic. For business purposes, the four personality types are usually identified with the following terms: Expressives, Drivers, Analyticals and Amiables.

Expressives are the party people. They love to have a good time, are highly enthusiastic and creative, and operate primarily by intuition. They have little tolerance for those who are not like themselves and find it a great sacrifice to have to put up with them. Because expressives are easily bored and highly creative, keeping them on task is a job in itself. They have a tendency to go off on tangents, and as a result often seem somewhat "flaky."

Drivers are strong, decisive, result-oriented types. They provide strong guidance for those who need it (and, unfortunately, for those who do not). They can appear to be overly pushy at times, demanding of themselves and of others. Drivers tend to keep their emotions to themselves, are highly self-critical, and resent those who waste their time with idle chit-chat and non-business oriented gossip.

Analytical people have a tendency towards perfectionism. They deal with facts, data, logic, details. They are sometimes slow to make decisions because they need to be sure they know what they want before taking action. As a result, they may appear overly cautious and not good risk-takers. On the other hand, the decisions and information they provide are usually accurate and thoughtful. Feelings and emotions are kept inside and not revealed to others.

Amiables are the "warm fuzzies" of the world. They are God's gift to the other personalities. People and friendships mean the most to them. They like to get people involved in activities and are usually good at recruiting others as well as juggling multiple tasks. They are genuinely concerned with the feelings of others and go out of their way not to offend. They are just as opinionated as others, but they are not inclined to share what is on their minds. They are likely to send out lots of cards for all occasions and are personally hurt or offended when others don't show similar consideration.

To help you determine what your behavioral style is, circle all the words below that you feel describe your behavior when you are at *work.*

Entertaining	Optimistic	Precise	Skeptical
Spontaneous	Animated	Suspicious	Perfectionist
Cheerful	Interrupts	Analytical	Unforgiving
Loud	Gregarious	Introvert	Reliable
Enthusiastic	Creative	Serious	Deep
Decisive	Confident	Low Key	Worrier
Frank	Domineering	Adaptable	Patient
Direct	Demanding	Supportive	Loyal
Impatient	Quick	Shy	Listener
Practical	Adventurous	Consistent	Stable

Once you have finished, divide the word list into four equal rectangles. That is, divide the word list between rows two and three and then again divide the list across, between the fifth and sixth line of words.

In which of the four corners are the most words circled? In which of the four corners are next to the most words circled? The top left corner has more *Expressive* descriptor words; the top right corner has more *Analytical* descriptor words; the bottom left corner has more *Driver* descriptor words; the bottom right corner has more *Amiable* descriptor words.

Determine your primary and secondary style of behavior. Your primary style is the quadrant with the most words circled and your secondary style is the quadrant that has the next highest number of words circled.

To communicate effectively with styles different from yours, it is important that you identify their styles, value them like your own, and learn some basic techniques to communicate within their comfort zones.

When two opposite behavioral styles are in a negotiating situation, hostility and miscommunication can develop. It is like trying to communicate between two people speaking totally different languages.

The following section will help you communicate with various behavioral styles.

With Expressives, you should:

- Become their friend first
- Use the time to be entertaining and fun
- Be fast moving
- Talk about their goals and what they find stimulating
- Provide supporting examples from people they see as important
- Deal with the "big picture," not the petty details
- Offer special deals, extras and incentives

With Drivers, you should:

- Use their time efficiently, stick to business, don't chit-chat
- Be brief, specific, and to the point
- Present information in a well organized package, with all necessary, supporting material included
- Plan your presentation to present the facts clearly and logically
- Provide alternative solutions and let them make the decision

- Never direct them, or order them around (They will rebel.)
- Persuade by referring to results
- Leave quickly after talking business--don't linger

With Analyticals, you should:

- Be formal, very organized and accurate
- Be direct, stick to business
- List pros and cons to any suggestion you make
- Draw up a scheduled approach; use time-table for any action steps
- Take your time, but be persistent
- Provide guarantees over a long period of time, but give options

With Amiables, you should:

- Start with some personal comment to break the ice
- Show sincere interest in them as people; find areas of common interest
- Listen and be responsive
- Be nonthreatening, casual, and informal
- Ask "how" questions to draw out their opinions
- Provide assurance that their decision will minimize risk

Concept 1 should be invaluable in learning to negotiate through reading and relating to people. Now we are ready to examine another important aspect of getting the results you want.

Concept 2: To negotiate effectively, use the breakthrough strategy of success.

The breakthrough strategy is one that cuts through the obstacles that exist when two parties begin to negotiate. It requires you to do the opposite of what you naturally feel like doing in difficult situations. When the other side stonewalls (postpones), dodges (avoids discussion), Mother-May-I's (has to check with someone else before they give you an answer), Scrooges (makes you give in before he will) or attacks, you may feel like responding the same way.

Playing the other side's game by their rules leaves you frustrated; therefore, your single greatest opportunity as a negotiator is *to change the game.* Instead of playing their way, use the breakthrough strategy to negotiate successfully. Rather than pounding in a new idea from the outside, you encourage them to reach for it from within. Rather than telling them what to do, you let them figure it out for themselves. That is the breakthrough strategy. It clears the barriers that lie between their *no* and the *yes* you want for a cooperative negotiation.

In the breakthrough strategy the following four techniques need to be applied:

1. *Don't React:* Human beings are reaction machines. The most natural thing to do when confronted with a difficult situation is to react--to act without thinking. The power of not reacting is one of the strongest assets of negotiating successfully.

   When confronted with a difficult situation, our most common reactions are to strike back (fight fire with fire), to give in (we feel if we give in just this one time, we'll get them off our back), or to break off the relationship altogether (resign from a job, get a divorce, dissolve a joint venture).

   Objects react. Minds can choose not to. O. Henry's story, "The Ransom of Red Chief," offers a fictional example of the power of not reacting. When their son was kidnapped, the parents chose not to respond to the kidnappers demands. As time passed, the boy became such a burden to the kidnappers that they offered to pay the parents to take the child back. This story illustrates the power of refusing to react in disarming the opponent.

Instead of reacting, pause and say nothing. By saying nothing you give them nothing to push against. Your silence may make them feel a little uncomfortable. The job of keeping the conversation/negotiation going, shifts back to them. Since they are uncertain of what is going on in your head, they may respond more reasonably.

2. *Don't Argue:* A mistake of negotiations is trying to reason with a person who is not receptive. Your words will fall on deaf ears or be misconstrued. You are up against a huge barrier of emotion. The other side may feel distrustful, angry, or threatened. Convinced they are right and you are wrong, they may be unwilling to listen.

Before you can discuss the problem, you need to disarm the person. Your challenge is to create a favorable climate in which you can negotiate.

A favorable climate can be created only by defusing their hostile emotions. This means getting them to hear your point of view and getting their respect. They don't need to like you, but they do need to take you seriously and treat you as a human being.

The secret of disarming is to step to their side. This can be achieved by doing the opposite of what they expect you to do. If they are stonewalling, they expect you to apply pressure; if they are attacking, they expect you to resist.

Stepping to their side involves three things:

A. *Listening:* You need to acknowledge their point by paraphrasing what they have said. Sum up your understanding of what the other side has said and repeat it back in your own words. Paraphrasing gives the other side the feeling of being understood; that you see it their way.

B. *Acknowledging:* Acknowledging the other's point of view does not mean that you agree with it; it means that you accept it as a valid point of view among others. By letting them tell their side of the story and acknowledging it, you create psychological room for them to accept that there may be another side of the story.

Perhaps the most powerful form of acknowledgment is an apology. This is a lesson we all learn as children. If we say the magic words, "I'm sorry," we can usually continue playing the game. Unfortunately, this is a lesson we often forget when we become adults.

Even if the other side is primarily responsible for the situation that you are in, consider apologizing for your share. Your bold gesture can set in motion a process of reconciliation in which they apologize for their share.

C. *Agreeing:* You don't need to concede a thing. You need to simply focus on issues on which you already agree. Look for any opportunity to agree, even if it is only in a humorous way.

The key word in agreement is "yes." "Yes" is a magic word; it is a powerful tool for disarming the other side. Use sentences like: "Yes, you have a point there." "Yes, I agree with you." Say "yes" as often as possible, and you will see their disposition change.

Agreement can be nonverbal too. Much of your message comes across in the form of your conversation. Observe the other side's communicative manner. If they speak slowly, you may want to slow down your own speaking rate. If they talk softly, you may want to lower your voice. Observe their body posture also. If they lean forward to emphasize a point, consider leaning forward too.

People also use different sensory languages, when talking. These sensory languages vary depending on whether they primarily process information through their eyes, ears, or feelings. If the other side mostly uses visual terms such as "Can't you see what I'm saying?" or "Let's focus on that," try to match them with similar phrases: "I do see your point," or "I can picture what you are saying." If they use primary auditory terms such as "Listen to this," you should respond with a phrase such as, "I hear you." If their language is oriented around feelings, as in "That doesn't feel right to me," you should answer with phrases like, "I'm not comfortable either." Using sensory languages helps you to connect with your counterparts.

3. *Ask for their advice:* Use questions such as, "What do you think is best for you?" (Sales negotiation) "Do you like the blue one or the white one?" (Sales negotiation) "What do you think will happen if we don't agree?" (Credit payment negotiation) "What would you do if you were in my shoes?" (Payment negotiation)

   Instead of treating the other side's position as an obstacle, you should treat it as an opportunity to complete the negotiation successfully. When they tell you their position, they are giving you valuable information about what they want.

   It is always flattering to be asked for advice. By doing this, you are acknowledging the other side's competence and status. It not only disarms them, but it also gives you a chance to educate them about your feelings in the negotiation. This turning point should be used to educate the other side that the only way for them to win is for both of you to win together.

4. *Sharpen the choices:* Once they have offered their advice on how they think the situation should be handled, build on that information. Use some of their solutions and keep sharpening the choices. First, highlight the cost of no agreement; then highlight the benefits of agreement. Your job as an effective negotiator is to keep sharpening the choices by listing advantages of agreement and disadvantages of no agreement. Building this sharp contrast between consequences and benefits helps the other side recognize for themselves the correct choice to make.

As you negotiate, look for ways to make it easy for the other party to agree. Offer escape routes that tactfully let the other side see that your suggestion is the answer. Plant the seed of an idea, and let the other side nurture it until they take ownership of it. A timely planted, well-cared-for seed will grow into a strong, sturdy tree that can withstand anything.

Your last negotiating problem follows: Once there was a very old man who left seventeen camels to his three sons to be divided in the following manner. Half of his camels were to be left to his oldest son, a third to his middle son and a ninth to his youngest son. After the old man's death, the three set out to divide their inheritance, but soon were in a state of despair with their inability to negotiate a solution. The sons couldn't divide the seventeen camels by two or three or even nine.

After much discussion and disagreement, the three sons approached a wise old woman in their city and asked for her help. After pondering the problem, the old woman also could not come up with a solution. She said to the young men, "I have an old camel; why don't you men take it and I think you will be able to make the division as your Dad had planned."

The sons then had eighteen camels. The eldest son took his half--that was nine. The middle son took his third--that was six. The youngest son took his ninth--that was two. Nine and six and two make seventeen. The sons went about happily and gave the eighteenth camel back to the wise old woman.

Like the seventeen camels, some negotiations will seem impossible, stubborn, and hard to work out; you will feel as though you are pulling roots of trees to get to cooperation. It is almost as though you "can't see the forest for the trees." In most cases, you will need to step back from the negotiation (forest), look at the problem (tree) from a fresh angle, and find an eighteenth camel.

Thoroughly understanding others, applying effective listening techniques, using positive body language, and concentrating on negotiation strategies are your eighteenth, nineteenth, twentieth and twenty-first camels. They will allow you to reach solutions for problems you once thought had no answers.

Answers to Test Questions Concerning Listening:

1.
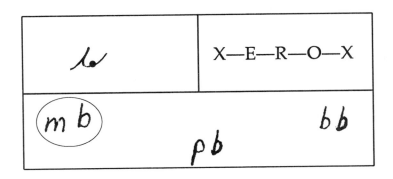

    a.   Place a dot *ON* the i, not above it.
    b.   *IN* the blank spaces.
    c.   There's no such thing as a female bull.

2. Henry

3. a.   23 passengers
    b.   5 stops
    c.   You

CHAPTER 10

Presenting Yourself: Developing Articulate Body Language in Presentations

Did I ever tell you the one about the Louisiana cajun who had a chance to visit the Phil Donahue show?

On that particular day the subject was ghosts. Phil began by asking his audience if anyone present had ever seen a ghost. Seventy-one people stood up, including Lovelace Boudreaux from Lafayette, Louisiana. Phil then asked of those standing if anyone had ever talked to a ghost to remain standing. Seventeen people were still up, including Lovelace Boudreaux from Lafayette, Louisiana.

Phil's last statement was, "Have any of you that are still standing ever kissed a ghost?" Everyone sat down, except Lovelace Boudreaux from Lafayette, Louisiana. Phil Donahue then said, "Sir, I'd like to know your name and where you are from?"

The cajun then answered, "Well, I'm Lovelace Boudreaux from Lafayette, Louisiana."

Phil Donahue then said, "So you mean to tell me, you have kissed a ghost?"

"Ooooh," the cajun replied, "I'm so sorry, I misunderstood you, I thought you had said a goat!"

These two people are in a situation in which they supposedly should understand each other. But they don't. That's how difficult communication is!

Not only in the conversations we have with each other, but also in the signs we read everyday, there is some confusion. Haven't you seen these . . .

CLEAN RESTROOMS AHEAD   Does this mean we must scrub the basin?

DRAW BRIDGE Does this mean we need to begin sketching?

T. G. I. F. Toes go in first?

E. S. P. Error some place?

NEW ORLEANS LEFT Does that mean everyone left the city?

I have long believed that the difference between a person's competence and a person's effectiveness can be directly measured by his ability to communicate, to present himself verbally and nonverbally.

Estimates are that 94% of our day is spent in communications-related activities, and 53% of these communications involve face-to-face meetings. Yet, fewer than 1% of people focus any attention on developing their presentation skills.

Presentation skills aren't just for top executives and CEO's anymore. They're necessary for any person who wants to get the point across clearly, confidently, and without nervousness.

Granted, speaking before a group is the number one fear of people (see list below), but it is a fear that can be lessened with proper training, practice and determination. All people have the actual skills needed for good presentations; all the training that is needed is transferring these skills to work before audiences.

What Do You Fear Most? The following list gives the answer. From *People's Almanac Presents the Book of Lists*

1. Speaking Before A Group
2. Heights
3. Insects & Small Bugs
4. Financial Problems
5. Deep Water
6. Sickness
7. Death
8. Flying
9. Loneliness
10. Dogs

The one reason people would rather die than speak in public is that they have not been trained. Fortunately, proper training can give you the confidence you need to get in front of any audience. Good communication is a skill. It is learnable!

You've got what it takes to be a good presenter. Try this checklist.

1. You use the word "you" more than "I".
2. You have a good memory.
3. You've listened to your own voice, just to see how it sounds.
4. You like to tell people what you've learned.
5. You like the feeling of being "in control."
6. You tend to "act out" what you are talking about.
7. You are an optimist.
8. You were in the senior play in high school.
9. You look people in the eye when you talk to them.
10. While watching TV panel shows, you sometimes answer the questions before the experts do.

If you answered "yes" to at least half of these questions, you have much potential to become a superb presenter. If you scored less than half, all is not lost. At least you're honest, and that is clearly the most important prerequisite of all.

You've been asked to make a presentation. Great! Congratulations! Somebody thinks enough of you to ask you to present your thoughts on a particular subject to others. If this happens to you, you have entered a charmed circle. The majority of people are never asked. You let the idea of speaking in front of others enter your head, but the event seems so far away that you just put it on your "plan ahead" schedule.

Several days before the actual presentation comes the unsettling question, "What have I let myself in for?"

In struggling to deal with this issue, some people have even been known to admit, "I'm not sure I know what a presentation is. It sort of sounds like something that should be done in costume."

It's not the costume one wears; it's the enthusiasm, wit, warmth, credibility, and genuineness of the speaker that makes or breaks the presentation. Let's define it here and now. At one end of the spectrum, there is what is loosely called a speech. The very word send chills up the spine. When people say, "You're not going to make a speech, are you?" they really and truly hope that you will not.

Most speeches have very little impact because they don't ask you to do anything. The very definition of the word *present* is "to bring . . . to give a gift to." That implies a giver (a presenter) who's tuned in to what the recipient (the audience) wants. What response do we get when we give someone a gift of something they really want? What response do we get when we give someone a gift that they really don't like? The difference in these two is the difference between sharing a meaningful message and delivering a speech. Audiences hate to be talked to; they are waiting for the speaker to drive home a specific point or idea that they can really use.

In any presentation, two things are happening simultaneously:

1. The presenter is making a commitment to the audience. The presenter is working to prove something that will win the support of the audience or that will generate action.
2. The audience is making a judgment on the presenter and the commitment. They are asking, "Do I really trust this person?" "Does this information make any sense?" "Are those facts accurate?"

By the final moment of the presentation, if the presenter has fulfilled his or her mission, the audience will unfold its arms and say, "By golly, I see what you mean; I understand your points; I'm going to use this information in my life."

By the same token that the audience is measuring the presenter, the presenter can also measure the audience to see how his presentation is doing, every step of the way, by merely looking at the audience's body language. Signs of acceptance, evaluation and interest are clearly evident in the body movements of the audience.

The following paragraphs will disclose the various types of presentations and reveal the secrets of effective presenters. You will learn how they prepare their messages using key points and supporting material, what to wear for a winning presentation, and the most effective way to use body language to project authority, confidence, sincerity and enthusiasm. We will also examine signs a presenter can look for in his audiences that can help him "shift gears," if necessary, during his presentation.

Types of presentations:

- An attorney stands before a jury to summarize the reasons that his client, accused of stealing, should be allowed to return "to his rightful place in society." He is making a presentation.
- Two candidates for high office stand on a platform and try to win the votes of the people in the auditorium. The candidates are really making competitive presentations to the audience.
- An instructor at a small eastern college reads a section of one of Henry Wadsworth Longfellow's poems to his class and explains imagery in writing. He is making a presentation.
- An economics student stands on a small platform in front of his Marketing 101 class and dissects a case history. Summarizing, he tells what the bankrupt subject should have done. He is making a presentation.
- The group manager of a major oil company appears before the company's board of directors to recommend that a new refinery be acquired in Africa. He is making a presentation.
- A motivational speaker stands behind the podium at the annual Stewart Title Appreciation banquet and inspires the audience to develop to their full potential. He is making a presentation.
- A third grade student nervously stands in the front of his classroom to give a book report on *Snow White*. He is making a presentation.

No matter what type of presentation one has to deliver, the first step is to develop the content of the message. This is usually the point at which many people get hung up. It's the very reason preparation is often put off until the last minute. The potential speaker just stares at a blank sheet of paper and develops writer's block. He is frightened to begin. This does not have to happen.

As you prepare the content of your message, structure the information in an orderly and logical manner. In this way, you make it easier for people to follow, digest, and retain what you are saying. If the audience has difficulty following your train of thought, your message won't get or keep their attention.

The skeletal structure of any speech should be:

INTRODUCTION

    Opener

        Objective

        Preview

BODY

    Key Point 1

        Supporting material

        Transition

    Key Point 2

        Supporting material

        Transition

    Key Point 3

        Supporting material

        Transition

CLOSING

    Summary

    To Do

Formulating an achievable and clearly stated objective is crucial. It provides the whole focus for preparation and guides you in determining what to include in the body of your message.

Stating the objective when you present is equally important. Doing so lets your audience know what to expect. It readies them for what they are about to hear. An objective must always be stated in conversational terms. For example, it might begin like this, "Today, we'll explore . . .," or "I'll help you understand . . ."

With the foundation (objective) in place, we are ready to outline the body of the presentation. Key points are those that "unlock the door" to your subject. They let the audience in on the most important content areas of your message.

Notice, we list three key points. It has been said that every great message contains at least one, but not more than three, key points. The rule of three should be applied to every presentation you make. It forces you to think through your material and distill the most significant points.

Three or fewer points keep it simple for listeners. Did you ever notice how we remember things in groups of threes, fours or sevens. When someone asks for your telephone number, you answer with a set of three numbers and a second set of four: 392-3458. Elementary school teachers never present material larger than in groups of sevens. Think of meaningful sevens: Seven Wonders Of The World, Seven Seas, Seven Dwarfs, etc. The way we store and recall information represents the brain's effort to organize and combine data, making it easier to remember.

This same principle applies to the body of the presentation. Simplifying it provides the audience with a message that they will be better able to assimilate and retain. Think about speakers who have rambled endlessly, on and on. Or, have you ever attended a day-long seminar that runs from 9 a.m. to 5 p.m. and offers 120 ideas for self improvement. At 5:15, the audience is leaving, pumped up, yelling, "Boy, that was great!" Two days later, they remember very little except perhaps the color of the speaker's suit or a new business contact they made.

If you want your presentation remembered, follow the rule of grouping. It doesn't mean you always have three points, at times you may have two, at times you may have nine, but the real importance on focusing on a few is that it produces a better, more concise presentation.

Supporting material for each key point can be obtained by using:

- Examples
- Stories
- Quotations
- Findings
- Comparisons

When you find your supporting material to use, consider balance. Do not just use quotations or findings; a combination of sources and types will produce the most persuasive presentation.

Since supporting material accounts for most of the content of a presentation, it generally takes the most time to identify, collect, and develop. Again though, try to keep in mind the rule of three. If you present too much material to support your key points, your significant points will get lost in the maze of rambling information. On the other hand, too little supporting material may not be sufficient to substantiate your points, and your presentation will not be convincing.

Next, let's look at the transition statement. A transition is simply a statement that acts as a minisummary or minipreview within the body of a presentation. It announces the end of one point and introduces the next. Transitions help your listeners stay with you, making your message easier to follow and remember. Without transitions, you could be halfway into your next point, while some of your listeners are still trying to figure out what this has to do with what you were talking about before.

A sample transition statement might be:

"Now that we have studied x, let's go on to look at y."

People are most readily persuaded by what they hear frequently and recently; therefore, your summary should include a capsule of your key points in brief sentence form. This review drives your message home to the listener.

Most trainers apply the formula T x 3 (tell them 3 times) when delivering a message:

Preview: Tell them what you're going to tell them.
Body: Tell them.
Summary: Tell them what you told them.

All that remains in the presentation's structure now is the Opener and the To Do. The Opener needs to open up the audience and the To Do needs to motivate the audience into some kind of positive action.

Openers need to invite the audience to come in and listen for more. Therefore, it is one of the most important elements of a presentation. It needs to capture attention. To do this may take some creativity.

Types of openers that can capture people's attention are:

- An authoritative quotation
- A scenario
- A question
- A declarative, factual statement
- An amusing anecdote
- A combination of two of the above

A presentation should rarely be started with a joke, especially in a business or professional setting. Speakers need to establish credibility with the first words that come out of their mouths for a favorable first impression.

The first ninety seconds of any presentation are crucial. Maybe the audience has never seen you before. Their eyes are taking snapshots of you and impressions are being registered as to character and temperament. Think back to the times you have heard someone in the audience say, "I knew in the first couple of minutes it wasn't going to be any good." Or opposite, "The minute she started, the very first minute, I just knew it was going to be sensational."

Never, never, never begin a speech by saying, "You don't know how I have dreaded this moment," or "Probably the worst hour you will have spent today is listening to what I have to say." Tell your audience that you are delighted to be there and you have been looking forward to this moment for a long time. What does that say? It says that you are prepared, confident, eager and enthused about sharing this particular subject with this particular group of people.

Since the first moments of a presentation seem to be the most anxious, nervous moments for the speaker, sometimes to rid yourself of this feeling you can turn the attention on the audience. This can be done by giving a few introductory remarks about yourself, then asking the audience a question, giving them a test, or asking them to jot something down. During these moments, the speaker can catch his breath, take a broad view of the audience, and regain some of the composure he may have lost when approaching the stage.

The last thing you want to impress on your audience is something to do, how they can use the information you have given them to bring about meaningful change in their lives. It is your measure of success as a presenter. Bringing about the response you want is likely to entail a change in the way people think or a change in the way they behave.

To Do's can be accomplished by suggesting things like, "I am trying to be the best me that I can be and I *challenge* you to be the best you that you can be," or "I *encourage* you to . . .;" these are both courteous and comfortable ways to ask the audience to do something.

Once the guidelines for writing a presentation have been established, the next consideration needs to be which approach will best reach your audience. Understanding your audience optimizes your effectiveness as a speaker. To "reach" or "land" an audience, a presenter may take one of several approaches. Which approach is the best is often based on numerous factors. The age, educational level, occupation, setting, mood and expectations of the audience all need to be considered.

Approaches with audiences can be directly related to approaches made by an aircraft when landing. Airplanes must consider such factors as other aircraft traffic in the area, weather conditions, and the condition on the ground. But no one approach is used all the time. Alternate avenues of arriving at the destination still enable the pilot to adapt to various circumstances and land the plane, just as alternate approaches to various audiences can also help a presenter land a point.

The parallel between the airline and the speaker extends even further. Sometimes their actions have the opposite effect than what they intended. Hostesses make announcements concerning "your final destination," "the terminal phase of your journey," and "in case of an emergency landing;" all which could make a passenger (audience participant) not be able to sit back, relax and enjoy the ride.

Make your audience participants comfortable with your presentation. Fasten their seat belts, fulfill their need for knowledge, and a successful landing is bound to emerge.

Seating arrangement of audience participants also plays an interesting role in the success of your presentation. Close, compact seating can enhance a group's participation, agreement and harmony. A presentation in a large, spacious room where participants are seated far apart can only weaken the rapport a speaker is trying to create. This can best be illustrated in the following analogy: Putting two pots of water on a stove to boil;

one pot is very large and the other is very small. The smaller pot boils much quicker than the larger. The same idea works for audience participants; the more compact the group, the quicker they begin to "get cooking" and accept the speaker's message.

In order to give a powerful, effective presentation, it is essential that the presenter know his audience. Taking the listener's perspective into account can help a speaker decide which approach is best to achieve the desired results.

Some questions a speaker should consider before a presentation are:

- What is the age and gender distribution of the group?
- Are they attending voluntarily?
- What is the audience expecting?
- Are decision makers present? Who are they?
- How will the audience be feeling? (Time of day, after meal, etc.)

All audience participants want to learn something from your presentation; they attend to gain knowledge, wisdom, facts. When participants enter the room, they are all tuned into Radio Station WIIFM (WHAT'S IN IT FOR ME). Each person is listening to you in terms of his or her own vested interests. When key points stimulate their brains, they are more apt to listen, participate, and accept the information being presented.

Understanding the brain and how it functions is the key in allowing the presenter to communicate fully with his audience. The brain is a glorious, remarkable instrument. It is capable of housing everything you've ever seen, heard, touched, smelled or thought. Its capacity is limitless. The glory of the brain, also, is that it can put "value" on information. No computer, no calculator, no printer can do this; to those instruments, information is information.

Many of us have never learned how to fully access our brains or the brains of others. Psychologists estimate that we tap less than one percent of our brain's potential.

The reason for this lies in the fact that we have not yet "met" our brains. Consider what happens during a presentation. A presenter's brain talks to the brains of the audience members. Research also tells us that the average presenter speaks at a rate of 135 words per minute, yet the human brain can listen and understand at a rate between 400 and 600 words per minute. What happens with all that excess time?

Unless we reach the "whole brains" of our audiences, we run the risk of having only half the impact we could really have. All communication is "brain-to-brain" communication. As you read the words on this page, my brain is generating a message to your brain through your eyes.

In examining the brain, we must first consider the two hemispheres, two sides, and how they each process information. Dr. Roger Sperry, in the 1970's, conducted the pioneering research leading to the popular notion of "left-brain" and "right-brain" thinking. (This is further explained in Chapter 11 - Brain.)

If you will put each of your hands into a fist and join your hands at the knuckles and palms, you will see the approximate size of your brain. It weighs roughly 3.5 pounds and just because someone may have a bigger brain than you, it does not mean that they are smarter than you. Your brain closely resembles what your hands look like when they are in this position. There are two definite sides, with small fibers that run across the top to make connections.

The left hemisphere primarily processes logic, language, details, mathematical reasoning and analysis, while the right side deals with color, imagination, rhythm, visuals and intuition.

Unfortunately our education system grooms us from a young age to favor left-brain activities. Reading, writing and arithmetic are the first subjects most of us study, and students who excel in these left-brain dominance skills are considered those most likely to succeed.

Meanwhile, students who excel in painting, creative doodling, daydreaming or singing are viewed in a different light. These expressive, imaginative children are often labeled as behavioral problems, and are often reprimanded if they daydream or use humor to get attention.

Because of the notion of left-brain supremacy, we usually assemble a factual presentation and assume that it will be well received by the audience. However, while presentations must be factual and informative, they also need other facets to be compelling--like variation in pacing, articulate body language, and an abundance of vivid verbal and visual imagery.

Research has proven that audience members tend to key-in on the body language, rhythm and imagery that speakers create more than on the words they say. These "right-brain" elements are more engaging than the words themselves. No audience member has ever left a presentation and remarked, "Wow, what a good presentation; it was filled with facts." Facts with no animation and enthusiasm will never make a presentation memorable. The integration of imagery and intuition with logic and analysis is the answer to a great presentation.

A "right-brain" element that has tremendous impact on the audience is the speaker's body language. Research shows that 55% of a person's impact during a presentation is determined by posture, gestures and eye contact, 38% by his voice tone and inflection, and only 7% by the content of his presentation.

To develop articulate body language, one must understand that all its main elements--posture, movement, gestures, hands, eye contact, voice, platform behavior, and presence--are all intimately related and interdependent. For example, if posture is rigid, it leads to stiffness of movement, tightness of voice and restriction of gestures. The overall coordination of the various components of body language can make or break a successful presentation. If body language is not synchronized with the message being given, it loses credibility.

In developing articulate body language, we must examine:

- Basic posture
- Movement
- Gesture
- Hands
- Eye contact
- Voice
- Platform behavior
- Presence (clothing & color)

POSTURE: Your posture is the most foundational statement you make with your body. An upright posture communicates a message of confidence and integrity. A slumping posture communicates cowardice and meekness to an audience. The basic posture for a speaker is feet placed approximately shoulder-length apart, weight on ball of feet for easy movement from side to side, and hands resting easily at sides.

This simple posture is incredibly powerful. It projects confidence, power and dignity. Many actors work years to master this stance of dignity. With feet in this position and weight on balls of feet, motion in any direction can be accomplished easily.

MOVEMENT: Swaying, rocking, or pacing distract and annoy audiences. Examples of natural, expressive movements might include walking toward your audience when emphasizing a point, or walking away, leaving them to contemplate a question you have just asked.

If speakers are not sure of where or how to move, they should return to their basic posture stance. The best cure for stopping yourself from swaying or rocking is to watch yourself on video. Once you see how distracting a certain movement may be, your awareness of that movement increases, and you will learn to use it in moderation or not at all.

GESTURE: Gestures can be tremendously powerful. When they are natural and expressive, they are the key to a successful presentation. Trained gestures, performed because you think one is needed at a certain point, appear robotic and insincere.

Speakers need to develop their own gestural vocabulary. Play with the following exercises in front of a mirror or video camera, saying each phrase and watching which gestures you naturally use to express each one. Go ahead, have fun!

- There are three gestures that we do with our left hand that indicate secretiveness or lying.
- To eat spaghetti you must stand your fork up and twirl the noodles around it. This is most easily accomplished when you use a spoon as a base for the noodles.
- Please help me!
- I really don't know what the answer to that question is.
- As I walked into this enormous room, I was stunned by its massive, dome-shaped ceiling and its glowing chandeliers.
- Happiness is like jam. You can't spread even a little without getting some on yourself.

Now for the advanced portion of the exercise, recite the following passages aloud and experiment with your gestures in front of a mirror or audience.

- In this lifetime, I should far, far rather possess eyes that know no sight, ears that know no sound, hands that know no touch, than to ever possess a heart that knows no love!
- How high I am, how much I see, how far I reach, depends on me.
- From birth to age 18, a girl needs good parents, from 18 to 35 she needs good looks, from 35 to 55 she needs a good personality, and from 55 on she needs cash!
- If I don't know laughter, all I can teach you is tears;
  If I don't know wisdom, all I can teach you is ignorance;
  If I don't know giving, all I can teach you is selfishness, and,
  If I don't know love, all I can teach you is hate,
  But everything I know, I can teach you and share with you,
  And still possess an abundance of it!

In addition to practicing these exercises, begin to study gestures in everyday communication. Watch television without the sound, play charades, or watch American sign language to expand your use of gestures.

HANDS: Hands often speak louder than words. Hands resting on hips during a question/answer session can say, "I don't really like that question. In fact, it's stupid, but I'll answer it anyway."

Speakers love to twiddle with their hands. They twiddle hair, electric cords, chalk, pens or pencils; all indicating nervousness and uncertainness. In fact, the less times a speaker touches himself (adjusts tie, plays with rings, adjust cufflinks, plays with neck chain, etc.) while speaking, the more confident he can appear. Every action made by speakers is an indication of something they are feeling or thinking; placing hands in pockets is a sign of dejection; jingling loose change in pockets, indicates a concern about financial affairs.

The most confident gesture that a speaker can make during a presentation is the steeple. That is, the tips of all five fingers of each hand are touching in a steeple position at his chest, at his waist, or lowered near his hip area. It is the kind of inconspicuous gesture that gives a speaker a boost of confidence to go on with his presentation.

Speakers can learn to keep their hands quiet and calm. One solution is to practice speaking with a large book in each hand. As you stand in front of a mirror and begin to talk, your hands will each raise every now and then with a gesture, even though the books are heavy. Those are the *real* gestures. These are the ones to be saved to be used during your talk, all the others are nervous gestures that need to be eliminated.

The second solution is almost a secret; it's so small. Speakers tend to build confidence in themselves when they can touch both of their hands together and feel awkward when their hands just fall loosely on their sides. If a speaker feels a need to "get in touch with himself" for support and confidence, all he needs to do is let his hands hang comfortably at his sides, then touch thumb and forefinger to each other on each hand.

This slight touching of your fingers—feeling the warmth of your own body heat—has the same effect as hands touching each other in any of the steeple positions at the front of the body.

EYE CONTACT: Eyes are the windows to our souls. They indicate happiness, sadness, tiredness, nervousness; in fact, all of our emotions. If in your soul you don't like what you are doing, it will show in your eyes. However, if you are enthused about your subject and care for your audience, your eyes will reflect that also.

Eye contact is the humanizing element in an often impersonal world. Making eye contact with your audience draws their attention, helping them feel more personally involved.

In small audiences, it is easy to make eye contact with all participants, but with very large audiences, the speaker has to learn how to create the impression of making eye contact with everyone by using a technique whereby he sweeps the audience with his eyes. As you present, picture the room like the face of a clock and make a point of addressing the major points of the clock: 12, 3, 6, and 9.

Avoid repeatedly following a clockwise pattern, or the pattern will become obvious. Vary the directions in which you move your eyes around the face of the room. Focus on points 12, 3, 6, and 9; then 6, 12, 9, and 3, and so on.

One of the best ways to make a whole group of people think you are looking directly at each one of them is to hold your eyes on one person in a large group for approximately 3 seconds. It gives audience members in that area the appearance that you are in direct eye contact with each one of them.

To handle notes and still keep eye contact with your audience, observe newscasters. They keep their heads up and maintain eye contact with their viewers. They very inconspicuously handle note sheets. They don't lift the papers up (visual distraction) or ruffle them (auditory distraction); they continue to speak and maintain eye contact while very quietly slipping the top sheet of their notes to the side and under the others. They are very subtle, and polished professional speakers should demonstrate that same kind of subtlety when they speak.

Not only is eye contact necessary for a successful presentation, but eye expressions are equally important. Learn to express yourself using only your eyes by looking into a mirror and expressing these feelings and emotions:

- Surprise, anger, love, intensity, confusion, boredom, playfulness, sincerity, and confidence.

VOICE: Your voice is your primary tool of communication and has the potential to have a tremendous effect on your audience. This depends on the inflection you place on certain words, when and how long your pauses are, and the proper use of tone and volume control.

Voices can be refined by recognizing and eliminating unnecessary elements, such as uhhh's, uhmm's, and ok's. Listen to yourself on tape and actually count the number of the unnecessary elements that are in your presentation. Speakers should also be keenly aware of the correct pronunciation of words and the diction of sentences. The incorrect pronunciation of a word can leave a very negative impact on audience members.

Use your voice to its fullest potential. Learn to sincerely express emotions through words, tone, and pacing of your sentences. Learn to pause effectively and to whisper for certain parts of your presentation that need special emphasis. Raising and lowering your voice appropriately is essential to effective speaking.

For practice, try saying hello, in a way that communicates each of the following feelings:

- Surprise, anger, love, intensity, confusion, boredom, playfulness, sincerity and confidence.

For further practice with volume control, first read the following in a whisper; second, read it in an ordinary conversational tone, as though you were speaking to a group of ten people; and third, read it as though you were speaking to a group of fifty people without straining your voice.

"The key in all this is not *WHAT* do you want, but what do *YOU* want."

Introducing singing, other languages, and mimicking of various accents into your presentations can also have dramatic positive effects on audience members.

PLATFORM BEHAVIOR: The movements a presenter makes are collectively termed, "platform behavior." Platform movements give emphasis and energy to a presentation and serve to sustain the audience's attention. Imagine a mime and how he uses his gestures and movements to convey his entire message. That's superb platform behavior.

Gestures and movements also serve to minimize barriers that may exist between a presenter and the audience. One such barrier is a solid wood podium. It creates a wall between the presenter and his audience. If you can, avoid standing behind a podium or against a projector. In cases where you must be behind a podium, leaning forward and casually moving from one side to the other at appropriate points, helps create the impression of connecting with your audience.

When on the platform to speak, stay up on you feet. In some settings, speakers use a presenter's stool, which seems to inhibit gestures and movement, and diminishes energy. When we sit, we tend to slump, which diminishes our breathing and makes our energy supply drop. During a presentation, you need all the energy you can muster; therefore, remain standing.

PRESENCE: "Presence" is something the audience "feels" about the presenter. It is an attitude of positiveness that guarantees the audience that "the speaker can handle anything." Presence is felt when nothing about the speaker is tentative. They don't fuss with things; they are determined about their mission; and they are decisive and well prepared.

Speakers are judged even before they take the platform. Their behavior as they eat their meals at the head table or mingle with others in the room before the presentation, are carefully observed by audience participants.

What one wears when making a presentation is the first consideration in establishing "presence." The attire for presenters should satisfy two requirements. It should contribute to the perception you want to create and it should not distract from your message. After a presentation, you want people thinking and talking about what you said--not about how you looked or what you wore.

Your clothes are pure, nonverbal communication. Skirts, blouses, shirts, trousers, and even colors speak volumes. Shoes talk. Open-toe sandals say one thing, closed-in pumps say another. Wingtips, scarves, jewelry, and eyeglasses all make a presentation of your taste and personality.

Your style of dress should be an extension of your greatest strength, but you should avoid anything that may hinder or dominate your presentation. Be careful of jewelry that is too dangly and noisy, clothes that are too tight, hair that is unkept, or coats and slacks that are mismatched or in need of a good pressing.

Compliment your audience by what you wear. Let your clothes communicate that you think your audience is important; that you thought they were worth getting dressed up for. The visual message you create is so powerful that it actually accounts for more than half of the impact you have on your audience. Before you begin to speak, if someone comes to you and says, "You must be our speaker today," you know you have arrived!

Not only are the styles of dress you choose an important visual message, so are the colors you choose. Color appeals to emotions; the right colors can promote attention, evoke moods, create desire, and even generate a favorable response. On the contrary, the wrong colors can generate a negative response.

Following are meanings we commonly associate with different colors:

Black	authority, death, strength, mystery
Blue	faith, cold, truth, tenderness
Brown	action, earthiness, fellowship
Green	envy, health, leisure, youthfulness
Red	passion, excitement, love, fulfillment

Orange	warmth, action, aggression, fury
Purple	dignity, royalty, frugality, melancholy
White	holiness, purity, cleanliness, professionalism
Yellow	playfulness, knowledge, esteem, confidence

Colors are attention-getters. Often we buy products on the basis of how they are packaged. This is an important point to keep in mind the next time you "package" your presentation. Package yourself and even your visual aids with color in mind. Both have a tremendous effect on your audience's attention, response and mood.

Since capturing the audience's attention and setting the right mood are deep concerns of every speaker, let's examine how to read your audience right. What messages are *they* projecting to you? Understanding facial messages and body positions can help presenters be more aware about reaching audience members.

Furrowed forehead	means	problems with acceptance
Furrowed eyebrows	means	problems with acceptance
Entire head held in palm of hand	means	boredom
Hand stroking chin	means	critical evaluation
One finger raised at temple	means	evaluation
Knuckles rapping on chair	means	boredom
Pulling on ear	means	resistance to what he is hearing
Deep, heavy sighs	means	"How much more can I endure"
Head tilted slightly	means	interest
Examining glasses, squinting through lenses	means	responsible for what he sees, how he feels
Arms crossed, legs crossed	means	"I'm not listening to a thing you're saying"
Keeps looking at watch	means	Time's up—ready for this to be over
Eyes		best indicators of interest

Mouth turned up   means agreement
Mouth turned down means disagreement
Mouth straight   means judgment pending

Your audience is your mirror. Where you lead, the audience will follow.

- If you're funny, they will laugh. If you're not funny, and try to be, they will be embarrassed for you.
- If you're a nervous wreck, they will be uncomfortable.
- If you are bored, they will be bored and drift off.
- If you wish you were back at the office, they will wish the same.
- If you are having a good time, they will smile and enjoy themselves.
- If you like them, they will like you.
- If you tread upon their toes, they will withdraw.

The audience follows the presenter, no matter what. Actually it goes even further; once in a great while, the audience not only reflects the presenter, the audience becomes one with the presenter. All of us have seen audiences, on TV or in live auditoriums, that have given themselves over to the presenter. Physically, emotionally, mentally. You can see it in their faces, read it in their body language. The presenter can do no wrong. Every line is a winner. Every story is a smash. Every little wink of the eye, every little smile, everything that a presenter says and does is relished, treasured, identified with.

You, also, have the capacity to do just that; train yourself to "capture" others with your imaginative thoughts, your creative ideas, your powerful words, and your enthusiastic actions!

CHAPTER 11

How to be Twice as Smart:
Using Both Sides of the Brain

Georgie's letter arrived today, and now that I've read it, I'll place it in my cedar chest with the other things that are important to my life.

"I wanted you to be the first to know." He began every letter with that phrase and as I thought about those words, my heart swelled with pride.

I haven't seen little Georgie Taylor since he was a student in my fifth grade class, fifteen years ago. The teaching profession was fairly new to me; I was in my third year.

I really didn't notice Georgie the first day of school because everything is so hectic, but on the second day, I observed him carefully. His hair was long and dirty, and he had to swing his head to one side to get it out of his eyes as he wrote. His clothes were soiled, his nails were filthy, and he smelled.

By the end of the first week, I knew Georgie was clearly behind the other students in the class. He wasn't only behind the others, he was just plain slow. I think it was on that day, that I began to withdraw from Georgie.

Even though we're not supposed to admit it, any teacher will tell you that it's more pleasurable to teach bright, eager young students, than slow, unresponsive ones. That year, I concentrated on my best students and hoped the others would follow along as best as they could. Ashamed as I am to admit it, I took excessive pleasure in using my red pen, and when Georgie's papers came up, it seemed I marked them larger and darker than was necessary.

Georgie was very well behaved and extremely quiet; thank goodness. I know he felt that I didn't like him, but I didn't have time to care. My job was to teach children, not concern myself with those who couldn't learn.

As the Christmas holidays approached, I knew that Georgie would never catch up in his studies and be promoted to sixth grade with the rest of his classmates. He would fail.

To make myself feel better, I decided to check his cumulative folder. I observed that he had very low grades in three of his first four years of school, but had never failed. I couldn't understand how his other teachers passed him. His skills were extremely low. I scanned the personal remarks. His situation was sad; still, he was a poor learner and I couldn't help that.

First grade: Georgie is a good student, makes good grades and is extremely interested in learning, but has a poor home situation. Second grade: Georgie could do better. Mother terminally ill. He receives little help at home. Third grade: Georgie's such a sweet boy, but he's too serious. He grasps information very slowly. Mother passed away at end of year. Fourth grade: Georgie seems to be constantly daydreaming. Father shows no interest in his schooling.

What a tough situation, but that still doesn't answer his learning problems. He made it through four years, but he will certainly have to repeat fifth grade. "It will do him some good," I said.

It was the last day of school before Christmas holidays. The children and I had worked steadily to get our room ready for the big day. Construction paper snow flakes and Christmas bells hung from our ceiling. Our miniature tree, with twinkling lights and paper chains, was propped up on the reading table with presents scattered all around.

It seems there were more presents than there were students for every one of them had brought me a gift. Each one I opened brought cheers of delight, and I showered the proud giver with elaborate thank-yous.

When I picked up Georgie's gift, I knew without looking who it was from. It was wrapped with a brown paper bag and he had colored Christmas trees and red bells all around it. It was held together with masking tape.

It read, "To Miss Hargrave-from Georgie."

Suddenly my students were silent. As I tore off the last bit of masking tape, two items fell on my desk, a gaudy rhinestone bracelet with several stones missing and a small, half-empty bottle of dime-store cologne.

I could hear the snickers and whispers, and I wasn't sure I could look at Georgie. "Oooooh, this smells great," I said as I sniffed the perfume. "Isn't this pretty?" I asked as I placed the bracelet on my wrist. "Georgie, would you help me clasp it?"

I then dabbed some of the cologne behind my ears and asked the little girls if they wanted some too. First, one girl came up alone. Then I made such a big fuss about how good it smelled, all the other little girls lined up for a dab behind their ears.

I continued to open the presents until I reached the bottom of the pile. We ate our refreshments and the bell rang.

The children eagerly left the room and shouted, "Merry Christmas, see you next year!" But Georgie waited at his desk. Once the others left, clutching his books and gift to his chest, Georgie walked towards me.

"You smell just like Mom," he said softly. "Her bracelet looks real pretty on you, too. I'm glad you liked it." He hurriedly left the room.

I hurried after him, but it was too late. I locked my door, sat down at my desk, and wept. I decided at that moment that I would make up to Georgie what I had deliberately deprived him of, a teacher who cared.

When he returned from Christmas holidays, I spoke to Georgie and told him that if we worked hard together, we could probably bring his grades up. He gave me a shy smile and said, "I'd like that."

Georgie and I worked every afternoon. Sometimes we worked together, other times he worked alone while I worked on lesson plans or graded papers.

Slowly but surely, Georgie's grades got better. Gradually he caught up with the rest of the class. To my surprise, his final averages were among the highest. He and his Dad were moving at the end of the school year, but I knew that wherever Georgie went to school the next year, he would be fine. His study habits had improved tremendously, and his successes had created a renewed self confidence in him.

I didn't hear from Georgie until seven years later, when his first letter arrived as a graduation announcement with a note inside.

Dear Ms. Hargrave,

I wanted you to be the first to know. I am graduating from high school as Salutatorian next month. It's been tough, but I made it.

Very truly yours,

Georgie Taylor

I sent him a small card of congratulations. I wondered what he would do after graduation. Since he finished second in his class, I presumed he would go to college.

Four years later, Georgie's second letter arrived.

Dear Ms. Hargrave,

I wanted you to be the first to know. College has not been easy, but I was just informed that I will be graduating first in my class. I'll keep you posted on my progress.

Very truly yours,

George Taylor

First in his class, that's great! I sent him a good pair of monogrammed cuff links and a card of congratulations.

Now today, Georgie's third letter arrived.

Dear Ms. Hargrave,

I wanted you to be the first to know. As of today I am George R. Taylor, M.D. How about that‼??

I've been dating a wonderful lady for some time and we are to be married October 23. I wanted to ask if you could come and sit where my Mom would sit if she were here. I'll have no family there as Dad died last year.

Very truly yours,

George Taylor

I'm not certain what kind of gift to send a doctor upon completion of medical school and state boards; I suppose I'll just wait and take a wedding gift, but my letter to Georgie can't wait.

> Dear George,
>
> Congratulations! You made it, and you did it yourself! I am so proud of you.
>
> I'll be at that wedding with bells on!
>
> Jan Hargrave

My experience with Georgie taught me a valuable lesson. Because of him, I view learners in a different light and have come to realize that certain children begin to fail even kindergarten because of learning disabilities or the problems in their lives.

Yet, every student has the ability to become a thinker. Thinking is not as natural as one might suspect, and does not always develop on its own; it needs to be taught, and practiced.

The principle "if people do not learn the way in which we teach them, we must teach them the way in which they learn," has great bearing on Georgie's story. Because of our specific generic inheritance, our family life, and our early training, each of us gathers and processes information in a different way. Understanding these processes gives us insights to maximizing our creativity and productivity, and the often unrecognized, talents of others.

Class begins in five minutes. Is your "thinking cap" in place? This will be a real workout; get ready to perspire.

Stretch your arms upward, bend from your waist to your right; now bend to your left. Straighten up; reach for the sky with your hands. Get up on your toes, go down, up again, and now down again. Tie a sweatband around your forehead. Let your mind float backward through space and time until you are very young. Now, remember your earliest memories as a child. Think of the house you lived in when you were four years old. Did the front door face the north, south, east or west? What did the rays from the sun touch as they came through the windows of your room? Now, stretch your mind forward and picture yourself twenty years from today. What color is your hair; look at your shoes, what are they like; observe your surroundings;

what color are the walls, the floor; is there a mantle with pictures, if so, who do you see? We're beginning our Brain Aerobics class. If this is your first time, don't strain yourself; the exercises get easier with each practice session. Body aerobics keep our bodies fit and healthy; mind aerobics keep our brains flexible and stimulated.

Of all the subjects that intrigue our modern society, none is more fascinating than intelligence. Understanding how to make your mind work for you, to reach into your subconscious and extract your thoughts, is our focus. We will discuss the functions of each side of the brain. We will examine: What do we mean by intelligence? What are the types of intelligence? How are they measured? Does the American education system acknowledge and constructively address the difference between the way in which right-brain dominated people learn as opposed to the way in which left-brain dominated people learn?

Intelligence tests, although accurate in the type of predictions they can support, do have limitations. They measure intelligence only as defined by convergent, as compared to divergent, ways of thinking. Convergent thinking is the kind of mental process used to arrive at answers which are predetermined, factual and numeric. It is the kind of thinking that is fostered in school and the one prized in many families. It is the type of thinking that largely comprises measured intelligence.

Divergent thinking, on the other hand, is the thought process associated with creativity. The inability of intelligence tests to measure divergent thinking, along with society's emphasis on convergent thinking, often stands in the way of identifying intelligence and giftedness. History confirms the abilities of certain individuals who have proven to be highly gifted and talented or of genius ranking, yet scored low on tests.

Noted poet Ralph Waldo Emerson graduated in the bottom half of his class. Thomas Edison was told that he was too stupid to learn. Albert Einstein did not talk until he was three years old, learned to read much later than most children and did very poorly in school. Eleanor Roosevelt was viewed by teachers as a withdrawn daydreamer who came out of her shell only during selfish attempts to be the center of attention. Ludwig van Beethoven's music teacher considered him a washout as a composer. These divergent thinkers were believed to have little or no ability because they were different.

Is there genius potential in you? You bet there is. Your mind contains convergent and divergent thinking skills that haven't even been tapped. Let's learn to tap into these skills by exercising our whole minds, rather than only one preferred side. Clench both hands into fists, bring your hands together by having your first and second knuckles touching each other with your thumbs toward your body (first position for Brain Aerobics). Your fists in this position are the approximate size of your brain, unless you have the hands of a wide receiver. There is a strong similarity between your brain and your hands in this position. The bumps created by the knuckles, veins, and scars on your hands represent the outer layer (neocortex) of your brain. The more folds and creases it has, the more information it stores. During medical examinations, upon the death of someone, the more wrinkles found on the outer layer of the brain, the greater the person's intelligence level. A baby's brain is nearly as smooth as its bottom because it has not yet experienced learning.

While your hands are in this position, notice how the knuckles meet. The two halves of your brain (hemispheres) meet just like this. These two halves are joined together and communicate by tiny fibers (corpus callosum). We have two distinctive thinking processes, one on each side of these tiny fibers. Housed in the left half of the brain are the analytical and verbal processes, and our intuitive and visual processes are seated in the brain's right hemisphere. Ordinarily, we use our left hemisphere when we are adding numbers or remembering a person's name and our right hemisphere when we're enjoying the beauty of a sunset or listening to our favorite music.

We shift back and forth between these hemispheres as we change activities. You're driving home from the office, your mind a thousand miles away, thinking about the vacation that you're going to soon take. You picture a sandy beach; you feel the sunlight warming you; you smell the salt air and the suntan lotion; you hear the waves lapping at the shoreline. You're humming to yourself when suddenly someone cuts in front of you without so much as a horn beep. You instantly come back to reality, braking just enough to avoid a collision.

You have just moved from your imaginative right brain to your logical left brain. In a split second we are able to shift into hemispheres in a way that is vastly superior to that of the most sophisticated computer. Some of us make these shifts easily;

others move hesitantly between them, or in the wrong hemisphere. To understand how this shifting process affects both your private life and your job performance, we need to know the exact functions of the two halves of your brain.

Dr. Roger Sperry, noted psychologist at the California Institute of Technology who won the 1981 Nobel Prize for Physiology and Medicine, is credited for his "split-brain" studies on the functions of the two brain hemispheres. He and his associates performed the first "split-brain" surgery on a soldier in World War II who had parachuted behind enemy lines, was taken prisoner and sent to a P.O.W. camp where he was constantly hit in the head by a rifle butt. The wounds damaged his brain so much, that once released, he began to experience devastating seizures that made normal life impossible.

The soldier had not responded to medical efforts to improve his epilepsy. In a desperate effort for recovery, the doctors decided he was to be the first split-brain patient. The plan was to cut the minute fibers that joined the two hemispheres (surgery known as commissurotomy) and allowed the seizures to transfer from one side of the brain to the other. The surgery would leave each hemisphere isolated so that when seizures occurred in the damaged hemisphere, they could not spread to the other side.

This cutting would reduce the severity of the seizures and the patient could then be treated with medication. The surgery was successful and soon another patient, and then ten others, were helped. This research continues today and some patients still return periodically to the California Institute of Technology to allow researchers to study the effects of the surgeries.

When the two hemispheres of the brain are severed, one side cannot communicate with the other. It is as if, within every person, two separate minds were operating. With each hemisphere in isolation, researchers were able to determine which tasks are performed by the left hemisphere and which are performed by the right.

Your left brain is your logical hemisphere. It is dominant for the following tasks:

1. Verbal: The left hemisphere is the side of the brain that is involved in language skills. This is the side that controls speech and is able to read

and write. It remembers facts, recalls names and dates, and knows how to spell.

2. Analytical: The left hemisphere is your logical, analytical side. It can evaluate factual material in a logical way.
3. Logical: Knowing right from wrong is a function of the left side of the brain.
4. Mathematical: Numbers and symbols are comprehended in the left hemisphere. Working advanced mathematical problems takes place here.
5. Organizational: The left hemisphere emphasizes organization and neatness. It allows you to perform tasks step by step.
6. Precise:The left brain is concerned with exactness. It plans ahead, likes schedules, and urges you to arrive on time for meetings.
7. Controls movements of the opposite side of the body: If you wiggle your right thumb, it is your left brain that gave the instruction.

Your right brain is your intuitive hemisphere. It is dominant for the following tasks:

1. Visual: The right brain receives information through images instead of words.
2. Emotional: The right hemisphere reacts to feelings. When we cry or laugh, we are experiencing a right brain task.
3. Intuitive: The functions involving perceptions are processes of the right hemisphere. Your right brain knows how to work jigsaw puzzles and enables you to find your way around without getting lost.
4. Musical: Musical talent, as well as the ability to respond to music, are right brain functions. NOTE: Extensive musical education can only result with left hemisphere involvement.
5. Imaginative: The right brain is capable of fantasy; it makes up stories, daydreams and visualizes.
6. Artistic: Drawing, painting and sculpting are talents of the right hemisphere.

7. Sexual: Making love is a right hemisphere experience.
8. Spiritual: It is the right hemisphere that is involved in worship and prayer.
9. Controls movement on the side opposite the brain: If your wiggle your left thumb, it is your right brain that gave the instruction.

Although these are the primary functions of one particular side of the brain, it has been proven that there are small or minor areas in both hemispheres that are capable of carrying on the activities generally centered in the opposite half. For example, some language activity may be centered in the right brain and some musical skills may be centered in the left brain. It should be noted that the reversal of the usual functions of the brain are likely to occur in persons who are ambidextrous, that is neither right- nor left-hand dominant.

The information concerning split-brain research will be of much greater value to you when we translate it into personal terms. I invite you to take the following test to determine your hemispheric dominance. Do not analyze the questions. Answer them quickly by circling the correct response. These responses will be transferred to an actual drawing of a brain for you to conceptualize their impact on the way you think.

BRAIN DOMINANCE TEST

1. You feel that daydreaming is:
   A. Amusing and relaxing.
   B. A real help in problem-solving and creative thinking.
2. When you want to remember directions, a name, or a news item, and have nothing to write on or with, do you:
   A. Visualize the information.
   B. Repeat the information to yourself or out loud?
3. In an argument, do you tend to:
   A. Push your chair, pound the table, throw off your glasses and talk louder.
   B. Find an authority to support your point.

4. Can you tell fairly accurately how much time has passed without looking at your watch?
   A. Yes.
   B. No.
5. In school, did you prefer:
   A. Algebra.
   B. Geometry.
6. When you are asked to speak extemporaneously at a meeting, do you:
   A. Make a quick mental outline, then begin speaking.
   B. Shift the focus to someone else or say as little as possible.
7. Do you learn new dance steps better by:
   A. Imitating someone doing that dance.
   B. Learning the sequence and repeating the steps mentally.
8. When trying to recall a song you've once heard, do you begin to:
   A. Hum parts of the melody.
   B. Recite certain lines from the song.
9. You find crossword puzzles:
   A. Easy to solve.
   B. Difficult to solve.
10. The handwriting position that most closely resembles yours is:
    A. Regular right-hand position.
    B. Hooked right-hand position (fingers pointing toward your chest).
    C. Regular left-hand position.
    D. Hooked left-hand position (fingers pointing toward your chest).
11. Using your right-hand pointer finger while keeping both eyes open, point to a corner of the room. Holding that position, it will look as though you are seeing double. Close your left eye? Did your finger appear to move?
    A. Yes.
    Close your right eye? Did your finger appear to move?
    B. Yes.
12. Clasp your hands comfortably in your lap while seated in a relaxed position.
    Which thumb is on the top?
    A. Left.
    B. Right.

13. In the presence of someone speaking, you:
    A. Focus on their message.
    B. Listen and watch their nonverbal signals.

Transfer your answers to the diagram of the brain. Darken the circles to the accompanying questions.

ITEM	A	B	C	D
1.	L	R		
2.	R	L		
3.	R	L		
4.	L	R		
5.	L	R		
6.	L	R		
7.	R	L		
8.	R	L		
9.	L	R		
10.	L	R	R	L
11.	R	L		
12.	L	R		
13.	L	R		

LEFT/Analytic   **RIGHT/Global**

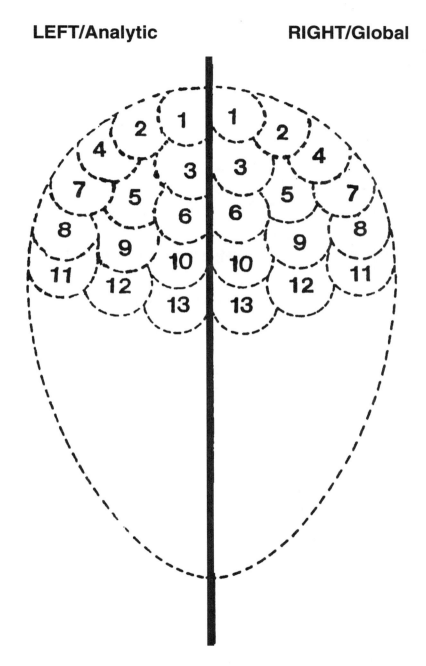

Chap. 11, Fig. 2

Add the number of darkened circles on the right side of the brain and those on the left side of the brain and insert the numbers in the score formula below:

SCORE FORMULA:

Analytic (left) Total: _____
Intuitive (right) Total: _____

SUBTRACT:

Higher Total: _____
Lower Total: minus _____
Degree of Dominance
in _____ Hemisphere: _____

Use the chart here to determine your degree of hemisphere preference.

Analytic (left)	Integrated (both)	Global (right)
10 9 8 7 6 5 4 3 2 1	0 1 2 3 4 5 6	7 8 9 10

Chap. 11, Fig. 3

The questions in this self-test cover the most noticeable differences between dominant rights and lefts. There is nothing good or bad about your brain preference score. It is simply a way of understanding your thinking style through an awareness of the general thought pattern prevalent in all areas of your life. Recognizing and understanding the components of this pattern allow you to evaluate which characteristics you enjoy as they are and which you may want to alter.

To help interpret your brain preference score, an analysis of each question follows.

Question 1

- A. Left-brain types find daydreaming and intuition only entertaining.
- B. Extreme right-brain individuals typically place their trust in daydreaming.

Question 2

- A. Right-brain types do better with visual and emotional clues. They picture numbers, remember what people wore, who they danced with, what they drank. Their directions consist of: "turn at the big yellow and green neon sign, go until you see a two-story brown building, etc."
- B. Left-brain people remember best by recording or repeating information. Lefts need directions in specifics: "two blocks north, one south."

Question 3

- A. Right-brain individuals are more emotional, tend to get upset easier than left-brain people.
- B. Left-brain types are analytical and factual. They believe their point is right and they will find someone that can prove this for them.

Question 4

- A. Lefts are very conscious of time and schedules and tend to become impatient with time-consuming meetings and committees.
- B. Rights frequently are oblivious to the passage of time and get lost in personal interaction.

Question 5

- A. Left-dominant types find algebra easier because it is the mathematics of logic and deduction, using analysis and comparison.
- B. Right-dominants understand geometry better because it is more graphic and visually comprehensible.

Question 6

A. Because lefts' verbal skills are more highly developed, they feel more at home talking than do rights. Left-brain types know what they think and they're glad to tell you.

B. In public speaking, right dominants are prone to wander, often failing to reach a conclusion. They relate information to personal experiences.

Question 7

A. Right-brain types thrive on freedom and having fun. They'll initiate others to learn the dance, then add some movements of their own.

B. Left-brain individuals play with competitiveness and goal-setting. Whether it is dancing or playing golf, lefts must get it right or they don't enjoy doing the activity at all.

Question 8

A. The creative, musical side of the brain is in the right hemisphere. It conceptualizes feelings by using sounds.

B. Left-brain dominant individuals focus on words and their intense meanings. The great composers, though, extensively use both sides of their brains. They are able to write meaningful lyrics and can invent melodies. They play instruments (right) and read music (left).

Question 9

A. Left-brain individuals remember facts, names, dates, enjoy problem solving, and are logical and competitive.

B. Right-brain types are not as disciplined as left-brain individuals and sometimes can't sit still long enough to even read the directions to solving a crossword puzzle.

Question 10

A. Left-brain types write in the regular right-hand position.
B. Right-brain individuals write in the hooked right-hand position.
C. Right-brain types also write in the regular left-hand position.
D. Left-brain types also write in the hooked left-hand position.

Question 11

A. If your finger moved less when you closed your left eye, it is evident that you are right-eyed. If you are right-eyed, you are likely to be left-brained dominant.
B. If your finger moved less when you closed your right eye, it is evident that you are left-eyed. If you are left-eyed, you are likely to be right-brained dominant.

Question 12

This question is used by hypnotists to determine how easily a person can be hypnotized. People who are more comfortable with the right thumb on top are more easily hypnotized than those who prefer the left thumb on top. Since right dominants are more suggestible than left dominants, the thumb test is also an indication of brain dominance, therefore:

A. If your right thumb was on top, it indicates right-brain dominance.
B. If your left thumb was on top, it indicates left-brain dominance.

Question 13

A. Left-dominants focus on words and message when listening.
B. Right-dominant types take a more general approach when listening, incorporating body signals, emotional tone, and facial expressions.

From birth to approximately four years of age, most of us are predominately right-brained. We create imaginary friends, we fabricate stories, we paint, we draw, and we laugh heartily. Upon entering kindergarten or first grade, instruction begins to favor left-hemisphere brain functions. We memorize, we recite, we calculate. In fact, learning, throughout middle school, high school and college favors the left hemisphere. Creative writing classes, drama classes and music classes, which stimulate the left brain, are scheduled by only a few students.

We live in a society that shows most respect for people who are left-brain dominant. The left-brain dominant school girl who remembers names, adds numbers properly and works diligently is praised and gets a star beside her name. The right-brain dominant child who daydreams, stares at the ceiling, and makes up stories rather than learn her lesson is sent home with a disciplinary note.

One goal of major universities is to get people back to whole-brain thinking.

When the hemispheres function properly, the cooperation between them is a perfect partnership. There is harmony in their goals and they avoid getting in each other's way. Each is supportive of the other and each does what it does best.

In business partnerships, when one partner gets too aggressive the result is usually disastrous. The brain has similar problems with partnership. The left hemisphere becomes too assertive and so aggressive that it tries to do jobs that are best accomplished by the right side of the brain. When that happens, the brain's partnership is in trouble.

If a person relies too heavily on the left hemisphere, he may lose the intuitive powers of the right side of his brain. Just as a muscle will atrophy from lack of use, the right hemisphere of the brain also suffers when its use isn't encouraged. Even though this creative side is underdeveloped, that doesn't mean that it can't be revived.

The person who relies solely on the left brain for everything usually has trouble in personal relationships, because the more sensitive hemisphere is needed for harmonious interaction with others. To solve problems, most of us tend to rely only on one approach or the other, rather than from a clear understanding of which hemisphere is best suited for the job. In the last few years researchers have indicated that when solving a problem, conscious effort to use the specific hemisphere for the problem's solution can alter performance favorably.

Let's continue with our Brain Aerobics class. Stretch your mind to the future, then back to the past. The following exercises have been devised to lead you directly toward untapped creativity in your right brain. When you finish the exercises you will be able to understand how creative people (Einstein, Emerson) learned to tame and make use of their creative energy from the right-brain.

People are most receptive to right-brain exercises when the body is relaxed and the mind is free from internal chatter. Therefore, sit in a quiet place, in a comfortable manner, and begin to quiet your mind. Inhale deeply and slowly breathe out, again, and again.

Exercise 1: "In The Distant Forest."

Imagine that you are walking alone in the woods. The trees are thick and beautiful.

Can you see them?

Imagine the colors . . .

Listen to the sounds . . .

Notice the smell of the trees . . .

How does the air feel against your skin . . .

There is a narrow stream running nearby. Enjoy the sound of the rushing water for a moment. Now, cross to the other side by stepping on large, flat stones that protrude above the water.

Walk slowly through the forest until you come to a beautiful

meadow, where you sit down to rest. Be intensely aware

of what you see and feel.

Are the colors different here? The sounds?

Sit quietly for a while and notice the specific details of the

meadow.

Create the scene as clearly as you can . . .

Feel the grass beneath you . . .

Smell the freshness . . .

Feel the wind in your face . . .

There is a sound at the end of the forest . . .

Identify that sound . . .

Walk toward the sound . . .

Feel the texture of the ground beneath your step . . .

Walk faster . . .

There's a house in the clearing . . .

Move closer, the door is slightly open . . .

It's all right to enter, you're not intruding . . .

Step inside, you're alone . . .

Look around, what do you see . . .

Explore . . .

Go to the open window and look out . . .

What do you see . . .

Walk down the hall . . .

Down the hallway to the closed door at the end . . .

Open the door, look inside . . .

Seems empty . . .

In the corner, what is it . . .

A child asleep . . .

Describe your experience on paper. Did you see the trees, feel the ground, hear the water? Write a description of the outside of the house. Describe the child and the emotion you felt upon seeing him. Let the power of your emotions direct your words.

Exercise 2: "From A Distant Past."

Look at the shoes you are now wearing. Close your eyes and visualize those same shoes in your mind. Think of a pair of shoes you had a year ago. Let time roll back even further and imagine a pair of shoes you wore on a special occasion, tennis shoes, dancing shoes, wedding shoes or . . .

Think of the shoes you wore in high school . . .

In grade school . . .

Let your imagination take you back to the shoes you wore
in first grade . . .

Imagine your feet are the same size that they were when
you wore those shoes . . .

Imagine your height, the shape of your little body . . .

What color are your socks . . .

Walk out of your house . . .

Follow a familiar path . . .

Notice the colors around you . . .

The smell of the air . . .

Let your shoes take you to a place in your memory that was
happy . . .

Do you see yourself . . .

Are you alone or with friends . . .

Close your eyes and visualize . . .

Enjoy the experience . . .

Write your memories of this experience on paper.

Exercises that explore feelings and touch upon memories and desires help develop the imaginative right hemisphere. You are creative. Decide on the most effective way you can incorporate these types of relaxing, right-brain exercises into your work schedule. Daydream, fantasize, visualize, exercise this neglected powerful source of intelligence.

Left brain exercises are next. Prepare yourself to compute, analyze, and evaluate.

Exercise 3: "Read My Mind."

Pick a number from 2 to 9. Multiple that number by 9. After multiplying, you have a two-digit answer. Add those two digits to each other. From that single digit, subtract 5. Let's correlate your answer to a letter of the alphabet. If your answer is a 1, use A; 2, use B; 3, use C; 4, use D; 5, use E; and so on. Next, think of a European country that begins with that same letter. Think of the spelling of that country. Picture the last letter of that country and think of an animal that begins with the same letter as that last letter. In your head, you should have a country and an animal.

Write your answer here: _____

Exercise 4: "The Hungry Worm."

On a bookshelf in a library, there are five books, each containing 100 pages. A worm begins to eat through the cover of the first book, eats through the second book, through the third book, through the fourth book, and through the back cover of the last book. Through how many pages and covers has the worm eaten?

Write your answer here: _____

Exercise 5: "Concentration."

1. The famous Fibonacci Sequence is:
    1,1,2,3,5,8,13,21,34,_____.

2. A phone number sequence: 428-6339, 286-3394, 863-3942, 633-9428,_____.

3. Does Lincoln face left or right on the U.S. penny?
    _____.

4. Without looking, does your watch have Arabic or Roman numerals? _____
    Does it have all the numbers, or just 12-3-6-9? ___

5. What letter comes next in this series?
    W   L   C   N   I   T   _____

6. Which of the five is least like the other four?
   Artist   Golfer   Newscaster   Dancer   Mechanic
   (a)   (b)   (c)   (d)   (e)
7. Which of the five makes the best comparison?
   YYZZZYZZY is to 221112112 as YYZZYZZY is to:
   221221122   22112122   22112112   112212211   212211212
      (a)   (b)   (c)   (d)   (e)
8. Which of the five is least like the other four?
   Squash   Pumpkin   Tomato   Cucumber   Corn
     (a)   (b)   (c)   (d)   (e)
9. Which of the five is least like the other four?
   Wichita   Dallas   Canton   Topeka   Fresno
     (a)   (b)   (c)   (d)   (e)
10. The person who makes it sells it.
    The person who buys it doesn't use it.
    The person who uses it doesn't know it.

What is it?
(Answers are at end of Chapter.)

Following are suggestions for providing significant shifting between hemispheres.

LEFT TO RIGHT	RIGHT TO LEFT
1. Shift phone to left ear for emphatic listening.	1. Shift phone to right ear for analytic listening.
2. Doodle, draw, print.	2. Work crossword puzzles, solve math problems.
3. Sing, hum, tell jokes.	3. Ask questions, make puns.
4. Breathe deeply with the intent of relaxing.	4. Stride purposefully, perform calisthenics.
5. Take a minivacation at your desk; lean back, close eyes, daydream.	5. Go off alone and write a memo describing anger or a problem.
6. Be aware of colors, aromas, sounds, your emotions.	6. Value your decisions and foresight.
7. Make eye contact with others, notice body movements of others.	7. Focus on messages from others.

8. Talk to yourself in a positive, supportive way.
8. Take notes.

9. See things through other people's eyes.
9. Organize, set priorities.

Human beings are the only creatures who can think about how they think. If you are to extend your brainpower, you must identify how it feels to be thinking in certain ways. When you identify these thinking experiences, you can purposefully alter, heighten, or move between them.

We're nearing the end of our Brain Aerobics class. Get ready for cool down. Take a deep breathe, exhale through your nose. Another deep breathe, exhale again. Bend your neck to the right (ear towards shoulder), hold for a few minutes; bend your neck to the left, hold for a few minutes. Bend your chin to your chest, hold a few minutes. With your chin down, slowly swing your head to the right, now to the left; back to your right, now back to your left. Lift your head, open your eyes.

Class dismissed.

Answers to Brain Aerobics:

Exercise 3: "Read My Mind."

1. Isn't it strange that there are no kangaroos in Denmark.

Exercise 4: "The Hungry Worm."

1. 302 (Stand the books up on a library shelf, where is the cover of the first book? It faces the second book, therefore, the worm just eats the front cover of book one, all 100 pages in books two, three and four, and one page from book 5, the back cover.)

Exercise 5: "Concentration."

1. 55
2. 339-4286
3. Right
4. Look at your watch.
5. S   The letters are the first letter of each word in the sentence.
6. C   All the others must use their hands and/or body but not words to perform their jobs like the newscaster must.
7. C   Substitute numbers for letters.
8. E   Corn. The others grow on vines. Corn grows on a stalk.
9. A   All the others have but six letters, Wichita has seven.
10. A   Coffin

EPILOGUE

If you set about the task of applying the skills of nonverbal communication to life as you live it day by day, you'll actually notice a major shift, not only in the quality of your communications, but within the context of your relationships. In many ways, the quality of your life is the quality of your communication.

Willingly improve your communicaton skills and help others to improve theirs. I end by sharing this heartfelt story with you.

MY FATHER'S HANDS

His hands were rough and exceedingly strong. He could wrestle an ornery horse into harness or dig post holes all day. At times, though, his hands appeared gentle as he delicately pruned fig trees. I remember his hands well. Sometimes they would tap me on the shoulder and point to a flock of geese flying overhead, or again tap me on the shoulder and point to a rabbit asleep in its nest.

They were great hands, hands that served my father well. Still they failed him in a very important way. They never learned to write. My father was illiterate. It pains me— pains me— to think of my father and the struggles that he went through by not being able to read or to write.

It began in first grade, where the remedy for the wrong answer was ten slaps across an extended hand. For some reason, numbers and words never fell into the right pattern inside his six-year old head. He struggled through first grade, second grade, third grade. Then, during his fourth year of school, his Dad said, "I'll take you out of school and put you on the farm to do a man's job."

Years later, my Mom with her twelfth grade education would try to teach him how to read, but again to no avail. He took great pride in *my* reading, though, and would sit for hours as I struggled through my first grade reader. On Sundays, when he thought no one was looking, I'd watch him at the kitchen table leafing through the paper as if by some kind of miracle the words would enter his head.

When my Mom left for a holiday to visit her sister, Dad said he had a surprise for us for dinner. The meal was perfect, and when time came for dessert, Dad said he had an even bigger surprise. He rose from the dining table, and went into the kitchen where I heard him open a can. Then everything was quiet. After a few minutes, I heard him mumble the words, "The picture looked just like pears to me." He then went out the back door for a solitary walk.

I immediately arose from the table and ran to see what had happened. I picked up the can and it read "Whole White Potatoes," but the picture on the label looked like pears to me, too.

After my Mom died, I begged my Dad to come live with my family and me, but he insisted on staying in his small farm house on the edge of town, with a few farm animals and a small garden plot. His health was failing. In fact, he had been in and out of the hospital with several mild heart attacks. Old Doc Green said it was nothing to worry about and gave him a prescription for nitroglycerin tablets to put under his tongue should he feel a heart attack coming on.

My last fond memory of my Dad is watching as he walked across a hillside meadow, his hands now worn with age, resting on the shoulders of my two children. That evening, my family and I departed for a new job, a new home, a new life. Three weeks later, my Dad died of a heart attack.

I returned home alone for the funeral. Old Doc Green told me how sorry he was. He couldn't understand it. He had just written Dad a prescription for nitroglycerin tablets, the druggist had filled it, but it was not found on Dad's person.

About an hour before the funeral, I walked for awhile in my Dad's garden, where a neighbor had found him. As I stooped to trace my fingers through the soft earth where he had been planting, my hand rested upon a half-buried brick, which I aimlessly lifted and tossed aside, before noticing underneath it the battered, yet unbroken plastic bottle that had been beaten into the soft earth.

As I held that bottle of nitroglycerin tablets in my hand, the scene of Dad struggling to remove the cap and in desperation trying to break the bottle with the brick flashed painfully before my eyes. I knew then why my Dad had lost in his struggle to live. For there on the cap read the words, "Child-Proof Cap—Push Down and Turn to Open."

I knew it was not a purely rational act, but I immediately ran down to the corner drugstore and bought a pocket-size dictionary and two gold ball-point pens. As I told my Dad good-bye, I placed them in those big old hands, once so warm and strong, that had served him so well, but had never learned to write.